Firesong

The Wind on Fire III

Firesong

William Nicholson

EGMONT

First published in Great Britain 2002
by Egmont Books Limited
239 Kensington High Street
London W8 6SA

Copyright © 2002 William Nicholson
Cover illustration copyright © 2002 Mark Edwards

The moral rights of the author and the cover illustrator
have been asserted

ISBN 0 7497 4955 5

10 9 8 7 6 5 4 3 2 1

A CIP catalogue record for this title
is available from the British Library

Typeset by Avon DataSet Ltd, Bidford on Avon, B50 4JH
Printed and bound in Spain
by Graficas Estella

Contents

Prologue: Bounce on, Jumper		1
1	The view from the sourgum tree	10
2	Drunkenness	29
3	Sisi's kiss	42
4	Walking the storm	59
5	The winner chooses a bride	81
6	Farewell to childhood	95
7	The dying of the last fire	110
8	Fatness is happiness	131
9	Talking with pigs	150
10	Captain Canobius's feast	167
11	Winter dawn	181
12	All my loves	193
13	The egg's song	213
14	Pinto grows up	229
15	Bowman flies	249
16	Ira sees the future	270

17 The meeting place   286

18 Into the beautiful land   306

19 The wind on fire   317

    Epilogue: A betrothal   325

Prologue: Bounce on, Jumper

Albard lay undiscovered among the ruins for three days and nights. All this time he remained in a half sleep, a waking dream, too weak to move or call out. He saw the sun pass overhead, and then the stars. He grew cold, and colder. The flesh dwindled on his great body as he starved. He knew he was dying, and knew there was nothing he could do now to save himself; nor did he wish to. He was only puzzled that it was taking so long, and a little afraid about what would happen in that mysterious final moment when the dying, which is after all a kind of living, came to an end. So at last he composed his mind and prepared himself to sing the song all Singer people sing at the end, for the release of their spirit. Unlike most of the Singer people's songs, this one had words. Albard's lips did not move. No sound came from him. But in his mind, he sang:

Joy of my days, let me go

> *Days of my life, let me go*
> *Life of my heart, let me go*
> *Let me go, let me go, far away . . .*

His own voice sounded sweet to him, and peaceful, and he thought he would sleep soon. The pain was all gone, and the ruined city around him was silent. He had no idea what time of day it was any more, or what time of year. It was for him the end time.

> *Heart of my life, let me go*
> *Life of my days, let me go*
> *Days of my joy, let me go*
> *Let me go, let me go, far away . . .*

Then as the song came ever fainter in his fading mind, he heard a new sound: the sound of footsteps approaching. They came in bursts, as if this unseen visitor was hopping and stopping, hopping and stopping. Through the fog of his own dying Albard heard a voice, a shrill chirpy voice that talked to itself.

'Bounce on, Jumper!' the voice said.

Leave me alone, said Albard in his mind. *Leave me to die.*

But it was no use. The newcomer couldn't hear him, and would have paid no attention even if he had. He was getting closer. Any moment now he would stumble right onto Albard's body.

'He's here somewhere, and I'm here, so when his here meets my here, I'll find him. Bounce on, Jumper!'

No! cried Albard, deep within his fading mind. *Not*

him! Not the jolly one! Now, death, now! Come quickly!

It was too late. Though his body was cold and his eyes long closed, stubborn life lingered in his core: and so the one who called himself Jumper found him, and cried out in joy.

'Oh happy day! Albard! My dear companion, I have found you!'

Go away.

'You don't look at all well.'

I'm almost dead, you clot.

'Never mind! We'll soon have you up and smiling, eh?'

Drown yourself, moonface.

'That's the spirit! You know you can do it! Who's let himself get cold? Dear oh dear! Rub-a-dub-dub! We'll soon have you warm again.'

The little fellow set himself hammering over the dying man's great starved wreck of a body, beating heat back into the icy limbs. Albard felt the tiny spark of life within him flicker and grow stronger.

His eyes opened.

'Well, hello, stranger!' beamed Jumper. 'Welcome back to this wonderful world!'

Albard did not speak. He let his great grey eyes stare his outrage and his contempt.

'You don't have to thank me,' said Jumper. 'Making people happy is my reward.'

What a moonface clot it is, thought Albard to himself, as Jumper chafed his limbs. He felt the first painful thrill of returning sensation. And what sort of thing is he anyway? Is he man or woman? Or something else altogether, for which we need a new name?

You're a blob, he decided. *A silly smiling blob.*

The creature was certainly human, though smaller and more short-legged and round-bodied than the usual sort. He was equipped with the standard number of limbs and eyes and ears, and had hair on the top of his round moonish head. But was the hair fair or dark? Long or short? The odd thing about Jumper was you couldn't quite get a fix on any part of him, except perhaps for his ever-cheerful voice. Sometimes he looked like a little middle-aged man, sometimes like a ten-year-old girl. He was known as Jumper not only because of his bouncing, hopping manner of getting about: there was something jumpish about him altogether. No part of him ever came to rest, but was always changing, becoming something else. It was no use asking Jumper himself who or what he was, because he would only reply, with his eager-to-please smile,

'What would you like me to be?'

To children he was an indulgent grandfather, to women he was a playful child, to men a willing friend. To Albard now, he was saviour, servant, and nurse. He scavenged food and drink for him among the ruins, and in the chill night he slept pressed tight to Albard's body, warming him with his own life's heat.

It was hard to complain. Above all, Jumper was so good-tempered. He was relentlessly, unstoppably good-tempered. As Albard returned to strength, he lay and plotted remarks that would offend him, but never with any success.

'Believe me, Jumper, I would rather die than have to endure one more day of your baseless optimism.'

'Oh, would you rather I was gloomy? I can be gloomy if you like.'

He hung his round head and turned down the corners of his mouth and shuffled about sighing to himself,

'Sad and lonely, sad and lonely.'

'And short and ugly,' said Albard.

'Sad and lonely, short and ugly,' echoed Jumper.

'And dull and fat.'

'Sad and lonely, short and ugly, dull and fat,' said Jumper, beating his breast. But then he spoiled it all by looking up with a radiant smile and asking, 'Did you like that? Did I do it right?'

Very much against his will, and due entirely to Jumper's devoted care, Albard recovered.

'Thank you, Jumper,' he said bitterly. 'Thanks to you, my life, which has no purpose left to it, nor any prospect of happiness, will now drag on a little while longer.'

'Oh no,' said Jumper. 'You're entirely wrong. Your life does have a purpose. You're to train the boy.'

'What boy?'

However, Albard knew well enough. There was only one boy who mattered: the boy who was to rule after him. Of course he must be taught. The boy he hated and loved, the boy that was his enemy, his rival who had taken from him all his power, his successor who would be his inheritor. Albard envied him his youth and his future. He hated him for his victory over him. He loved him like the child he never had. He felt a wild pride in him. He longed with a burning desire to see him again, and just once, before the end, to hold him in his arms. So many emotions, and all so violent: and all because this moonface spoke to him about the boy.

Jumper, apparently knowing none of this, answered simply,

'His name is Bowman Hath.'

'And what am I to train this boy to do?'

'To carry out his new duties.'

'And why am I to do this?'

'Because,' said Jumper, beaming, 'because you're the best of us.'

'I'm the best, eh?'

Albard knew what they said on Sirene. The best and the worst, that's what they said of him. The greatest of all the Singer people ever to have kissed the Prophet's brow, the one in whom the powers had been most perfected, and the only one ever to betray their calling.

'Well, so I am. What of it?'

'So you're to train the boy. You see how it all comes out right in the end?'

'In the end we're all dead.'

'That we are, and how glorious that will be!'

Albard sighed and gave up. There was no denting such wilful contentment.

'Where is he, then? This boy?'

'He's on his way to the mountains, with his people. We must hurry. They've been gone many days, and the wind is rising.'

'The wind is rising, is it? And will you be there at the end, little Jumper? Will you be singing the firesong, with the wind on your back?'

'Oh, yes! Of course I'll be there! How blessed we are to

be the generation that will know the wind on fire!'

'Not me. I made my choice long ago. I've had my day, and now it's over.'

He looked round him at the burned ruins of what had once been the most beautiful city in the world.

They didn't deserve it. I gave them perfection, and they feared it. They loved their mess. Now they have it back.

'Sirene sent you, moonface?'

'Yes, of course.'

'Sirene hates me. Sirene wants me dead.'

'Not at all. You've played your part, like all the rest of us.'

'Played my part!'

Albard let out a big bellowing laugh. That was rich! Albard the rebel, the traitor, the mutineer, had played his part in Sirene's plans! No, he was the breaker of rules, the defier of authority, the one who had split away from the rest and forged his own world, where he alone had been the Master. Singer people never sought power in the world. Only Albard, the best of them, had broken the rule of rules.

'I played no part in any plan of Sirene's, little Jumper. They call me the lost one. I am Sirene's failure.'

He spoke with a certain pride. What else had he left, now that his city was gone and he had not been allowed to die?

'We must go,' said Jumper. 'Are you strong enough?'

'Getting stronger all the time. But not what I was. You should have seen me in my day! I was immense! Now my skin hangs loose about me, and I rattle as I walk. Ah, mortality!'

'But you feel your powers returning?'

'A little. Yes.'

He looked round. There on the ground, near the hole into which he had crawled to die, lay a short sword. It had fallen from the hand of some poor fool who had died doing his will, and now lay beneath a layer of dust and stones. Albard fixed his mind on the hilt of the sword, and with great effort, he caused it to stir beneath the debris. More he could not do.

With a sigh, he stooped down, and scraping away the stones, picked it up with one hand. Jumper beamed his approval.

'There! That's a start, isn't it?'

'And if I were to cut your throat with it, that would be a finish, too.'

'Oh, you won't do that. I'm no use to you dead.'

'You're no use to me, Jumper. There's nothing you can give me I want. There's nothing you can do for me I need.'

He slipped the sword into the rope with which his plain woollen robe was belted, and turned his great beak of a nose northwards.

'But we'll find this boy, and set him on his path, and then what has been begun will be completed. Not because Sirene plans it, you understand, but because I choose it. Sirene has no control over me. I'm the lost one. I'm the one who goes his own way.'

Albard was facing the causeway across the lake, his gaze fixed on the hills to the north, and so he did not catch the look that passed briefly over Jumper's round and foolish face. It was the indulgent smile of the parent who allows his wilful child the last word, knowing the child cannot choose but to obey.

'So you are, if it pleases you,' said the curious young-old creature, hopping along after him. 'Bounce on, Jumper!'

1

The view from the sourgum tree

The column of weary marchers made slow progress. The land was rising, and the day was cold. The two horses pulling the heavily-laden wagon kept their heads down and held to a steady plodding pace, but everyone could see that they were growing thinner every day. The wagon's driver, Seldom Erth, walked beside them to lighten their load. He was the oldest of the marchers, well over sixty years old, but he strode along as determinedly as the younger men, watching the track as he went for stones too big or ruts too deep for the wagon's wheels. The ones who found it hard to keep up the pace were the children. Miller Marish's little girl Jet was only six years old. From time to time Seldom Erth swung her up into the wagon, to sit with the cat on the pile of folded tent-cloth at the back, and rest her little legs.

There were thirty-two people of all ages on the march, as well as the two draft horses, five cows, and the cat. Hanno Hath, the march leader, had ordered that they must keep within sight of each other at all times, so the column proceeded at the pace of its slowest members. These were dangerous days. There were rumours of bandit gangs that preyed on travellers. Young men with keen eyes and ready swords loped ahead of the straggling column, watching for danger; but Hanno knew his people had little experience of combat, and had been marching for days on reduced rations. When he fixed his eyes on the horizon ahead, it was not only bandits he feared, but the coming of winter. They carried food and firewood in the wagon, but every day the supplies grew smaller, and they were crossing a bleak, barren land.

'Have faith, Hannoka,' said his wife Ira, walking steadily beside him. She used his childhood name to comfort him, as if she was his mother as well as his wife, knowing how great a burden he bore. 'Have faith, Hannoka.'

'I worry about the children. How much farther can they go?'

'If they get tired, we'll carry them.'

'And you?'

'Do I slow you down?'

'No. You march well. You still feel it?'

'I still have the warmth on my face.'

She would not admit it, but he could see how she grew weaker every day, and her pace grew slower. He adjusted the speed of the march so that she would not fall behind, pretending to himself he was doing it for the children. He hated to see her grow thinner, and quieter. She had always been a noisy woman, a woman of quick passions and short temper. Now she was quiet, conserving her energy for the long march.

Have faith, Hannoka.

He understood her well enough. She was telling him to believe they would reach the homeland, that one day they would be safe for ever. But she was not telling him she would join him there.

He shook his head, a quick angry jerk, to send the dark thought skittering away. No good to be had looking that way. His care and his diligence were needed now, today, leading his people over the cold land towards the distant not-yet-seen mountains.

Bowman, his fifteen-year-old son, strode along at the head of the column, with his friend Mumpo by his side. The time was a little short of noon, and the young men knew that soon now the march would be called to a halt, for a rest to weary legs, and a share of the dwindling rations. But Bowman's sharp eyes were fixed on the near horizon, the crest of the rising land ahead. He could make out a straggling fringe of trees.

'Trees!'

'Not many.'

'Could be nuts. Berries. Firewood.'

So little grew on these rocky plains that even a few lone trees gave hope. They quickened their pace, opening up the gap between them and the rest of the march.

'We might see the mountains from there,' said Mumpo.

'We might.'

They were well out of earshot of the rest now, so as they strode up the sloping hillside Mumpo took the chance to say what he had been planning to say all day.

'I talked with the princess again. She asked about you.'

'She's not a princess.'

'She thinks you avoid her. She doesn't know why.'

'I don't avoid her.'

'You do. Everyone sees it.'

'Then let them look aside,' said Bowman angrily. 'What has it to do with them? What has it to do with you?'

'Nothing,' said Mumpo. 'I won't speak of it again.'

They went on in silence, and so reached the trees. Their feet crunched on the stony ground. Bowman stooped to pick up one of the dark-brown husks that littered the earth beneath the trees. He smelled it: a sharp, unpleasant smell. Disappointed, he let it fall again, and followed Mumpo to the crest of the hill.

'Do you see the mountains?'

'No,' said Mumpo.

Bowman felt the weariness close about him like a heavy coat. Standing at Mumpo's side, he looked north and saw how the barren land sloped down, and then rose again, another in the series of endless waves that limited the horizon. They were crossing an ocean of rolling waves, forever denied a sight of the farther shore.

He turned to look back at his people. He saw his father and mother, walking as always side by side. Behind them a straggle of people, in twos and threes, his twin sister Kestrel with the one Mumpo called the princess. The wagon rumbled steadily along after them, drawing Creoth and his five cows in its wake. Behind the cows he could make out the plump shape of Mrs Chirish waddling along, and behind her, holding hands in a chain, his younger sister Pinto and the other small children. At the back came little Scooch and the lanky teacher Pillish; and guarding the rear, Bek and Rollo Shim.

Bowman felt Mumpo's silence, and knew he had been too sharp with him.

'I'm sorry,' he said. 'It's just hard to explain.'

'That's all right.'

'I think I'll have to leave you. All of you. Someone will come for me, and I'll have to go.'

'Who will come for you?'

'I don't know who, or when. I only know why. There's a time coming called the wind on fire, which will burn away the cruelty in the world. And I must be part of it, because I'm a child of the prophet.'

He knew as he said the words that they would mean very little to Mumpo. He felt for a different way to explain.

'You know the feeling of not belonging?'

'Yes,' said Mumpo. He knew it well, but he was surprised to hear Bowman speak of it. Bowman had his family. He had Kestrel.

'I think I was born not to belong, so that I can leave you all, and – and not come back.'

Mumpo hung his head in sadness.

'Will Kestrel go too?'

'I don't think so. I don't know. The one who comes for me will say.'

'Perhaps he'll say I'm to go too. Like before. The three friends.'

'No,' said Bowman. 'They need you here. Promise me you'll protect them. My father and mother. My sisters. Everyone I love.'

'I promise, Bo.'

'You're strong. They need you.'

The chain of small children had broken up, as they

raced each other up the slope to the trees. The bigger Mimilith boys were there ahead of them. Before Bowman could stop him, Mo Mimilith had picked up one of the nuts on the ground and started to eat it.

'Yooh!' he cried, spitting it out. 'Yooh! Bitter!'

'Do you see the mountains?' called Hanno.

'No. No mountains.'

A sigh of disappointment ran down the length of the column. Hanno ordered a rest halt among the trees. Pinto came up, panting from running to the top of the hill, and took Bowman's hand.

'How much further do you think we have to go?'

'I don't know,' said Bowman.

'I don't mean I'm tired. I was only wondering.'

Pinto was seven years old, and had to make two steps for every one of Bowman's, but she hated it if anyone took pity on her.

Now Kestrel joined them, beckoning Bowman aside for a word in private. Her companion, the young woman who had once been a princess, met his eyes and immediately looked away. She had always been proud. Now that she had nothing, now that even her beauty had been taken from her, she was still proud, but in a different way. Her great liquid amber eyes now watched the world go by saying, I ask for nothing, I expect nothing. But those scars! Those two soft mauve wounds that ran down her cheeks, two diagonal furrows from the cheekbones to the corners of the mouth, they fascinated Bowman. They changed everything in that once so sweetly pretty face. The man who had cut her had said, 'I kill your beauty!', but in its place had come a new beauty: harder, older, more remarkable.

Kestrel turned his attention towards their mother, who was just now reaching the resting place.

'Look at her, Bo. She can't go on like this.'

'While she can walk, she'll walk,' said Bowman. 'That's how she wants it.'

'You know what it is that weakens her.'

Of course he knew. The prophet Ira Manth had said, *My gift is my weakness. I shall die of prophecy.* This was the secret that all knew but none spoke. Ira Hath, their own prophetess, was dying of the warmth she felt on her face.

'It's how she wants it,' said Bowman again.

'Well, it's not how I want it.' Kestrel felt trapped and angry. She heard in Bowman's voice the same note of resignation that now softened her mother's words: as if they had both decided to suffer for the good of others, and so refused to do anything to help themselves. 'I'd rather never get to the homeland than have her like this.'

'I don't think any of us have any choice.'

'Then let it happen soon, whatever it is. Let it come soon.'

Dock! Dock! Dock! It was the sound of Tanner Amos's axe ringing out over the cold land. He and Miller Marish were felling one of the trees for firewood.

Kestrel returned to the women by the wagon, where a fire was already burning. Mrs Chirish, rooting among the husks on the ground, picked up one kernel and after a short inspection declared,

'Sourgum. These are sourgum trees. We can eat this.'

Branco Such had already tried.

'Eat them? They're vile! I shouldn't be surprised if they were poisonous!'

'You have to boil them first, don't you? Strip off the husks and boil the kernels. That's how you get the gum.'

'The gum is edible?' said Hanno.

'Certainly it is. A rare treat, too.'

So Hanno set the children to gathering the husks and shelling them, while the biggest cook-pot was half filled with water and put on the fire to boil. The Mimilith boys spotted that here and there in the bare branches of the trees were other husky nuts that had not yet fallen, so they raced each other up the knobbly trunks to pull them down.

'Be careful, boys! Make sure the branches can take your weight!'

'Stand back! She's coming down!'

Tanner Amos's warning cry was followed by a long rending crash, as the tree he had been felling toppled at last. He and Miller Marish and Mumpo then set to work with axes and cleavers to cut up the branches into cord-wood.

Mrs Chirish sat over the pot and stirred the sourgum kernels as the water seethed. Seldom Erth unharnessed the horses and let them join the cows, grazing the sparse wiry grass. A group of women found places round the fire where they could lay out their blankets and their needles and thread, and get on with the making of bed-rolls against the coming cold weather.

Bowman stood apart, looking towards the group of sewing women, telling himself it was better for all of them if he kept his distance from her. The Johdila

Sirharasi of Gang, once a princess, now plain Sisi, sat beside Lunki, the stout woman who had been her servant, and who still, despite the changes, insisted on serving her. Sisi held her back straight, her head bent over her work, and did not speak. Every day Bowman expected her to fail under the hardships of the march, but she proved him wrong. She bore more than her share of the tasks, ate less than her share of the food, and never complained. Bowman reflected on what Mumpo had said, that he seemed to be avoiding her. That was not right.

He crossed over to the women by the fire. For a few moments, as if warming himself by the fire, he stood near Lunki and her mistress. Sisi was stitching the heavy blankets with small tight stitches, working with care and concentration. He could see from the groove the needle made in her fingertip how hard she had to push to drive the point through the stiff fabric. He could also see the smooth curve of her neck, and the rise and fall of her breast as she breathed.

'That's good work,' he said. 'That'll keep out the cold.'

She looked up, her eyes grave, questioning.

'The tailor taught me,' she said. 'I'm doing my best.'

'Hard on the fingers.'

'Is it?' She looked at her needle-finger as if unaware of the pressure she was putting on her soft skin. 'Oh, that doesn't matter.'

Bowman heard the clatter of falling nuts, and looking up saw that Pinto had joined the Mimilith boys in the sourgum trees. They had already stripped the lower branches of nuts, and were now climbing higher, each in an adjoining tree. He could think of nothing more to say to Sisi, who sat, head bent, steadily sewing, so he moved away once more. As he passed the wagon, Mist the grey cat uncurled himself from his bed on the tent-cloths, and jumped down to rub against his legs.

'Well, boy,' he said. 'Are we nearly there?'

'No, my Mist. First we must reach the mountains.'

The cat did not speak aloud, nor did Bowman answer him aloud. But they understood each other well. The cat asked this question every day, and every day received the same answer. There were never any mountains to be seen, so Mist had come to believe that Bowman chose to conceal their true destination. Mist knew that Bowman had great powers, greater even than his former master, Dogface the hermit, who had been able to fly. If the boy had such powers, he could not possibly be leading all these people with so much effort for so long, without knowing where he was going. Therefore their destination was a secret. So reasoned the cat, clever but not wise.

'And on the other side of the mountains, your homeland.'

'Yes. We believe so.'

'It must be something very wonderful, this homeland.'

'We shall see.'

'Do the cats there know how to fly?'

'I don't know, Mist. I don't know that there are any cats there. But if there are, I doubt if they can fly.'

'I shall teach them.'

Bowman smiled and stroked the cat's head. This annoyed Mist. It had always been his heart's dream to fly, and just once he had made a jump that was so immense that it must have been flying. He had told the boy, and the boy had said he believed him, but the look in his eyes had shown that this was no more than a polite pretence.

'You don't believe me?'

'If you say you flew, Mist, then I believe you.'

'Well, I did fly.'

The truth was, he couldn't be entirely sure. The time he had flown, it had only been a short distance. A short flight is very like a long jump.

'Take care, Pinto!'

This was Hanno, calling out in warning. Pinto had seen a plump husk on a very high branch, and she reckoned she was light enough to reach it without danger. Looking across to the neighbouring tree, she saw that Mo Mimilith was also climbing, and he saw her. At once, instinctively competitive, they began to race each other.

Mo Mimilith was three years older than Pinto, and much heavier. At first his greater strength enabled him to outclimb her. But then he felt the branches bending beneath him, and realised he was at his limit. Pinto kept on climbing, her skinny little body easily supported by the upper branches; and so was the only one to reach to the very top of the tree.

She looked down and saw the wagon, with the horses among the cows, snuffling out what coarse grazing they could find. She saw the huddle round the fire, where the sourgum was being boiled, and she smelled its strange sharp-sweet smell. She saw her mother, seated on the ground with her father beside her, holding her hands and stroking them, as he so often did. Then she looked across and saw Mo Mimilith on his way down his tree.

I've won! she thought, exulting. I'm the highest one of all!

Only now, turning and looking up and ahead, did she think to take advantage of her high vantage point. There were the rolling hills, receding into the distance. But beyond them, far off, she could clearly discern through hazy low cloud a range of jagged white-capped peaks.

'Mountains!' she cried. 'I can see mountains!'

No one else would be able to climb so high. She must be the eyes for all. She looked and looked, and memorised.

Some way off, the rolling land levelled out and became rocky and craggy: it seemed to be a huge desert of cracked and shivered land, a rubble of boulders and fissures. On the far side of this broken plain, where the cloud lay low over the land, there was a belt of dark forest running from side to side of the visible world. Within this forest gleamed a river; and beyond the river towered the mountains. They rose through the cloud, to rear their bare-toothed peaks all along the white horizon.

Bowman called up to her.

'Can you really see the mountains?'

'Yes! Far, far away!'

People were gathering below, staring up at her.

'Be careful!' That was her father, who could see how the treetop swayed under her weight.

She came scrambling down, a little too fast, showing off, and grazed one arm. She pretended not to notice. The marchers gathered round her, eager to hear what she had seen.

'There's a river,' she told them. 'And a forest. But before that, empty land, for miles and miles, all full of cracks.'

'Cracks? What kind of cracks?'

'Like cracks in dried mud. Only much bigger.'

'Did you see any people? Any houses? There must be people living somewhere.'

'No. I didn't see anyone.'

'How far to the mountains?' asked the teacher, Silman Pillish.

'Miles and miles. Days and days.'

'Days and days!'

'And how far beyond the mountains?'

This question was addressed to Ira Hath. She was the prophetess, the one who knew the way to the homeland; though, as she told them again and again, she would only know it when at last it lay before her. She had seen it in a dream. They would find it on the other side of mountains, at the end of a path rising between steep slopes of land. It would be snowing. Ahead, the sun would be setting. Red sky, falling snow: and framed in the V of the hills, a land where two rivers ran to a distant sea.

'I'll know it when I see it,' she said. 'First we must get there.'

'It's just beyond the mountains,' the people told each other. 'The homeland!'

Even though the mountains Pinto had seen were so far away, this news gave everyone heart. They felt the end of their journey had been sighted. Their task now was to survive the getting there.

While Hanno Hath questioned Pinto more closely about what she had seen, Kestrel went up to Bowman.

'It's only mountains,' she said, very low. 'We don't know the homeland's on the other side. There might be a desert on the other side, or a swamp, and then more mountains, before we get to the sea.'

'There might.'

'So there's nothing to get so excited about.'

'No,' said Bowman. 'But people need hope.'

'I don't. I don't want hope. I want what's real. I won't believe we're getting to the homeland until I see it.'

'You don't really want to get to the homeland at all, do you, Kess?'

'Of course I do.' Kestrel was irritated that Bowman could think this of her. 'I don't want to be wandering about for ever, always tired and hungry. Why would I want that?'

'I don't know. I just feel that you're frightened of the homeland.'

'Oh, you feel. You're always feeling. Why would I be frightened of the homeland? It's the place where we all sit about being happy for the rest of our lives, isn't it?'

Too angry to wait for his reply, she took herself off to the far side of the trees, where Mumpo and Tanner Amos were chopping wood. For a few moments, as she listened to the *dock, dock, dock* of the axe, she thought how maddening her brother could be, with his assumption that he knew her better than she knew herself. Then as she calmed down she realised he was right. She was afraid of getting to the homeland; and not only because of what it meant for ma. There was something else.

She tried to make out the shape of her fear. She could imagine the journey ahead, but when she tried to imagine the end of the journey, all she saw was a blank. It was like a book without the last few pages. All at once there was nothing. That was what she was afraid of: the nothing. But nor did she want the journey to go on for ever.

What is it I want? she thought, shivering. What's wrong with me?

Tanner Amos and Mumpo between them filled the bed of the wagon with firewood. And now Mrs Chirish's sourgum was beginning to set. She dipped a spoon in the sticky froth and drew out a scoop of the amber-coloured gum, and waved it back and forth until it cooled. Then she nibbled at it.

'There it is,' she pronounced. 'Fetch some dishes.'

All the people round the fire had a taste. Some liked it and some didn't. It was odd, both sweet and sour at the same time, and it got stuck in the teeth; but it was edible, no question about it.

Guided by Mrs Chirish, they spread the gum over all the tin dishes they had, and let it cool. It hardened quickly in the cold air. Then when it was hard, they banged the underside of the tin plates with spoons, and the gum cracked off in clear amber fragments. The fragments were then packed in barrels, with layers of flattened husks between them to stop them sticking to each other. By the time they had done, they had filled four barrels, and there were enough crumbs left for everyone to have a snack.

Hanno was quietly grateful to Mrs Chirish. Their supplies of food were running very low. Now he calculated they could survive on a barrel of sourgum a day, which gave them four days to find the next supply of food. Water was another matter. He checked the level in the big water barrel, and made another simple calculation. The people must drink; the horses and cattle too. No doubt they would find a stream soon. But just in case, it would be wise to save all they could.

'From now until we find water,' he ordered, 'the ration will be two cups a day each. And no washing.'

'No washing!' exclaimed Lunki. 'How is my precious one to keep clean?'

'It won't be for long,' said Sisi. 'We'll find water soon.'

Hanno made his rounds, speaking softly to Creoth about the cows, and to Seldom Erth about the horses, saying nothing new, giving no instructions they would not have carried out for themselves, but showing a care for each person on the march. This was the nature of his leadership: not the shouting of orders, but the letting himself be seen as the link between all of them, the one to whom they all turned their eyes, so that as they went on their way, they went together.

Now he gave the signal to resume the march. The group round the fire put out the flames, stamping out the embers and rescuing the unburned faggots to be used again. Others bent down to lace up boots that had been loosened to ease their weary feet. Bowman moved to the front of the column as it formed, and took up his place as the lead watchman, his eyes alert for danger. So it was he who found the body.

It was not the first body they had passed on their long march. In these lawless times, the robber bands that attacked travellers on lonely roads often left their victims dead or dying; when what knives and clubs had begun was finished by the night cold. The Manth people could do no more than pause on their way, and cover the sad remains with stones, as an act of respect.

This was the body of an old man, lying face down on

the ground, his hands raised as if to cover or protect his face. Bowman knelt down by his side, and gently eased the body over, to satisfy himself that there was no hope of saving him; though the utter stillness of the body told him that life was long gone. The hands remained clutched to the dead face, concealing the features. Bowman let his sensitive probing mind reach gently into that lifeless skull, and as he did so he felt for an instant that something was moving within it; then the moment passed, and all was still. He took hold of the dead man's hands, and drew them away from his face.

The eyes were open, and unseeing. The old cheeks grizzled, unshaven. The dry lips apart, as if calling. But most shocking of all, the skin of his face, from brow to chin, was lacerated: scratched and torn into a hideous wreck, the blood dried black in the dead white skin.

Mumpo now joined him, and stood looking down at the dead man in silence.

'What would do that to him?' said Bowman.

'He did it to himself. Look at his fingernails.'

Mumpo had noticed what Bowman had overlooked: the dead man's fingernails were black with dried blood. For some terrible reason, as he was dying he had torn at his own face.

The rest of the marchers were approaching. Creoth came up to them, and looked.

'Oh, the wretched man!'

'Let's cover him,' said Bowman. 'No need for the others to see.'

He scraped up handfuls of stony earth and began to sprinkle it over the corpse. Mumpo and Creoth did the same. Bowman hurried to cover up the torn face. He thought again as he let the earth drop over that dead open mouth that something moved: a brief flurry in the air that shivered the falling dust. He thought he heard a faint whine pass close by his head, as of some small flying insect. But then the wagon was rolling near, and with it his father.

'Poor fellow,' said Hanno Hath, kneeling down to help with the roadside burial.

When the body was entirely covered, a dusty mound that would not long resist the wind and the rain, the Manth people stood round the stranger and Hanno Hath rose to his feet to speak the customary funeral words.

'We who are left behind watch you on your way.'

He fell silent for a few moments. No one spoke or moved. Then he went on with the old words in his quiet clear voice.

'The long prison of the years unlocks its iron door. Go free now, into the beautiful land. Forgive us, who suffer in this clouded world. Guide us and wait for us, as we wait for you. We will meet again.'

He bowed his head, and they all repeated,

'We will meet again.'

They could do no more. Hanno gave Bowman a quick sad smile, and turned to his wife. Bowman caught the faint whine he had heard before, and the quick shimmer in the air. He saw his father give a small start, and raise one hand to his throat. Bowman suddenly felt the close presence of danger.

'What is it, pa?'

'Nothing. Some little stinging insect. Nothing to worry about.'

He turned away, a little too quickly.

'Pa, look at me.'

Hanno turned back, frowning with annoyance.

'I'm alright, I tell you. We have to get moving. We've wasted enough time already.'

For the last time Bowman looked down at the long mound by the roadside, and wondered fearfully what would make a man tear at his own face. But now the column was reforming, and it was time to go.

2

Drunkenness

While the wagon had been stationary, Seldom Erth had loosened the horses' harness, and Mrs Chirish had decided to wrap the cook-pots in an extra layer of cloth, afraid that the shaking of the wagon-bed would shatter them. The cows had drifted off in search of grass. Many of the people had sat down.

Now that it was time to move off again, Hanno Hath started to shout at them.

'You! Cowman! If you can't control your animals we'll have them for dinner!'

Creoth was speechless with surprise. Hanno never spoke like that.

'You! Old man! Did I say you could unharness the horses?'

Ira Hath, aware that something was wrong, tried to take him aside.

'Hanno –'

'Not now, woman. Come along, everybody! We've wasted enough time!'

Kestrel heard him, and reached out for Bowman with her mind.

What's wrong with pa?

I'm not sure. Something bad's happened to him. I need to feel him.

Come on. I'll help you.

Kestrel knew what her brother meant when he said he wanted to 'feel' their father: he wanted to enter Hanno's mind. For that he needed close physical contact, preferably brow to brow. But Hanno was moving fast, never staying in one place for long. The twins didn't want to alarm everyone by making a direct attack on their father.

'Pa,' said Kestrel. 'Before we set out again, let's have a wish huddle.'

'No time,' said Hanno.

'Please. It won't take a moment.'

'Ma! Pinto!' called Bowman. 'Wish huddle!'

Hanno turned on them, eyes blazing with anger.

'I am the head of this family! You heard me say we have no time! How dare you disobey me!'

Pinto had come running.

'But I'd like a wish huddle, pa –'

Smack! He struck Pinto across the face with the flat of his hand.

'You will do as I say!'

The blow hurt. Pinto bit her lip to stop herself crying, not understanding how her gentle father could hit her so hard.

'I'm sorry, pa.'

Hold him! Don't let him move!

Bowman and Kestrel hurled themselves forward in the same moment. Bowman got his arms round his father's chest, pinning his arms to his side, while Kestrel wrapped herself round his legs. Hanno struggled, and fell to the ground, but Bowman did not let go. He pressed his head to his father's head, and summoned all his power to force his way into his father's mind. He found it at once, felt its shape without seeing it: it was like a grub, curled up tight, with a thick and slimy skin. He tried to grasp it, but it was slippery, and it wriggled out of his grip. It was strong, and growing stronger, feeding on its host that was his father.

Bowman set about flooding his own mind into his father's mind, filling him up, leaving the grub no room to breathe. None of this was apparent to the others, who saw only that Bowman and Kestrel had fallen to the ground with their father in their arms, and were holding onto him. They crowded round, not sure what to do.

'Leave them!' said Ira.

Bowman found his father's brow at last, and pressed his own brow against it, and the force pulsed from him in waves.

Out! Out! Out!

Suddenly he felt all resistance cease. His father's body gave a juddering jerk, and went limp. The creature was gone.

Hanno Hath let his head fall. Bowman released his hold. He took his father's face and turned it, so he could see it. It was mottled with pink blotches, and beaded in sweat. Bowman gathered up his loose sleeve and wiped his father's brow. Kestrel let go of his legs, and moved to his other side, resting his head on her lap. Ira sat down close by, as did Pinto. Hanno's eyes opened. He looked dazed.

'Are you alright now, pa?' asked Pinto.

'Yes, darling.'

Bowman stood up, to reassure the anxious crowd.

'He's alright. Nothing serious.'

As he spoke, he looked round all the watching faces, searching for signs of any others who had been attacked in the same way. But everyone seemed as they had been before.

Hanno got up off the ground, shaking his head and smiling.

'Well, well, well,' he said. 'I don't know what that was all about.' His eyes fell on Pinto, whose cheek still bore the red mark of his blow. 'Did I hit you?'

'Yes, pa.'

'I didn't mean to, my darling. It wasn't me that did that. I'd never hurt you.'

'I know, pa.'

Hanno smiled at the staring faces all round.

'I'm not as strong as I thought I was.'

'What was it?' they asked him. 'What happened to you?'

'I seem to have been stung by some kind of poisonous insect. There may be more of these insects in the air around us, and they may sting you.'

The people began to look nervously about them.

'They're too small to see. Even the sting is tiny. You hardly feel it. It's like an itch.' He touched his throat.

'What does it do, Hanno? Will it harm us?'

'It doesn't exactly do any harm. What it does is bring on a kind of drunkenness. I don't know how else to explain it.'

'Drunkenness!'

The younger men laughed, and nudged each other. Rollo Shim waved one arm in the air and called out,

'Here I am! Sting me!'

'It's not pleasant,' warned Hanno gravely. 'Please, if you think you've been stung, go to my son Bowman. He has a way of dealing with it.'

A sudden gust of icy wind reminded them all that this was no time of year to stay still, for those with no sheltering homes. So the marchers prepared to set off once more. Before taking up their places in the column, Hanno and Bowman exchanged a few brief words alone.

'I think whatever it was came out of the dead man,' said Bowman.

'You saved me, Bo. I do know that.'

'It made you shout, and give orders. Not like you at all.'

'No. I'm happiest in my own small quiet world, aren't I? With my family and my books. I don't want to make people fear me. I'm only leading our people now because I believe in Ira's gift. Nobody is obliged to follow me.'

Bowman could hear the puzzled note in his father's voice, and realised that he was not as sure as he wanted to make out.

'They follow you because they respect you.'

'All I mean to say, Bo, is I don't set myself up as wiser or more important than others. Who am I, to tell them what to do?'

'You're our leader, pa.'

Hanno gave him an odd smile. Bowman reached gently into his father's mind, and was surprised by what he found there. He heard a chatter of thought-voices saying, *What an absurdity you are! Go back to your library,*

*librarian! Nobody pays you any attention. Speak more
softly or people will laugh.* But deeper than these sounds,
like a steady beat below the cackle of interference, he
caught another voice, that whispered, *I do know more, I
am wiser, they would do well to follow me.*

What is this fly that came from a dead man's mouth?
Bowman asked himself. What does it do to us? How can it
reach such deep and hidden passions?

He remembered then how he too, long ago, had been
touched in just such a way. In the halls of the Morah,
when he had looked into those eyes that were the eyes of
a multitude, he had felt the stirring of wild desires within
himself, and he had been changed. Was this stinging fly a
creature of the Morah?

He felt a sudden lurch of fear.

I'm not ten years old any more. I have powers of my own.

The Morah comes from us, he told himself. The Morah
is ourselves. This stinging fly has no poison; unless it takes
poison to discover to ourselves our own hidden passions.

This last thought was almost the most frightening
of them all. What if all of us are quite different inside?
What if some tiny insect, with a momentary scratch, can
transform us into this alien self? My gentle father becomes
a shouting dictator. And I, I become a killer –

He shook his head. Better not follow that path. Whether
the insects came from the Morah or not, he was the only
one who could protect his people from their poison, and
that was his task. That was all he needed to know.

As the march was resumed, Hanno Hath's strange
drunkenness was on everyone's mind. The people looked
out for the flies, slapped their own arms and faces every

time they imagined something had settled on them, and watched each other for evidence of strange behaviour. Mrs Chirish complained that the pace of the march was too rapid, saying, 'It makes my legs jabber.' Was that a sign of drunkenness? Creoth answered her, 'If the cows can keep up, madam, so can you.' That seemed unnecessarily harsh, coming from the kindly Creoth, the very man who had helped to carry Mrs Chirish on the slave march. Had he been stung by the invisible flies? Then young Ashar Warmish started to giggle, and couldn't stop; but it turned out that she and her friend Red Mimilith had been making moonish faces at the Shim brothers, and it was this that made her laugh.

Little Fin Marish, who was eight years old, took advantage of the general excitement to run ahead to the front of the column to march by Mumpo's side. She adored Mumpo, as did all the smaller girls, because he was tall and strong and slow in his speech, and believed everything you ever said to him.

'Mumpo,' she said, 'did you know you talk in your sleep?'

'No,' said Mumpo. 'What do I say?'

'You say, "Pooa pooa Pinto! Hubba hubba Fin!"'

'Do I? Do I say that? I wonder why.'

'Because you hate Pinto,' said Fin, 'and you love me.'

Miller Marish came looking for Fin, and scolded her sharply for leaving her place in the column. Fin responded by pointing an accusing finger at him, and crying out in a shrill high voice,

'My papa's become a horrid monster! I think the flies have stung him!'

The effect of so many false alarms was that quite

quickly they all became tired of the matter, and stopped believing the young people with their games. After the first hour on the resumed march they had forgotten that they were to watch out for each other's behaviour. No one else had been stung, and their spirits were high. The going was easier than it had been for some time, because they were making their way down a gentle slope; and now that the mountains had been sighted, there was a general feeling that the long trek would one day have an end after all.

So the wagon wheels crunched on over the stony ground, and the horses clop-clopped along, and each of the marchers fell into their own private dream of the life they would make for themselves when at last they reached the homeland. Creoth, feeling he had been a little sudden with Mrs Chirish, chose to tell her of the farm he planned to establish.

'Not a great deal of land. I'm not as young as I was. Just a meadow or two for the cattle to graze, with the river on one side, and the sea on the other. I shall have a little house for myself, just the one room, and a nice shady milking parlour that looks out to sea. To the east, if possible. Then I shall watch the sun rise during morning milking. Beard of my ancestors! There's a life to envy, eh, ma'am? The smell of fresh milk, and the light of the rising sun.'

'You may sit and shiver in your shed, sir. I shall be in my bed.'

'In your bed, eh?'

'My bed will be such a bed! Up on each side, and down in the middle, and fluffy as a nest! I shall lie in my nest like an egg, and my poor legs will never ache again.'

'Just lie there, will you, ma'am? And do nothing all the long day?'

'I might get up and eat a little this and that around noon, and stand on the porch and nod to my neighbours, and wish them good day. Then it's back to my bed.'

Silman Pillish, stumping along beside the wagon, told Seldom Erth about the school he would set up in the homeland. Seldom Erth showed no signs of wanting to hear this, but nor did he object, and this was permission enough for Pillish.

'In my school, the lessons will be a service to the children, not a burden. They'll come to me, you see, and tell me what they wish to learn – for example, a song to sing together – you never forget the songs you learn as a child, don't you agree?'

'I wouldn't know,' said Seldom Erth.

'I'll say, Ah, I can help you there! Then I'll teach them a song – perhaps "The Hen and her Chicks".'

He sang a line of the song in an unexpectedly sweet voice.

'Where have you gone, little chicks, little chicks? Oh! oh! and oh!'

These last exclamations were, it seemed, the lost chicks reappearing from behind Pillish.

'So you see, they'll come willingly to school. Yes, our homeland school will be a happy place. They'll love their teacher too, don't you think?'

'I wouldn't know,' said Seldom Erth.

Mumpo strode along at the head of the marchers, dreaming no dream of the homeland. The little girls had left him, and he must be alert, watching out for danger;

and anyway, he had no dream any more. He glanced back down the line, and let his eyes rest for a moment on Kestrel, who was walking with Sisi. For as long as he could remember he had loved Kestrel. He knew every line of that agile high-boned face, every mood of those restless eyes. But Kestrel did not love him. He accepted this, feeling it to be natural and fitting. Who was he, that Kestrel should love him? But without her, what was left? It was as if a hole had been cut out of the future. So he went on his way in a kind of puzzlement, not grieving, but without any real hope of happiness to come.

Kestrel was unaware that Mumpo had looked back and watched her. She was concerned about Sisi.

'You should be eating more,' she told her. 'We have a long way to go.'

'There isn't much food left,' said Sisi quietly. 'Let the children have it.'

'Then you'll get too weak to walk, and we'll have to carry you in the wagon. That just makes more work for the horses.'

'You can leave me behind.'

'Oh, Sisi. We'd never leave you.'

'I don't see why not. I'm not Manth, like you. I'm not any use to anyone. I'm not even – you know.'

'Not beautiful?'

'Not beautiful. Not a princess. Nothing.'

'You think people who aren't beautiful princesses are nothing?'

'You know what I mean.'

'Everyone admires you, Sisi.'

'Not everyone.'

Kestrel didn't pretend not to understand her.

'Bowman too?'

'Has he said so to you?'

'I know what my brother feels. He came and talked to you, didn't he?'

'I was sewing. He said I was doing good work.'

'There you are, then.'

'Oh, Kess, please! Don't you start pitying me too.'

It was a flash of the old Sisi. Kestrel took her arm affectionately.

'I like you better when you're cross.'

'No you don't.'

But she was smiling.

'Come on, Sisi, admit it. You're not as good and humble as you make out.'

'Yes, I am. I'm the simplest, humblest person in the world.' She smiled as she spoke, making Kestrel smile too. 'I'm the princess of simplicity. I'm grandly, beautifully, proudly, simple. I'm magnificently humble.'

She started to laugh, and couldn't go on. Lunki looked round approvingly.

'There, my pet. It does my heart good to hear you enjoying yourself.'

'You're very unkind, Kess,' said Sisi when she had calmed down. 'You make me say things.'

'So you'll stop starving yourself, will you?'

'I'll have what the others have.'

'Good. That's all I ask.'

'But Kess, I truly don't mind if I live or die. I'm not saying it to show off. Since I've been with your people, I've started to see everything so differently. It makes me ashamed of how I've been. You Manth people, you have such strong family feeling, and you're so considerate to each other. You're so serious, and thoughtful, and most of all, good. Such quiet, good people.'

'I think you're talking about one person.'

'Maybe I am.'

'He has his faults too.'

'Sometimes I think he's too sad, and keeps himself too much alone. But I don't see any faults.'

'Ask him. He'll tell you.'

'Oh, I wouldn't think of it!'

What Sisi didn't tell her friend was that secretly she believed she could make Bowman happy. But even as this thought was passing through her mind, she remembered that she was no longer beautiful, and so there was no reason why he should choose her.

'I keep forgetting. Everything's different now.'

She reached up as she did a hundred times a day, and touched the scars on her cheeks.

By now, everyone had forgotten the fly that had stung Hanno Hath. The marchers were in better cheer than they had been for days. Some even sang as they marched, a song of the road that went back to the earliest days, when the Manth people had been a wandering tribe. Kestrel joined her mother and father, and tried once again to persuade her mother to ride in the wagon, for at least part of the way. But Ira Hath insisted on walking with the rest.

'We'll be stopping at sundown. I can last till then.'

Bowman and Mumpo, far ahead, kept watch over the bleak land. Once Bowman looked back, and saw Kestrel walking close by his mother, holding her hand. He saw

Sisi too, walking steadily beside the wagon, her scarred face to the cold wind, her lustrous amber eyes gazing ahead at nothing.

Sisi never heard the faint whine in the air behind her. When there came a tingling itch at her throat, she reached up one hand to scratch it, and thought no more about it. For a little while afterwards there was a tender spot at the base of her neck, in the soft hollow between the collar bones.

3

Sisi's kiss

The cracks were becoming more frequent, and wider. They ran in random zigzag patterns all over the land, as if the ground had been baked too long in some distant summer and had shivered like a badly-glazed plate. At first the cracks were only inches wide, and inches deep; but as the column of the Manth people marched on north, the cracks grew in size, until they were too wide to step over, and they had to find a way between them.

There was no made road, but the path taken by other travellers before them was easy enough to see. Here the tough grasses had been beaten down by the tread of men and beasts, forming a winding route that made its way through the cracked land. After a while the path began to descend, and so entered a natural groove in the plain, which seemed to be the bed of some long-ago dried-up stream. This path, no more than a dozen yards wide at the base, snaked its way here and there between the sudden fissures, descending all the time. The downward gradient was barely noticeable, but little by little the slopes rose up on either side, until they were higher than the travellers' heads.

Hanno Hath didn't like this stream-bed of a road. He sent scouts up the side slopes to look for some other route, Mumpo to the west and Tanner Amos to the east. The surface of the sloping sides was crumbling and littered with loose fragments of stone, which made them hard to scramble up. Every step kicked free a few of the loose stones, which skittered down in miniature avalanches, picking up smaller stones as they went.

'What do you see, Mumpo? Is there another way?'

'No,' Mumpo called back. 'The cracks are too wide.'

From his viewpoint on the west slope, Mumpo could see that the land-cracks had increased and widened and deepened in every direction. The dried-up riverbed was the only way through.

By mid-afternoon, when they stopped to rest again, the road had cut deeper still into the land, and was now running down a steep-sided valley. Mumpo and Tanner descended the slopes, picking their way with care, then taking it at a run, racing the rolling rocks to the bottom.

'Still nothing?'

'Just cracks, everywhere.'

Hanno Hath turned to his son. 'Are we near water, Bo?'

Bowman shook his head. Sometimes he could sense the presence of springs or streams, but right now he felt nothing.

'I can't smell anything.'

'My dear?'

This was to Ira Hath, who had sat down and was composing herself on the ground, her back leaning against a wagon wheel. She closed her eyes. Several times a day she repeated this process, in order to make sure that they were going the right way. It was a little like sensing the direction of the wind, only it wasn't wind she felt on her upraised face, but warmth. The sensation was faint, but clear. It told her the way to the homeland. There was another part to the feeling, which was harder to describe: a sense of gathering hush, the prelude to a storm. Ira never spoke to the others of how much she feared this coming time. They could travel no faster than they were doing. There was no point in spreading panic. To herself and to Hanno, she called it the rising wind: every day, a little more every day, the wind was rising. They must seek shelter, they must reach the safety of the homeland, before the storm broke; or the coming wind would carry them away.

Her husband squatted down before her, and took her hands in his.

'Are we getting closer?' he asked.

'Yes. Closer.'

'And you?'

'I'll live to see the homeland. Haven't I said so?'

He gave her the last of the bread that he'd saved from his own ration, together with a cup of milk. She ate a little and drank a little for his sake, but she wasn't hungry.

'You're getting thin.' He pretended to be cross. 'You must eat what you're given.'

She smiled and watched his anxious face and thought what a good man he was.

'We each have our part to play, Hannoka. Then it will be time for us to go.'

'Not yet,' he said, like an order. 'Not yet.'

'No. Not yet.'

While the marchers rested, Sisi became more and more agitated.

'Sit, my pet,' said Lunki. 'We have two more hours of walking before sundown. Take the ache off your feet.'

'Lie down, I should,' said Scooch. 'Get your feet higher than your head. That's the trick.'

'Higher than your head?' Lunki was mystified.

Little Scooch lay on his back on the stony ground and supported his heels on the wagon's step-board.

'Like this. It makes all the heaviness drop off the feet.'

Lunki lay down beside him, with her heels on the step-board alongside his.

'Yes!' she cried, amazed at the sensation. 'I can feel the heaviness dropping off!'

She turned to urge Sisi to follow her example, but her mistress was gone. She was some way off, pacing round and round in restless circles.

'What's the matter with her? Why can't she settle?'

'Too thin,' said Scooch.

'Do you think so?'

'No doubt about it. A body needs padding, or the nerves stick out.'

'My poor baby! Her nerves do stick out, you're right. She feels things too much.'

What Sisi was feeling was a sudden and insistent need to go to Bowman, and talk to him, and – and she hardly knew what, except that it would end in humiliation. Her pride held her in check, but the longing was becoming more powerful all the time.

Bowman was some way off, talking quietly with Kestrel. He was as agitated as Sisi, but for very different reasons.

'I want it to be over,' he said. 'I want them to come for me, and for it to be over. Why don't they come? Every hour that passes, I feel it, the wind is rising. They must come soon.'

'They'll come for you when they need you,' said Kestrel. 'I don't want you to go before you have to.'

Kestrel knew her brother believed it was his destiny to join the Singer people, but she didn't understand how they could be parted.

We go together, she thought. *We always go together.*

Bowman heard her thought.

'I don't want to go. But I can't go on like this. You don't know what it's like.'

'I feel it, a little.'

She could feel the turmoil in him, his spirit a field of endless battle. Bowman was so open, he could resist nothing, he was like the sky, he absorbed all things. The nomad dreams of the Manth people, the fierce power of the Morah, the sweet wordless songs of Sirene, all swept the horizons of his mind, chasing each other like wind-borne clouds.

'I don't want to leave you,' he said. 'But I must be with them, when the time comes.'

'And after?'

'There is no after. Not for me.'

'Am I to go on without you?'

Don't ask. Forgive me.

As Kestrel received these unspoken words, she felt a

movement against her skin, beneath the fabric of her shirt. It was the silver pendant she wore on a string round her neck, that had once been the voice of the wind singer. She had worn it so long she had almost forgotten it was there. Now it stirred and pressed on her chest, and felt warm, as if it was part of her. At the same time, as she sensed its familiar shape and weight, a door opened in her mind, a door she had not known existed. Through the doorway she saw herself and Bowman together, just as they were now: but a little further away, in a time she knew had not yet taken place, she saw her brother without her, lost and heart-broken, calling her name.

He seemed so real, and so lonely, that she called out to him with her mind.

I'll never leave you. Even if I seem to be gone, I won't be gone. I'll always be with you.

Bowman heard her and was astonished.

'What do you mean, Kess? Why do you say this?'

'These things that are coming,' she said aloud, speaking slowly, finding the thoughts only as she formed the words, 'these things the prophet has written, the time of cruelty, the wind on fire, these things are greater than us.'

'Oh, yes. Far greater.'

'We aren't the makers and the un-makers of the world.'

'No.'

'Our task is only to play our small part, for our brief moment, in what must happen.'

'Yes.'

'Then we should neither hope nor fear. We must wait for the call, and then do what we must.'

'Yes.'

She stroked his cheek lightly, tenderly.

'It'll come soon enough, brother. Don't wish it any sooner.'

Sisi could control herself no longer. She must be with Bowman, whatever the consequence. Holding her head high, and looking before her with the distant imperious gaze she had so often used when she had been a princess, she stalked past the other marchers to where Bowman and Kestrel stood. Sisi knew that what she was about to do would shame her for the rest of her life, but the desire was too strong to be resisted. She would do it, and let the future take care of itself.

As she approached she saw both Bowman and Kestrel staring at her in surprise. Do I look so different? she thought to herself. Is it written on my face?

'Leave us, Kestrel,' she said. 'I want to talk to Bowman alone.'

'Yes, of course,' said Kestrel wonderingly. Bowman signalled her with his eyes, calling, *Don't leave me.* But Kestrel was already on her way.

He was alone with Sisi. Her eyes were fixed on him so intently that he felt himself blush.

'We'll be moving on any minute,' he said. 'We should rejoin the others.'

'Not yet,' said Sisi.

To his astonishment, she laid one hand lightly on his arm. She had not been this bold since they had left the Mastery.

'I know you can't love me,' she said, 'since I've lost my beauty. But I can love you.'

'Sisi, you mustn't speak like this.'

'Why not? All I have to lose is my pride. I'm tired of my pride.'

'You don't understand. Whether you love me, or I love you, it makes no difference. In a little while someone will come for me, and I'll leave with him, and you'll never see me again.'

'Oh, in a little while. Who cares about that? Here you are, and here am I.'

She stroked his arm.

'I don't know what I can do for you, Sisi.'

'I do.'

She made him meet her eyes: made him become still.

'Just for now, just for a few moments, pretend you love me.'

'Please, Sisi, I think this is –'

'Touch my scars.'

He stared back at her, filled with confused feelings.

'Do my scars disgust you?'

'No.'

'Touch them.'

So he raised one hand and touched one fingertip to the livid stripe on her cheek. He felt the residue of scar tissue, and the softness of new skin where the scab had crumbled away. He did it out of pity for her, and because her will was strong.

'Now touch my lips.'

He felt her lips: so soft, and moist.

'What do you want from me, Sisi?'

'I want you to kiss me.'

The great amber eyes gazed at him unashamed. For the first time, Bowman stopped thinking about his own confusion, and attended to the change in her. Sisi would never make such a request, so directly. Something had happened to her.

'Kiss you?' He needed time. 'Why?'

'Because I love you.'

'We're not betrothed.'

'I don't care. Do you care?'

This was not Sisi speaking to him, he was sure of it. This was the passion fly within her. He needed closer contact, to reach into her mind.

'Close your eyes,' she was saying. 'Then you won't see the scars. The kiss will be just as sweet.'

He closed his eyes. He felt her come into his arms. He felt her lips reach up to his. As they kissed, he felt a shiver of delight go through his body, and for a fleeting moment he was aware that he'd never kissed before, not like this. There was a closeness to it that was both tender and eager. He felt her body press against his, and the feeling of her body was part of the kiss. He held her tight in his arms, and his hands felt the shape of her slender back, and his lips moved against hers, sharing secrets –

No! He jerked his mind free. He reached through the kiss, beyond the kiss, into her desire-possessed mind. As he pressed closer, she kissed him ever more passionately, ever more desperately, as if only in kissing him was she safe. Pushing, probing, burrowing into her, he found it at last, the creature curled within her. He seized it in a firm grip, and still holding Sisi in his arms, he dragged it, tore it, ripped it out of her. One last spasm of resistance, and it let go. He heard the whine of its wings as it flew away.

Sisi went limp in his arms. He held her weight, not wanting to cause alarm among the others. He looked towards them to see if any had been watching, and had witnessed the kiss. Everyone was up and preparing to continue the march. If they had seen, they were not showing it now.

Sisi awoke, in confusion.

'What happened?'

She remembered, and blushed a deep red.

'Oh!'

'It wasn't you,' said Bowman quickly. 'Something got into you. It made you do things.'

'The stinging insect?'

'Yes.'

'Did it make me drunk?'

'Yes. In a way.'

Sisi looked down, ashamed.

'It made me kiss you, didn't it?'

'Yes.'

'I'm sorry.'

'That's alright. It wasn't you.'

Now the horses were being harnessed to the wagon, and the people were moving to their places in the march.

'Did it get into you too?'

'No.'

'But you still kissed me.'

'I needed to hold you close. To get it out.'

'Of course. To get it out.'

There were several curious glances directed at them as they returned to the others, and Bowman realised they had been seen. He would have to explain.

'The stinging insect is still with us,' he said. 'I've just taken it out of Sisi.'

'My baby! Are you alright?'

'Yes, Lunki, I'm fine.'

'Be on your guard!'

'To your places,' called Hanno. 'Lookouts, to your posts. We have an hour of daylight yet.'

The march set off once more.

Bowman marched in the middle of the column, and listened for the return of that telltale whining buzz. He heard nothing, and none of his companions were acting strangely. As the immediate danger faded, the memory of Sisi's kiss returned, and troubled him. He told himself it had not been her who had kissed him, but the thing that had possessed her: but it had felt like her, like the most intimate part of her.

There came a patter of feet behind him, and turning, he saw Kestrel running up to join him. He blushed, and feeling the blush, told himself it was because he should have thought to reassure Kestrel about Sisi.

'She'll be alright,' he told her. 'I got it out of her.'

Kestrel looked at him curiously.

'Will it come back?'

'Yes, probably, but I can't tell where. I've never even seen it. It's as if it doesn't exist until it stings someone. And then it's like it's a part of them.'

'I saw how it made Sisi drunk.'

'I had to touch her. To get it out.'

'Yes, of course. You had to touch her.'

Neither of them called it a kiss. The word hung in the air between them, unspoken. There had never before been anything they hadn't been able to say. Bowman felt his sister's silence, and it made him miserable.

'Something strange happened –'

'Bandits!'

Mumpo's urgent cry from the ridge shattered the private moment. Bowman span round just as there came a rumbling sound ahead, and what seemed to be half the hillside came sliding down, to crash into the riverbed in a cloud of fragments and dust.

'Halt!' cried Hanno. 'To your weapons!'

Bowman and Kestrel ran back to the wagon. A second grinding roar, this time behind them: a second rock fall now cut off their retreat. They were boxed in.

'Mumpo! Tanner! Come down!'

The lookouts came scrambling down the slopes to join the rest of the marchers, who were frantically taking out swords, hay-forks, and lengths of firewood, with which to defend themselves.

'How many?'

'A dozen. Maybe more.'

Within moments they were able to count for themselves. A figure appeared on the west ridge, tall, lean, and seemingly faceless; to be joined by another, then by three more. They stood looking down in silence, silhouetted against the white winter sky. They wore many layers of clothing, of many different kinds, like refugees who scavenge where they can. The loose garments were cinched at the waist and above the elbows and knees with ties of fabric. Round the shoulders and neck, round the face and head, each one had wound a long scarf, so that only the eyes remained uncovered.

'Bandits, sure enough,' said Hanno.

More and more were showing themselves along the ridges that walled the Manth people in. Bowman counted thirteen on the west side, and another eight on the east. They seemed not to be armed.

'They don't have swords,' he said low to his father. 'I think we can match them.'

But even as he spoke, one of the masked men drew a cord from his belt, and stooping, picked up a stone from the ground.

'Sling shots!' cried Rollo Shim.

The bandit swung the cord in rapid circles over his head, hissing through the air, building up speed at its weighted end. Then with a flick of the hand, he released the stone. It shot down into the valley and hit one of Creoth's cows on the side of its head, with such force that the beast fell dead without a sound. The Manth people were struck with terror. Creoth cried out, and ran to the side of the lifeless animal.

'Cherub! My Cherub!'

All along the ridges the bandits could now be seen to be holding sling shots at the ready. They neither moved nor spoke. Their posture of readiness said all that was needed.

Hanno made a rapid calculation. The bandits were above them on both sides. The horses and cows could not scramble over the steep landslides. They must fight or give in. If they fought, they could inflict damage on the bandits, but many of his people would fall as the cow had fallen.

'Lay down your weapons,' he said to the marchers.

He called to the one who had used his sling shot to such great effect, who he presumed to be the leader.

'We are Manth people! We mean you no harm! What do you want from us?'

The bandits stared back in silence.

'Do you want our cows and our horses? We have nothing else.'

The bandit leader signed to two of his men. At once they jumped over the ridge, and pushing small rock-slides before them, came skidding down to the valley floor. The rest of the bandits raised their slings, to show their readiness to strike should their companions come under attack.

'Don't move!' Hanno called to his frightened people. 'Stay still, until we know what they want.'

The two scarfed bandits now came among them, eyes glittering, and scanned the motionless marchers. One of them pointed to Kestrel, then to Sarel Amos. His companion took both by the arms and roped their wrists.

Mumpo growled a deep growl of rage.

'Don't move, Mumpo!' hissed Hanno.

He saw, and understood that they would have to fight after all, whatever the cost: but he wanted to give his people their best chance. He looked round, to calculate how many of them could find cover beneath the wagon. Even so slight a movement of his head was enough to signal his intention to the keen-eyed bandit leader above, and his sling whirred. Bowman saw the stone leave the sling and hurtle towards his father. At once he reached out with his mind to shield him, and himself rocked under the stone's impact, sending it glancing harmlessly to one side. Its force shocked him. He had enough strength to deflect a single shot, but he knew that if all the bandits were to strike at once he would be helpless.

The bandit leader, surprised that he had missed, was already reloading his sling.

'Bo,' said Hanno, 'do we have a chance?'

'No. They'll kill us all.'

As he spoke, one of the bandits on the valley floor was roping Ashar Warmish. Her father Harman Warmish drew his knife.

'Harman! Don't!'

A snap, a crack, and Harman crumpled to the ground, his skull smashed. Bowman gasped aloud. It had happened too fast, he had caught the flick of the sling too late.

Now for the first time the bandit leader spoke, calling down into the valley in a harsh voice.

'Must we kill every man among you? We've done it before.'

Harman Warmish lay unmoving on the ground, the blood bubbling from his head. His wife sobbed, but did not move. The bandit holding young Ashar Warmish pulled her, now limp and unresisting, to join Kestrel and Sarel. After her they picked out Seer Such, and Red Mimilith, and Sisi: all the girls who were no longer children, but were not yet mothers; though Ashar was barely twelve years old.

Kestrel allowed herself to be roped and led aside, because she understood exactly what danger they were in, even before the killing of Ashar's father. Bowman was speaking to her.

Don't resist. Not yet.

Sisi too understood that she had no choice. When her turn came she brushed the bandit's hand away with contempt, and walked of her own free will, head held high, to join the shivering group. Lunki tried to go with her, but the scarfed bandit pushed her back.

When the six girls were all roped together in a chain, the bandits indicated that they were to climb the slope. Their mothers and fathers began to groan, so that Hanno had to command them.

'Don't move! Our duty is to live!'

It was a pitiful sight to watch, the manacled girls half-scrambling, half-pulled up the slope, dragged by the rope from above, slithering to their knees, kicking for a foothold on the loose scree. But then it was done, and the bandits on the eastern ridge were already loping away.

'Don't try to follow us!' called the bandit leader. 'We go into the labyrinth. You'll never find us, and you'll never find your way out again. We wish you no harm. Take this warning, and go on your way.'

He gave a sign, and the roped girls were led away. Mumpo watched, groaning under his breath, his whole body shaking with controlled rage.

'I wish you harm!' he said.

'Don't, Mumpo!' said Hanno. 'You're no use to us dead.'

Bowman called silently to Kestrel.

I'll find you. We can't do anything yet. But I'll find you.

One by one the bandits on the ridge slipped away, leaving only the gaunt threatening figure of the bandit leader. Then suddenly he turned and was gone.

At once Mumpo and Bowman, Tanner Amos and the

Shim brothers, raced for the western slope. It was far harder to climb than they had supposed, watching the sure-footed bandits. Again and again their scrambling feet set off rock slides, which carried away the ground beneath them and sent those behind tumbling back down. Mumpo fell twice, and then took the entire hill at a run, hurling himself to the top by sheer force. The others, scrambling up behind him, called out to him.

'Do you see them?'

'No,' said Mumpo, standing on the ridge where the bandits had stood, looking west.

One by one the others joined him, and understood why he had fallen silent. From the ridge to the far off western horizon the land was riven by a maze of deep cracks. Here and there the jagged fissures met, or crossed each other, in a crazy network that extended for miles. The cracks varied in depth, some no deeper than a man, some seeming bottomless. From the surface they all looked the same: shadowy slits without any distinctive markings, without any visible plant life, without the marks of human habitation. The bandits and their captives had vanished into the labyrinth leaving not even a trail of footsteps on the hard windswept plains.

Bowman closed his eyes and turned his face to the west. He was tracking Kestrel by other means.

'They've not gone far,' he said. 'They're moving fast. But I can find them.'

4

Walking the storm

Kestrel felt the tug-tug-tug of the rope on her wrists as she followed the bandits down the cracks of the labyrinth. She hated them for what they were doing to her, but she also hated to be dragged like a roped calf, so she did her best to keep up with their jogging pace. Behind her she felt the tug of the rope that was pulling Sisi along, and behind Sisi the other girls, all strung like pendants on the same twitching string. When one stumbled all of them were jerked back a pace, and then lunging forward again, the stumbler was dragged back to full speed. Behind the chain of girls came the rest of the scarfed bandits, in silence but for the pounding of their running feet.

The rock walls forked before them, and they were led to the right; and then another fork, and a turn to the left; turn after turn, until there was no way of knowing which path they had taken. The cracks became deeper, the rock walls higher as they went: now the slot of sky seemed frighteningly far away overhead: but deep though they were into the ground, here and there their path ran alongside an even deeper crack, that seemed to fall away into bottomless darkness.

After an hour or so they reached a space where several cracks intersected, and here the bandit leader called a brief stop. The girls were untied, and the bandits removed the scarves from their faces; all but one, who kept silent, and remained unobtrusively at the back. Kestrel and Sisi and the others rubbed their wrists where the ropes had chafed them, and waited in fear to learn what was to happen to them.

The bandit leader too removed his covering scarf. He was an older man than they had expected, fifty or more, with greying hair and a deeply-lined face.

'I am Barra,' he said. 'I am the father of the klin. You are now my daughters.'

'We have fathers of our own,' said Kestrel.

'Where are they now?' said Barra, fixing her with his hard eyes. Kestrel stared back, not flinching before his gaze, but saying nothing more.

'You think you will run away,' said the bandit leader, moving his eyes to look at each one of them in turn. 'If you do so, you will be lost in the labyrinth. You will wander the rocky passages until you're too weak to go on. You'll lie down to rest.'

He felt in an inner pocket, and drew out a strip of dried meat. He looked up at the sky far overhead, and then threw the meat onto the rock floor a few paces away.

'You'll grow weaker. You won't be able to move. No one will find you.'

There came a sudden blur of wings, and a great bird

flashed down out of the sky, swooped on the strip of meat, and carried it away.

'But the scavenger birds will find you. They eat the flesh from starving animals while the animals are still alive.'

He saw the terror on the young faces before him, and nodded, satisfied.

'Stay with us, and you'll be fed, and protected.'

'What do you want with us?' asked Sisi.

'We are a warrior klin,' he replied. 'Young men join us, because we are strong. Young men need wives.'

The leader indicated the bandits on either side. Kestrel looked, and saw for the first time that they were indeed young, many of them even younger than she was herself.

'Are your young men so hated that they must take their wives by force?' she asked.

Barra's hard eyes locked onto Kestrel's once more.

'Hated, yes. And feared. As it's right that they should be.'

The intensity in that lined and weathered face scared Kestrel. He went on in a more controlled voice.

'The world is at war. Cities burn, people starve. Scavengers roam the countryside, taking what they can. The strong prey on the weak. These are dark, brutal times. You think we choose to live like rats in cracks in the ground? You think we choose to come courting with slingshots, killing for our brides? That is the world today! Our klin survives because we have no pity. Your klin has lost you because they're weaker than us. You belong to the Barra klin now.'

'And if we refuse?'

'Go. Go now. Leave our protection, and die.'

There was a silence. Kestrel looked from Sisi to Sarel Amos, to Red Mimilith and Seer Such and little Ashar Warmish. No one spoke. No one moved. The bandit leader was content.

'So we understand each other,' he said. 'When we get to our settlement, you will each be given a husband. Be good to him, and he will treat you well.'

He gestured to his men, and the ones in front set off once more down the endless passages. Kestrel and the other Manth girls followed. The bandit leader and the rest of his men came behind.

The atmosphere had changed. Kestrel became aware that the men were staring at them as they loped along, discussing them among themselves. From time to time they even tried to catch their eyes, and smile. The girls looked ahead or down, avoiding all contact. They caught fragments of conversation between the young bandits, and realised that already they were being compared and quarrelled over. Shortly two of the bandits started jostling and shoving each other, evidently squaring up for a fight to settle who was to get the preferred bride.

'Stop that!' cried Barra.

The jostling stopped at once.

'The brides will be chosen according to the way of the klin.'

The journey continued in silence, but for the patter of their feet over the rock floor. By now they had come so far down so many twists and forks in the labyrinth that Kestrel wondered if Bowman would be able to follow after all. Also they were deep in rock fissures, which would make it harder for him to sense her presence. Kestrel knew her brother would keep searching until he found them, but she began to realise the search could take many days. Somehow she and the others must survive until then.

The line of bandits, with the captive girls, now ran in single file along a curving ledge. To one side the rock face rose up a hundred feet, to the strip of paling sky above; on the other, the fissure fell away in a vertical drop, that vanished into contrasting darkness. Afraid of the drop, the girls pressed themselves to the rock wall, and found that it was wet. Thin threads of water were trickling down it, and finding grooves and runnels in the ledge, and trickling on down the falling rock face. Shortly this ledge brought them to a triple fork. They took the left-hand way. Here the path ran once again between high walls on either side. The walls slanted, becoming narrower as they rose, so that only a thin slit admitted the daylight above. Soon even this slit closed, and they found themselves walking on in a darkness broken only by the dim glow of light growing ever fainter behind them.

Here and there, barely able to see, they brushed against the sides of the fissure, dislodging loose flakes of stone from the crumbling surface to rattle to the ground. The path was formed out of fragments of the eroding walls, and it crackled and crunched under their feet. Just as the crack above had closed in, so now the walls seemed to be pushing closer, until the space between them was just wide enough for the bandits and their captives to walk in single file.

'Keep to the middle of the path,' said the bandit leader, his words echoing down the tunnel.

Kestrel touched the walls as she went, feeling the cracked and crumbling surface. Then her outstretched hand struck a timber post, and another. Feeling more carefully now, she learned that the tunnel was ribbed with timber supports, at first every few paces, then closer and closer to each other. They had been set at a slant on either side, to meet overhead, forming a triangular space. Between these timber frames, showers of small stones and dust fell as they passed.

Ashar Warmish began to sob, afraid of the tunnel and the dark. Sarel Amos, who was next to her in line, felt for her hand and squeezed it.

'Not long now,' said Barra gruffly.

The tunnel had become so tight they had to stoop to pass between the supports. There were beams all the way now, making a timber-lined shaft just big enough for a man to pass along at a crouching shuffle.

Then the bandit leader called into the darkness,

'Watchman ho!'

There came a faint answering cry.

'Aya!'

'Barra ho!'

They came to a stop. There was the slow creak of a heavy door opening – and sudden light.

The roar of water. The tang of wood smoke. The dazzle of sky. One by one the bandits and their captives emerged through the low doorway, past the waiting watchman. Kestrel found herself on a broad shelf cut high up in a sheer rock wall. Above her rose the flanks of a great split in the land, hundreds of feet high, unclimbable cliffs of stone. Below her, the forger of this spacious rift, a fast-flowing river, that came rushing from a crack in the far wall to tumble in a hissing spray into a turbulent rock-bound lake. At the far end of the rift the water was sucked boiling and gurgling down a succession of narrow slits. Her eyes searched for an escape route, but no other fissures entered this natural fortress. The only way in and out was the timber-sided tunnel through which they had come.

The river's waters completely filled the rift, from wall to wall. But on the water, supported by timber piles, the bandits had built a deck that extended all along one rock side. The deck was a good fifty paces wide, wide enough to hold a settlement of thatched huts. From it projected three broad jetties, over the widest part of the pool. At the end of each jetty, a fire was burning, and pots were boiling. People came and went between the huts and the fires; most of them were men, but there were some women, and some children.

Kestrel stood on the rock ledge and gazed down at the scene with a sinking heart. The bandits were far more numerous than she had expected, and their settlement far harder to attack.

The bandit leader gestured at his people.

'The home of the Barra klin,' he said. 'Your home.'

He led the way down the steep steps cut into the rock wall, to the timber deck below. Here he was greeted by a tall woman of his own age, her grey hair tied back with string. She studied the captured girls with a careful appraising gaze.

'Very good,' she said to Barra. 'Where are they from?'

'Travellers,' said Barra. 'From the Mastery, I'd guess.'

'Ah, well. There's all sorts there.'

She beckoned to the Manth girls to follow her.

'Come with me.'

She took them to one of the jetties, and told them to sit and warm themselves at the fire.

'Just take care not to fall into the river. It's ice cold. You'd be dead before we could get you out.'

Here they sat, shivering and fearful, while the young bandits who had captured them gathered on the main section of the deck and stared at them. The grey-haired woman went into the largest of the huts, and could be heard giving orders. Shortly two younger women with babies strapped to their backs came out carrying cups of water and plates of dried meat.

Ashar Warmish began to cry again. She cried quietly, out of fear, and grief for her dead father.

'I want to die,' she said between sobs. 'I want to die.'

'It's going to be alright,' said Kestrel, putting her arms round her. 'We just have to be brave.'

'They can do the dying,' said Sisi fiercely. 'I'll kill anyone who comes near me.'

'We do nothing at all for the moment.' Kestrel spoke to them all in a whisper. 'Eat and drink as much as you can. That way we'll last longer when we go back into the labyrinth.'

'Go back into the labyrinth!' Kestrel saw their frightened looks. 'We can't!'

'It's the only way. Trust me. I know how to find the others.'

So long as Bowman gets near enough, she thought to

herself; and so long as Bowman finds a way to get us back out of the labyrinth. But she said nothing of this.

'We can't go while they're watching us. We have to wait until dark.'

'Go into the labyrinth in the dark!'

'It's the only way.'

She saw the grey-haired woman returning.

'Let them think we've given up,' she whispered. 'Do everything they say.'

This was mostly for Sisi's benefit. The others were too shocked and frightened to offer resistance; but Sisi was angry, and her anger could make her act rashly.

'You've eaten? You feel refreshed?'

The girls nodded in silence. The grey-haired woman sat down.

'My name is Madriel. I'm the mother of the klin.' She saw the tears still wet on Ashar's cheeks. 'Don't cry. You're not prisoners any more. You're brides. You will be treated with respect and honour. Our klin has a wise father, and a strong one. He will punish anyone who harms you.'

Kestrel spoke up for all of them.

'Are we to be brides whether we want to or not?'

'You will want to,' said Madriel. 'It is how you will serve the klin. From now on, the klin is your home and your family. It will nourish you and keep you safe while you live, respect you when you grow old, and mourn you when you die. In return you will keep the fires burning for the hunters and warriors. You will give the klin baby boys who will grow up tall and strong; and become hunters and warriors in their time. That is the way of the klin.'

Sisi shook her head angrily.

'You don't like our way?' asked Madriel mildly.

'Do women have nothing more to do than give life to men?' said Sisi.

'Nothing more,' said Madriel. 'Just as men have nothing more to do than give life to women.'

The crowd of young men that had been staring at them now broke up, and moved away into one of the main huts. Madriel gestured across the lake, where a second deck ran along the far wall, beyond the rushing water. It was narrower than the platform on which the main settlement stood, and was reached by a long railed bridge that crossed the river at its narrowest point. All along this second remoter deck small thatched huts had been built, newly built by the look of them, each one barely big enough for two people.

'There are your bridal huts. Tonight you will go to them, with your new husbands, and there you will stay for five days and nights.'

The Manth girls stared at the little huts, and suddenly their fate seemed real and close. Red Mimilith looked back towards the young men.

'Are we to choose our husbands?'

'Choose your husbands! Of course not!' The klin mother was shocked. 'They will choose you.'

As she spoke, the young men came filing out of the communal hut to form a cluster at the far end of the broad deck. They started to stretch their arms and legs, as if limbering up for some violent activity. Among them Kestrel saw again the one who had kept his concealing scarf, and she wondered fleetingly why he chose to remain masked.

'The strongest will have first choice,' said Madriel. 'He will choose the healthiest and most fertile among you. In this way, he will give the klin strong and healthy babies. The second strongest will choose next. And so six of our young men will choose their brides. That is the way of the klin.'

'But that's all nonsense!' exclaimed Sisi. 'How is anyone to know who's the most fertile?'

'By the strength of their desire. When a young woman is most fertile, she is most desirable. Look at me. I'm like the flower whose petals have shrivelled and fallen. My child-bearing days are gone. No man desires me. But you' – this to Sisi – 'you are the unfolding bud.'

'Not me,' said Sisi, flushing and touching her scarred cheeks.

Madriel laughed.

'You think that makes you any less desirable in a young man's eyes? My child, every part of your body is heavy with the sweet scent of youth. You'll be the first to be chosen.'

'It makes no difference who chooses us,' said Kestrel. 'We know nothing of any of them.'

'You'll know them,' said the klin mother, 'when you see them walk the storm. A woman learns all she needs of a man by the way he walks the storm.'

Before they could ask more about this, a second woman from the klin now joined them, carrying a sleeping baby in a sling round her neck, and holding in her hands a shallow basket filled with strips of coloured fabric.

'The bride colours, mother,' she said, handing over the basket.

Madriel took the basket and picked out a blue-and-yellow ribbon. It was rough-edged, torn from the hem of some discarded garment, only a few inches long. She twisted it into a loose knot, and gave it to Sisi.

'Hold it where the men can see it. I'll tell you what to do when the time comes.'

One by one she took the cloth strips out of the basket and distributed them at random to the Manth girls. Some were striped, some were checked, some plain. Kestrel received the plainest strip of all, a fragment of light grey material, almost white. She felt oddly pleased to have so colourless a piece of material, and was sure the klin mother had picked it out for her on purpose.

'What is this walking the storm?' she asked.

'You'll see.'

There came a stir among the huts, and a group of older men came filing out. Each held in one hand a home-made weapon, a stick or a weighted cord or a whip.

'The fathers are ready,' said Madriel. 'Come.'

She rose, and the Manth girls rose at her command, and followed her. She arranged them in a line, kneeling or sitting as they chose, down the wide boardwalk that ran between the huts and the water. She showed them how to hold their bride colours open on their laps, where they could be seen. The older men, the ones she had called the fathers, some of whom weren't old at all, now formed two long lines before them, their weapons in their hands. They took their places quietly, eyes cast down, with grave looks on their faces; and so stood, legs apart, facing each other, in an ever-lengthening human corridor two paces wide, running parallel to the water, all the length of the deck.

While these lines were forming, the young men were making their final preparations. Each one bound onto his right upper arm a strip of coloured fabric corresponding to the bride colours. When this armband was in place, they wound long scarves round their necks and faces, leaving only the narrowest slit below the nostrils to allow them to breathe. From now on, they were blindfolded.

Kestrel picked out the one with the white armband, that corresponded to the knot of material in her lap. She saw his face before it was muffled in the concealing scarf: a broad face with a snub nose.

Not him, she thought. I won't marry him.

As soon as the thought formed in her mind, she chased it away. She had no intention of marrying anybody, from the Barra klin or anywhere else.

'I won't! They can't make me!'

This was Sisi, speaking aloud. She too had identified the youth wearing her colour, and she was outraged.

'Be patient!' said the klin mother, seeing how the Manth girls were growing agitated. 'No choices have been made yet. Soon now you will lay down your bride colour in the place I tell you. Later, when the young men make their choices, a bride colour will be given back to you.'

The blindfolded young men were now lining up at one end of the double row. Kestrel looked for the one she had puzzled over on the journey through the labyrinth, but now that all their heads were covered, she couldn't pick him out.

Barra came out of the meeting hut and strode down the

centre of the rows to the far end. Here he turned, and raising his hands above his head, he clapped twice. The fathers all stiffened, and lifted their whips and their sticks. The first of the blindfolded young men was led into the starting position. The Manth girls realised now what was about to happen, and forgot their own fears in horror at what was to be done.

The bandit leader clapped once more: this time a single clap. The first blindfolded young man set off down the lines, his boots clopping on the timber boards. The sticks swung hard, cracking onto his back; the cords lashed his arms; the whips cut at his legs. He staggered on, unable to see the blows before they landed, flinching at every sound, struggling not to cry out or to run. The blows rained down from either side, onto his head and chest and buttocks, brutal and unceasing. This first young man wore colours of black and orange, and gentle Sarel Amos, who clutched the same colours in her hands, couldn't stop herself from crying out at his suffering. She knew neither his name nor his nature, but the chance of the colours linked them, and it was enough to make her care.

He staggered on down the long line, but the relentless blows were taking their toll. They could hear him groaning now, and whimpering. Too slow to dodge, every blow landed, and with each one, he crouched lower and moved more slowly. Then a bull-hide whip sliced at his calves, and he stumbled to his knees, and did not rise again. The flailing arms of the older men fell still. Madriel gestured to Sarel.

'Lay your bride colour on the ground where he has fallen.'

Trembling, Sarel did as she was told. The older women

came forward and helped the beaten young man limp away. Now the stripe of orange and black lay on the deck to mark how far he had endured, in the ordeal they called walking the storm.

'Did I do well?' he asked, his voice breaking with pain, as they unwound his blindfold.

'You did well,' they told him. 'You passed the halfway line.'

The second young man was in place. The father of the klin clapped his hands. The grim beating began again, as one after another, the young men submitted themselves to the ordeal.

Some, caught by an unlucky blow, fell within a few paces of the start; and even though they were on their feet again within moments, the colour was laid where they had fallen, and their chance was gone. Others struggled on, crying out with the fear of the unseen blows as much as at the pain, until unable to bear it any longer they took the first opportunity to stumble, and so end the punishment. The one who wore the band of white was not one of these. As soon as he began his walk, Kestrel could tell he would be among the winners. He moved with a sure stocky gait, bowing his shoulders to the crack of the sticks, pushing doggedly onwards like a wounded ox. The whips couldn't trip his ankles and the weighted cords couldn't break his skull. On he stomped, breathing heavily, past the halfway line, maintaining the same steady speed. Kestrel found herself willing him on, for no other reason than that she held his colour in her lap; and then was ashamed of herself, thinking, Let him be clubbed to the dirt. What do I care?

And yet the klin mother had been right. Watching the young men walk the storm made Kestrel know them. The ordeal was the same for each one, but each one suffered it in his own way. This one with the white armband had tenacity, and courage, but he was not clever. He had no sense of how to avoid the blows, or reduce their punishing impact. He was a man who would be reliable, who would work hard, but who would never learn. His sheer determination took him to the three-quarter line, but here, worn down by the hundreds of blows he had endured, he was at last hammered to his knees.

Kestrel rose and placed her bride colour on the deck where he had fallen, and returned to her place. She caught Sisi's eye as she walked back. Sisi's face showed her distress, but whether for herself or for the young men who were walking the storm, Kestrel did not know.

The next youth was already on his way. The colours lay all down the line, showing how far each had got. Those for whom the ordeal was over were returning to watch and see how their companions fared, and to look at the row of waiting brides. These new-made veterans, bruised and aching though they were, held themselves with pride. They had walked the storm, and were now entitled to take their places as fathers of the klin.

At last there was only one bride colour remaining, the blue knotted strip held by the youngest of the Manth girls, Ashar Warmish. One young man waited at the end of the double line, wearing a blue band on his arm. Because he was the last, the atmosphere became more relaxed. His companions were starting to talk among themselves, and compare their wounds, while the leaders, the ones whose colours were furthest down the line, were already making their choice of bride. But first the final blindfolded youth must make his way down the lines.

Kestrel saw the difference as soon as he started. He was no stronger than those who had gone before him; nor was he nimbler at evading the blows. He simply cared less. He walked with his scarfed head held high, accepting the hammer-strikes to his back, reeling under the impact, finding his balance once more, and moving on: all as if he felt nothing. Shortly the others watching realised something unusual was happening, and their eyes turned from the brides to the blindfolded boy stalking down the lines. Already he was past the halfway mark, and he had made no sound. He turned his unseeing head towards the blows, seeming to invite them to strike him. Kestrel found herself thinking, How can he mind so little? Does he want to die? He walked on as if into the waves of the sea, turning always towards the higher wave and the higher, breasting the breakers and finding there an increase of strength. One club caught him full in his masked face with a sound of crunching flesh, but still he strode on.

Now in full silence all the klin watched, as he passed the three-quarter line, smashed and lashed but never brought down. Now he was past the white cloth marker, which was the furthest any of the others had got, and still he did not fall. Now the blows fell harder, and he staggered and tottered, but the big men with their clubs and their whips could not bring him down. Barra, father of the klin, stood at the far end, watching with his hard eyes, and the young man came nearer and nearer.

Why? thought Kestrel, as spellbound as the rest. Why take so much punishment? No bride is worth so much pain. And as she thought it, she knew, as everyone watching knew, that this was nothing to do with the brides, or even the klin. This, she said to herself, is a young man who chooses pain. He refuses to fall to his knees because he does not want his suffering to end.

On he strode, and now the entire klin knew he was going to the very end. Barra slowly opened wide his arms. The blindfolded boy, beaten and broken and barely conscious, walked on across the end line and into the klin father's embrace.

There he fell, and for a few moments it seemed he had paid the price for his foolhardy glory. Then Barra looked up and said,

'Aya! Honour him!' He barked out the klin's cry. 'Aya! Aya! He is the first to walk the storm to the end!'

Men and women, young and old, joined him, calling together, stamping the deck and beating their hands in time to the cry.

'Aya! Aya! Aya!'

Ashar Warmish, the blue bride colour in her hands, looked uncertainly towards Madriel. The klin mother beckoned her, took her hand and led her herself to lay the blue ribbon at the victor's feet. He was stirring now, finding the strength to hold his own weight.

'See to his wounds,' Barra said to his wife.

Madriel took the young man's arm, holding it gently, and herself unwound the long scarf that covered his head. As it came off, the onlookers saw that his face was disfigured and bright with blood. His nose had been crushed. One eye was swollen shut. One cheek was livid with a long dark bruise. But through the blood and the wounds, Kestrel still knew him, the minute the scarf came off.

It was Rufy Blesh.

She turned and saw that all the Manth girls were staring at him: Sarel and Seer, Red and Ashar. Only Sisi didn't know him.

'Who is he?'

'He's Manth, like us. His name's Rufy Blesh.' Kestrel spoke very low, so that they would not be overheard. 'When we were slaves of the Mastery, he ran away in the night. Twenty of our people were burned alive.'

'Because of him?'

'Yes.'

'Did he know they'd do that?'

'He knew.'

Sisi turned her beautiful eyes back to look at Rufy Blesh. He was standing unaided now, his face still a mask of blood, looking towards them. His one open eye was glazed, as if he looked but did not see. Kestrel understood that look. He was saying, Here I am, do what you want with me, I no longer care.

Barra, the klin father, raised his hands above his head and clapped for silence and attention.

'Stand by your colours!'

The young men, moving awkwardly, some limping, some clutching their bruised arms, came forward, and each stood by his coloured marker where it lay on the deck.

'Make your choice!'

No one moved. All eyes were on Rufy Blesh. As the one

who had endured the longest, he had the right to choose first. But he seemed not to know it.

The klin father nodded to him.

'The honour is yours.'

Rufy Blesh took up his colour, and stepped slowly across the intervening space to the line of Manth girls. He held the blue fabric strip in one hand. It was already stained with the blood that his hand had wiped from his battered face. Kestrel, watching in horror and pity, wondered that he could see to walk at all, through the mess of split flesh and drying blood.

He came to a stop a few paces away from them, and his head turned this way and that, so that everyone thought he was studying the brides, making his choice. But then, abruptly, he let his colour fall from his hand to the deck, and walked off.

He had chosen none of them.

Kestrel released her breath: not having realised until then that she had been holding it. Barra frowned. But already the young man who had placed second in the test was stepping forward, his white colour in his hand. He headed straight for Sisi, just as the klin mother had predicted, and laid his colour at her feet. Sisi looked at it, and then raising her elegant head, she looked away to one side.

'Take it,' said Madriel. 'Undo the knot, and tie it round your neck.'

Sisi pretended she hadn't heard. The third young man was limping towards them. He laid his colour before Sarel Amos. Kestrel found herself both relieved and irritated not to be chosen.

'Take the bride colour,' said Madriel to Sisi again, 'or be cast out of the klin.'

'Do as she says, Sisi,' whispered Kestrel. 'It means nothing.'

Sisi took the strip of cloth then, and with her slender fingers she loosed the knot, and drew it round her neck, and tied it at her throat. As she did this, she kept her gaze averted, looking far away to one side, as if it was someone else who was fixing onto her this shameful neckband, and she knew nothing about it.

Kestrel was chosen fourth. She glared furiously at the boy as he approached, hoping to make him change his mind, but he just grinned back at her. He was little and young, younger than her, she was sure, and had big sticky-out ears, and hobbled as he walked. Kestrel seethed and burned with humiliation as he laid his miserable colour before her. Pink-and-blue check! Even his colour was childish. To be chosen by a stranger was bad enough, but to be chosen fourth, and by a flap-eared baby, was unendurable. For a moment she was even angry with Rufy Blesh for not making a choice. He would have picked her, she was sure of it. They had known each other all their lives.

With trembling fingers, she tied the odious pink-and-blue ribbon round her neck. Not much longer, she told herself. Closing her eyes, she reached out with her mind.

Bo! Can you hear me?

There was no answer. He would be searching for them, she knew. So would Mumpo, and the others. It was just a matter of time.

Now the klin mother was beckoning them all to rise

and follow her. The choices had been made, each bride had her neckband in place.

'The men will rest after the trial,' said Madriel. 'You will wash yourselves. At sundown the klin will eat, and you will each serve your new husband with his meat and drink. At last light your husbands will lead you across the water to the huts they have built for you, and there you will stay with them. That is the way of the klin.'

As she heard this, Kestrel looked up at the sky above. The winter sun was descending. The shadow on the eastern wall was rising. Last light was approaching fast.

Bo, she called, *my brother, are you coming? Come soon! Come soon!*

5

The winner chooses
a bride

Bowman loped steadily along the edge of the great fissure, followed by Mumpo, Miller Marish, Tanner Amos, Lolo Mimilith, the Shim brothers, and Mist the cat. The young men carried such weapons as they had: short swords, knives, lengths of timber from the wagon bed. No one noticed the cat.

The fissure ran east-west. They were moving west, towards the sun as it sank in the white cloud-hazed sky. In every direction the rocky plains stretched away, unmarked except by the maze of cracks that broke the surface every few yards. Mostly the cracks were narrow enough to jump: but this great chasm was twenty feet across and widening all the time, and the stream they could hear rushing along its floor was deeper still. Bowman's acute senses told him that his sister and the others had been taken north, but until they found a way to cross the great fissure, they were being forced ever farther westward, and the trail was growing cold.

'We must go down into the cracks,' said Tanner Amos. 'It's the only way.'

'We'll get lost.' Bowman shook his head. 'Look how the cracks twist and turn. We'd lose all sense of direction. Even if we found them, how would we ever find our way back?'

He turned and strained his eyes to the south-east, to see if the flag was still in sight. The main body of the Manth marchers had made camp for the night in the dry river valley. They had erected a home-made flag on a pole raised on the western ridge, so that the search party could find their way back to them. The flag, a long band of fine white silk, flew bravely in the distance, catching the light of the descending sun.

Mumpo looked west, along the edge of the fissure, following its erratic path towards the distant mountains.

'I don't think we'll ever cross it,' he said. 'I think this is Crack-in-the-land.'

Bowman had had the same thought, but he had kept it to himself, not wanting to dismay the others. He and Kestrel and Mumpo had met Crack-in-the-land many years ago, and had crossed it, but then there had been a bridge. That great chasm had been far away to the north-west, and near the foot of the mountains, but it was possible this crack was its younger self, or a tributary crack, carrying its waters to the distant ocean.

He came to a stop. Back some way to the east they had passed another fissure, with crumbled sloping sides, that led into the greater crack. They had noted at the time that if need be they could climb down there, and enter the maze of passages the bandits had called the labyrinth. Should they go back?

'If only one of us could stay on the surface, to act as our guide.'

Bowman was thinking aloud: but it was impossible. No one following on the surface could go where they went, down in the labyrinth. There were too many cracks that were too wide to jump.

'Well, here's how it seems to me,' said Mumpo. He spoke slowly, as he always did, and quietly, not much expecting others to listen. 'If we go on the way we're going, we'll never cross the great crack. So that's no good. If we give up and go back to the camp, we've lost them for ever, and that's no good. But if we go down into the cracks, we've got a chance.'

Mumpo didn't say to the others that he would go on searching, whatever decision they reached. He would go into the labyrinth, into the depths of the earth, by day and by night, for as long as he lived, until he found Kestrel. And when I find her, he said to himself, I'll kill the men who took her away.

This was not an idle boast. Mumpo knew how to kill. They had taught him that when he was a slave in the Mastery.

Bowman did not share Mumpo's simple view of the choice that faced them.

'Think what my father would say. We've lost our young women. Are we to lose our young men as well?'

A silence fell. Then they heard a low mew. Mist had decided his time had come.

'Mist! How did you get here?'

'How do you think I got here?'

Bowman heard the cat's irritated answer, but of course

the others heard nothing. All they saw was that the cat had approached Bowman, and was now sitting down by his feet.

'It must have followed us,' said Miller Marish. 'That cat is devoted to you, Bowman.'

Mist gave Miller Marish a look of withering contempt, and turned back to Bowman.

'It's just as well for you I came,' he told Bowman. 'You go into the cracks below. I'll follow, and guide you from the ground above.'

'But Mist, you won't be able to follow us. The cracks are too wide for you to jump.'

'Too wide to jump. Not too wide to fly.'

The others waited, hearing none of this, but aware that some sort of communication was taking place.

'Look at its face!' said Rollo Shim. 'You'd think it was talking!'

'We're losing time,' said Tanner Amos.

Bowman stroked the cat's back.

'Oh, Mist. You know you can't really fly.'

Mist rose up, offended.

'So what did you think? I was making it up to impress you? Why would I want to impress you? I'm not a kitten.'

He stalked away.

'Do we go on?' said Bek Shim. 'Or do we go back?'

'We go back,' said Bowman. 'When we reach the slope down into the labyrinth, we'll decide whether to take it or not.'

So they turned about and jogged back east, at a steady trot. The cat followed some way behind, to indicate that he was not part of their group, but just happened to be heading in the same direction.

'I'll show them,' he said to himself as he bounded along. 'I'll show them.'

When they arrived at the crack with the crumbled side they stopped once more. As the others rested and got their breath back, Bowman reached out with all his senses for some indicator of which way Kestrel had been taken. He called to her, with little hope of an answer; and none came. By now she would be too far away. But the path she had taken still held the fast-fading print of her passing.

'I can feel her,' he said.

'Then we go after her,' said Mumpo.

'But Mumpo, even if we find her, even if we rescue her and the others, how do we get back? It's already dark down there. And my feeling won't reach far enough to get us back.'

There came a sudden pattering sound, and Mist appeared behind them, running at great speed. He raced over the ground to the edge of the crack, and there sprang into the air. Up he went, in a long high curve, at the height of which they saw him start to paddle with all four legs, exactly as if he was swimming: and astonishingly, instead of dropping down again, he sailed horizontally onwards, until, in a second gentle curve, he dropped down to the ground on the further side.

'How did he do that!' exclaimed Rollo Shim.

'He flew,' said Bowman.

Mist turned himself round on the far side of the wide fissure and looked back at Bowman.

'So, boy. It seems you don't know everything after all.'

'Can you do it again?'

'As often as you want. Once you have the knack, you don't lose it.'

'Then follow us, Mist!'

To the others, he said,

'Let's go! The cat will guide us back!'

Without further talk, the band of young men slithered their way down the sloping side of the fissure, and into the labyrinth.

The Barra klin held the marriage feast round the biggest of the fires, which was built on the middle jetty. Here the six Manth brides were allotted places in a circle, with the leaping flames between them and the icy water behind. Each was given a plate of food and a cup of sweetened water, not for themselves, but for their husbands; who were in the bachelor hut, cleaning themselves for the bridal night.

Kestrel watched the light fade in the sky high above, and knew that time was running out. Somehow they must delay the process long enough for her brother to find them. But even then, when he did at last come close enough for them to communicate, how were they to escape?

She studied the river rift again, as she had already done a dozen times, searching for a way out. Again she concluded, as she had done each time before, that there was no way to climb those sheer towering walls; that the icy rapids of the river would indeed kill them; and that the only way either in or out was the timber-propped tunnel at the top of the flight of rock-hewn steps. The klin had chosen their refuge well. Any attackers would be forced to enter singly, and would then have to descend the exposed rock steps, where they would present an easy target for the deadly slingshots. She saw the watchman standing on the high shelf by the tunnel door, and knew that this one small entrance would be guarded night and day.

How many would Bowman bring with him? Four? Five? There was no way that they could mount a successful attack on so well protected a fortress. Nor did she see how they, the captives, could escape unnoticed. The people of the klin would sleep soon. But their almost-husbands, lying with them in those tiny bridal huts, would feel them and hear them, if they attempted to creep away in the night.

Her thoughts broke off. The young men were coming now, filing out of the bachelor hut with their coloured bands on their arms. Each one sought out his bride, identified by the matching colour of her neckband, and took his place by her side in the firelight. The older people, the fathers and mothers of the klin, now followed; and the feast began.

It was humble enough. The Barra klin lived a hard spare life, with enough food for survival, and little more. There were no songs or stories, and little laughter. The Manth brides had no reason to celebrate either. They shrank back from the husbands seated cross-legged on the deck beside them, did as they were told, and avoided all closer contact. Kestrel could feel the boy with sticky-out ears gazing at her, and she had to exert all her self-control not to smash the plate of food into his face. But now was not the time for an outburst.

The older people started to drum on the deck with their feet.

'Aya! Aya! Aya!'

They were greeting the appearance of the honoured champion of the day's ordeal, Rufy Blesh. He nodded stiffly to acknowledge the greeting, and sat down on the boards alone. He had been cleaned up, but his injured face was still distressing to look on. Kestrel watched him closely: and at last found a plan forming, that might give them a hope of escape.

The klin mother was watching the new brides, guiding and correcting them in the proper manner of serving their menfolk.

'The wife feeds the husband before she eats herself,' she said. 'The wife gives the husband to drink before she drinks herself. That is the way of the klin.'

'Who is to feed the one who sits alone?' asked Kestrel. Her question was met with silence. 'He suffered the most. He proved himself to be the strongest. Where is his bride?'

Barra looked at Rufy Blesh, and turned back to Kestrel, and nodded his head.

'What you say is true. But he hasn't chosen.'

'He threw his bride colour to the ground,' said Madriel. 'He wanted none of you.'

'He was weary and in pain,' said Kestrel. 'He's rested now. Perhaps he wants to make his choice after all.'

'The brides have all been chosen.'

Kestrel was watching Rufy Blesh. He gazed back expressionlessly, with his one good eye.

'He is the winner,' she said. 'He may choose who he likes. Until he makes his choice, none of us are free. That is the way of the klin.'

Barra frowned, and thought for a moment in silence. Then he sighed and said,

'It is so.'

He turned with a grave look to Rufy Blesh.

'Do you wish now to choose a bride?'

Rufy Blesh kept his gaze fixed on Kestrel. Then, at last, he inclined his head.

A murmur rose up from the people round the fire. Such a thing had never happened before. Barra gave a sign, and the young men rose to their feet.

'Lay down your plates and cups,' said Madriel to the brides. 'Untie your colours.'

She gathered up the strips of fabric, and one by one they were given back to the young men. Rufy Blesh took his band of blue ribbon and stood facing the fire. The others formed up behind him in the order that their markers had been laid earlier. The one who had placed last now withdrew from the line, shaking his head and murmuring under his breath.

When all were ready, Barra said,

'Make your choice.'

This time Rufy did not hesitate. He stepped forward in the firelight, and laid his colour in Kestrel's lap. Barra, watching, nodded his reluctant approval. The young woman was clearly the leader of the Manth brides, and therefore the right partner for a future leader of the klin.

The others followed, each choosing as he had chosen before, with the exception of the boy who had chosen

Kestrel. When his turn came he gave a sulky shrug to show that he felt he had been hard done by, and picked the one who had been chosen last before, little Ashar Warmish.

All this took time, as Kestrel had intended. By the time the marriage feast was resumed, the great fire was burning lower, and night had fallen in the sky above. Kestrel handed Rufy his meat and his drink, as she had been shown; he ate and drank in silence, moving his jaws slowly, because of the bruised and torn flesh. He and Kestrel did not speak, or even look at each other. But when he had finished eating, and returned his plate to her, she took her finger and wrote in the grease that smeared its surface: HELP US.

He read, and looked up, and gave the slightest nod. It was enough.

Barra rose.

'Last light has come and gone,' he said. 'The fire burns low, and we're all weary. The bridal huts are prepared. Take your brides across the water.'

Kestrel knew she needed still more time.

'Father of the klin,' she said. 'We Manth people have our customs too. For us, the wedding night is the night when the child becomes a woman. On that night, we say farewell to our childhood, and cross the threshold into a new life.'

The other Manth girls listened, and exchanged surreptitious glances. They had never heard of this custom before in their lives. Kestrel was making it up.

Barra, not knowing this, was respectful.

'What is it you want to do, child?'

'According to the Manth custom, father,' said Kestrel, seeing he liked this title, 'the bride spends the first part of her wedding night alone with her husband in silence and stillness. During this time, their two spirits make friends with each other. Then the brides leave their husbands and gather together one last time, in what we call the bride huddle.' Kestrel was inventing as fast as she could, but her earnest face showed no sign of it. 'In the bride huddle, we say farewell to our childhood. Then we return to our husbands, and cross the threshold into our new lives.'

'I see.' Barra looked to his wife. She gave a shrug and a nod.

'There's no harm in it,' she said.

'You are no longer Manth,' said the klin father after some thought. 'However, I see no reason why you should not follow your custom for one last time. Say farewell in the Manth way to your Manth childhood, then start your new life in the klin.'

'Thank you, father,' said Kestrel. And casting her eyes down to show submission, she held out her hand to allow Rufy Blesh to lead her across the water.

Madriel spoke to the young men as they went.

'Show respect to your brides. Follow their customs.'

Couple by couple, they made their way across the deck to the narrow bridge, and over the bridge to the platform on the far side of the water. Here, lit now by pale moonlight, stood the line of bridal huts.

Kestrel turned and met the fearful eyes of her friends. They were all looking towards her, expecting her to say or do something that would spare them the coming ordeal. She looked back, trying to tell them without words that she had a plan, and they must be brave. Then she saw how Seer Such's hands were shaking, clasped tightly at her waist, and knew they were being brave, far braver than she, who knew that Bowman would find them soon.

'Sit still in silence,' she said. 'I'll come for you when it's time.'

Kestrel stooped and entered the low-roofed hut first. Inside, beneath the rough thatch, there was no light at all. She felt before her, and found a woollen blanket, laid out on a bed of dry grass. She sat down. Rufy Blesh followed, sitting close to her: not by choice, but because there was very little space. She could feel his knee where it touched her leg. He was trembling.

For a few moments, neither of them spoke. Kestrel's eyes adjusted slowly to the darkness. Through the arched doorway of the hut she could see across the water the older klin members kicking out the fires on the jetties and retiring to their own larger communal shelters.

She spoke low, so they would not be heard in the neighbouring huts.

'How long before the fathers sleep?'

'Not long.' His voice was so quiet even she could hardly hear him.

'When do they change the watch?'

'Dawn.'

Silence. Across the water the scattered embers of the fires crackled and died. The river rushed on in its everlasting way. No sound or movement came from the huts.

Kestrel was listening intently for Bowman. She had the beginnings of a feeling that he was approaching, but each time the feeling slipped away before she could hold it. Rufy Blesh was silent.

'My brother is coming,' Kestrel said. 'Bowman is coming.'

Then Rufy spoke.

'How many?' he asked.

Kestrel understood him. For a brief moment, before she could shut out the memory, she saw again the flames that filled the monkey cage, and heard the screams of the twisting figures caught behind its bars.

'Twenty,' she said.

He bowed his head. Then, even more softly,

'Who?'

'Amareth. Helmo.' Just names now: they died without a burial, without a memorial. Cruel times indeed. 'Old Sep. The Mooth boy.' She had never been able to recall his name, but for some reason it came to her then. 'Chaser Mooth. And Pia.'

'Pia!'

Of course: Rufy Blesh had been close to Pia Greeth once. There had even been talk that he would ask her to marry him. Then she had married Tanner Amos. And now, because Rufy had run away, Pia had died.

Rufy asked no more. He seemed crushed by what he had learned. Kestrel could think of nothing to say that would ease his suffering; in truth, she believed he deserved to suffer.

On the other hand, she needed him for her plan.

'Rufy,' she said. 'All that is in the past. Here, now, we need your help.'

'What do you want me to do?'

'We need weapons. Swords, knives, anything.'

'What's the use? There are too many of them.'

'Get us weapons. We'll find a way.'

Rufy fell silent. Kestrel waited, sensing that nothing more she could say would help. He was making his decision on his own; as he had done once before.

'There are knives in the kitchen hut,' he said out of the silence. 'Meat knives.'

'Can you get them without being seen?'

Rufy looked out towards the dying fires. The klin was sleeping.

'Yes.'

'Get one for each of us.'

'I know these people. They have no mercy. There are no old people in the klin. When they lose their strength, and can do no more work, they're thrown into the river to die.'

'Are you afraid?'

'Afraid? What have I to fear? No, Kestrel. I'm warning you. I want to help you.'

'Then go. And come back with the knives.'

After that, he spoke no more. He rose up and passed stooping through the doorway, and so on across the slender bridge. Her eyes followed him, a shadowy figure moving noiselessly in the faint moonlight. Then she looked up at the rim of the high rock walls. There, silhouetted against the silver clouds, she saw a cat.

6

Farewell to childhood

Bowman, Mumpo and the other young men had made good progress. The trail had grown warmer as they had gone along. Above them the cat had followed, running beside the high edges of the fissures, and whenever it became necessary, leaping across from side to side. Now, as Bowman felt his way along a curving ledge that hugged a high rock wall, he sensed that he was near enough to attempt a call.

Kess! Can you hear me, Kess?

There was still no answer. Glancing up, Bowman was surprised to see that the cat had disappeared from view. He beckoned to the others to follow, and padded on along the ledge. She had come this way, he was sure of it.

They came to the place where the fissure split three ways. Bowman paused to sense the way to go.

'We go left,' he said.

Again, he called to his sister.

Kess! Can you hear me?

This time there came an answer, faint, distorted, but recognisable.

Bo . . . you . . . are you . . ?

Not near enough yet, he called back. *We're coming.*

To the others, he said,

'They're there. They're not far. Let's hurry.'

And with renewed energy they followed the rising path, until the slit of moonlight closed overhead and they were moving in full darkness.

They jogged on, feeling the walls of the tunnel push closer on either side.

Bo! Take care! Don't let them know you're here!

Bowman stopped dead. Kestrel's voice was suddenly clear and close. The great barriers of rock had deceived his senses. They were far nearer than he had realised.

Kestrel! I heard you!

Where are you?

In a tunnel.

You've very close. I can feel you. At the end of the tunnel there's a door. There's a watchman stands guard beyond the door.

Just one man?

Just one man. But beyond him, sleeping, there's fifty and more. Stay still and silent. Do as I say.

Shortly after Rufy Blesh had returned to the bridal hut, Kestrel came out, wrapped in his long cloak. The night was cold. She straightened up, and stood looking across the water. Nothing was moving. Reassured, she set off along the line of bridal huts, stooping by each low doorway and whispering to her people within.

'Come! The time has come!'

One by one the Manth brides crept out of their huts,

and gathered in a shivering cluster on the deck by the bridge. The young men who were their almost-husbands came out too, and stood with Rufy Blesh, watching their brides and waiting.

'Form a circle,' said Kestrel to the young women. 'Arms round each other. We must share our strength, as we say farewell to our childhood.'

They wrapped their arms round each other and pressed tight together, so that their heads were touching. Within the concealment of the circle, Kestrel opened her cloak.

The young men watched and waited. They were doing as they had been told, but they didn't like it. For an hour and more they had sat patiently with their brides, forbidden to touch them or speak to them. The long day had wearied them; their bodies ached with the brutal punishment of walking the storm. They longed now for kindness, and soft caresses, and sleep.

At last the huddled group separated. They stood back from each other, but still they kept to their circle, facing inwards, their arms crossed over their breasts. A cloud crossed the moon, plunging the river rift into a deeper darkness. Kestrel called softly,

'Take your places behind your brides.'

Rufy Blesh led the way, showing the others what they were to do. He stood immediately behind Kestrel, who faced in to the ring, with her back to him. The other young men, following his example, found their places behind their brides, thus forming an outer ring.

The cloud passed, and by the soft light of the returning moon Kestrel saw the faces of her companions: tense, fearful, but determined.

'Are we ready?'

She saw them nod: sensed the keen edge of anger in Sisi's coiled body: and felt in herself a fierce bright thrill of passion. This is how warriors feel, she thought. This is how it feels to put your very life itself at stake.

Kess! We've reached the door!

Break the door! she called to her brother. *Kill the watchman! We're coming!*

Aloud she cried out,

'Farewell to childhood!'

She and Sisi, gentle Sarel Amos and chubby Seer Such, Red Mimilith and little Ashar Warmish, all turned at once, knives flashing in the moonlight. The young men of the Barra klin, taken entirely by surprise, did nothing to defend themselves from the furious stabbing blades. Bleeding, wounded, shocked, they fell to the deck, from where the women kicked and pushed them towards the ice-cold river.

From the high rock steps came a crash and a scream, as Mumpo burst through the tunnel door and sent the watchman flying into the water far below.

With that scream, Sisi began to scream. She was jabbing and jabbing with her meat knife into the man cowering at her feet.

'You want a kiss?' she screamed. 'This is how I kiss!'

Mumpo, Tanner Amos, and the Shim brothers were down the rock steps before the klin fathers, woken by the screams, had come out of their huts. Kestrel called to her friends,

'Quick! Run! Don't look back!'

She led them over the narrow bridge, while Rufy brought up the rear, fighting off those of the wounded young men who still had the strength to pursue.

'Up the steps! Make for the tunnel!'

Mumpo and Tanner and the Shim brothers stood before the hut doors striking with fury at the men within as they attempted to fight their way out. Miller Marish and Lolo Mimilith caught up with the running women and ran with them, along the edge of the deck, towards the rock steps. Bowman remained on the rock shelf high above, waiting for his moment.

Suddenly three men of the klin burst out through a side wall, smashing the timbers before them, and threw themselves, blades flashing, onto Rollo Shim. Rollo fell with an agonised cry, a long gash opening up down his back and thigh. Mumpo turned and struck, struck and danced and struck again, killing with each blow. He moved so effortlessly, seeming to melt before their swords, that they felt the hot cut of his blade before they saw him strike. Within moments all three were dying on the ground, and he was standing before the break in the wall holding back all who would follow.

Tanner Amos and Bek Shim seized Rollo by either arm and dragged him away towards the steps. Mumpo held the gap in the wall for a few minutes longer, but now other gaps were appearing, on all sides, and the men of the klin were pouring out. Some moved close to surround Mumpo, while others loaded their sling shots to pick off the Manth fighters as they ran.

Bowman saw the slingshots circling in the air, and concentrating all his mind's strength, he tracked the stones as they flew, to send them glancing away against the rock walls.

The young women were on the steps now, the Manth men racing close behind. The brief advantage of surprise was gone, as more and more men of the klin came streaming out into the open. More and more stones were flying, and Bowman could feel his powers draining away, even as Sarel Amos passed him on the high shelf and gained the cover of the tunnel, with the others close behind.

Mumpo too was on the move now, but he was like a stag at bay, ringed by hounds. He leapt and struck, ducked and struck, slipped out of reach and sprang back to strike again, fighting the way he had been taught to fight in the dance of death called the manaxa. He offered himself to the blades only to spiral away, leaving bloody wounds in his wake. But even he could not escape the press of so many swords for long. A slash of searing pain across one shoulder, and he felt the warm slick of blood down his back. He moved out of range, but too slowly, and took a blade in the gut that made him gasp the breath out of his lungs. He turned and saw the steps, not far off now, and felt himself stumble. Dimly, from far off, he felt the pain of his wounds, felt himself growing weaker, knew he must fall –

Suddenly there was space opening up round him, and there was another fighting with him, a wild thing, a creature masked in blood. With one great howl of rage, Mumpo exploded through his tormentors, and sprang up the stone staircase, urged on by Bowman, followed by the wild one.

'On, Mumpo! Run!'

Bowman cleared the way for Mumpo, and saw behind him the wild one who wore the bandits' dress, climbing the steps backwards, fighting off his own people. He heard him shout, saw him turn his bloody head and shout –

'Go, Bowman! Pull down the tunnel timbers behind you! Go!'

Bowman didn't know who this stranger was who fought so hard for them. All he could see was a hideously disfigured face and a ferocious arm wielding a long serrated blade.

'Come with us!' he cried. 'Hurry!'

Now the stranger was up on the ledge, pushing Bowman into the tunnel.

'Go! I'll hold them! Destroy the tunnel!'

It was the voice Bowman recognised at last.

'Rufy! Rufy Blesh!'

'Go!'

'You'll be killed!'

Rufy turned on him, his hollow eyes staring out of his smashed face.

'I'm dead already, Bowman! Now go!'

Bowman turned and followed the others into the tunnel.

'Pull down the timbers!' he cried.

Jamming his sword blade between two of the support beams, he wrenched, and a beam came away. A tumble of loose stone fell, kicking up dust in the dark.

'Pull down the timbers!'

Now the others understood. Miller Marish on one side, Sisi on the other, they attacked the beams, and dragged them down, running back as the rock above came crashing to the tunnel floor. Back and back they went, and the more the tunnel collapsed, the more they could feel the rolling thunder of the rock above, as it settled down once more to fill the little thread of space that men had made.

When they came out at last, choking and dust-grimed, into the place where the fissure opened to the air high above, they stopped to regain their breath and take stock. Behind them they could hear the continuing rumble as the immense weight of the land above settled, closing the one exit from the river rift, sealing the Barra klin forever in its own icy fortress.

Bowman searched the faces of the young women, trying to identify them in the darkness and dust.

'All here? Do we have all of you?'

'Yes,' said Kestrel, almost crying. 'All here.'

Mumpo was bent over, clutching his stomach.

'Mumpo! Are you hurt?'

'Not too badly.' He looked up and forced a smile. 'You should have left me there. I would have killed them all.'

Rollo Shim's back and leg were bleeding copiously. They did what they could to bind the gash. There was no light to do more, and they wanted to move, to run, to be far from this terrible place.

'Can you walk, Rollo?'

'Yes. I'm ready.'

'Then let's go!' cried Bowman.

'Rufy!' Kestrel was hunting among the faces in the dark. 'Where's Rufy?'

'He held the gate for us,' said Bowman.

'They'll kill him!'

She saw Bowman's answering look and understood, and spoke no more.

They set off back down the maze of cracks and fissures,

moving as fast as they could. Above them there came the mewling cry of the cat, stalking the edges of the fissures, guiding them on their way. From time to time the cat seemed to cross overhead, in slow impossible leaps: but Kestrel had no energy left to wonder at such things. The night was dark, and the labyrinth was long.

As first light began to seep into the sky, the rock walls on either side grew lower, and the descending moon reached further down to lay the last of its silver light at their feet. Then there came the moment when the guiding cat was no longer high above, but was waiting ahead, on the same path they trod: and they knew that at the end of this long last slope lay the open land.

Exhausted, panting, drenched in sweat for all the chill of the night, they came out of the labyrinth and stood still, gazing at the sudden great distances reaching to the dark horizon. It was like a return to life after burial in the tomb. Endless space, brightening sky, the fresh sting of the wind.

Not far off, flying high above a ridge, they saw the white flag of their people.

Pinto was awake, and had been for some time. She was too young to share the watch, but she knew she would not go back to sleep, so she chose to sit here, under the flagpole, and look out over the labyrinth. Somewhere out there were her brother and sister, and Mumpo who she loved more than either of them.

It seemed to her a whole lifetime since they'd gone away, but it was only one long night. Her father and the others had buried Harman Warmish under a cairn of stones, and she had helped. With every stone she had laid she had thought about Kestrel and the others, and Ashar Warmish, who was only a few years older than herself.

The capture of the young women had had a strange effect on Pinto. It had frightened her terribly, and she still shivered as she thought about what might be happening to them. Her mother had told her they had been taken to be wives. But how could anyone be forced to be a wife? Pinto tried to imagine one of the scarf-masked bandits forcing her to be his wife, and it just didn't make any sense. It was like forcing someone to be your friend. It couldn't be done.

The absence of Kestrel and the other young women had brought about a change within their group that Pinto felt acutely. Somehow she and Fin and Jet Marish, none of them more than eight years old, had become young women. No one had said this: it was just how it felt. As if in any group of people there must be some who were the young women, and now she was one of them.

After the burial they had all set to work clearing the rock fall that blocked their way. She had worked with the rest, glad to be occupied. They had made a fire, and cooked the meat from the dead cow. Then somebody had said something, something about weeping. What was it?

Mrs Chirish had given her some of the meat to take to Creoth, and he had refused to eat it, because he was sorrowing for the cow's death. Mrs Chirish had not been at all sympathetic. She had said to the grieving cowman,

'It's bad about your cow, but things have a way of dying. People weep for a while, and then they stop.'

Pinto sat under the flag in the faint light that preceded

dawn and wondered if that was true. Mrs Chirish had given Creoth no reason to feel better, but her words had seemed to help him.

People weep for a while, and then they stop . . .

If they never come back, thought Pinto, if Bowman and Kestrel and Mumpo never come back, I'll weep and I won't stop. I'll cry myself to death.

She heard a faint sound behind her, and turned to see who was coming. There was nobody. The other lookouts were a little way away from her along the ridge. The rest of her people were sleeping under and around the wagon. Then she felt a brief tickle at her neck, and reached up to scratch it. There came a lurching feeling inside her, that for a few moments made her feel she was going to be sick, followed by an entirely different feeling, a feeling that she could do anything she wanted in the entire world.

She stood up, and reached her arms high, and pranced up and down for sheer joy.

I can do anything! I can have everything!

All at once she caught a movement in the dark land; and another. Figures were appearing in the distance. She strained her eyes, and made out the familiar shape of her brother, and behind him, taller, shoulders slightly hunched, Mumpo.

'They're back!' she yelled. 'They're back! They're back!'

As Bowman led rescuers and rescued to the ridge, the Manth people woke and came scrambling up the far side. Running and cheering, they ran to take them in their arms. Rollo Shim, who was in more pain than he had admitted, collapsed in a faint. The cheer faded on the watching people's lips. Ira Hath hurried forward, and kneeling, peeled away his blood-crusted shirt to expose the wounded flesh.

'Water! Quickly!'

'Mumpo's hurt!'

Mumpo remained standing, but he staggered as he stood, and clutched his stomach. Pinto cried out in panic.

'Mumpo! You're not to be hurt! You're not to die!'

Bowman spoke sharply above the mounting cries of fear.

'We're all alive. We're all back.'

Branco Such held his daughter in his arms and sobbed aloud. Ashar Warmish hugged her mother, who was weeping uncontrollably. Hanno Hath embraced his son, and spoke to him low.

'Are they still following you?'

'No,' said Bowman. 'They'll never hurt us again.'

Little Scooch set himself to cleaning and bandaging the wounds, helped by Lunki and Mrs Chirish. Lunki was impressed by Scooch's neat dressings.

'It's very like pastry work,' he said by way of explanation.

Kestrel satisfied herself that the wounded men were being well looked after, and then sought out her brother. For a long moment they stood in silence, arms round each other, feeling the fear retreat, and the knowledge that they were together again fill up the space it had occupied.

I knew you'd find me. I knew it.

'Did you see Mumpo fight?'

'And Rufy Blesh. We'd never have got away without them.'

A low mewling sound came from the cat.

'And Mist. We'd never have got back without Mist.'

The cat turned his head aside, as if to show he needed no thanks. Nevertheless, he felt that what the boy said was no more than the truth. It was right that the others should know it.

Nearby, Lunki was now listening to Sisi's account of their capture and escape, her eyes wide with terror.

'Oh my pet! Oh my sweet one!'

'I killed him, Lunki.' Sisi's eyes glowed at the memory. 'The one who dared to call me his bride. I killed him.'

She looked up at the flag, still streaming in the night wind. She knew it well. It was her former wedding dress.

'I'll never be a bride now, Lunki. I'm a husband-killer now.'

Pinto, still in her strange state, stayed close by Mumpo, clinging to one of his arms. Mumpo stroked her hair, touched by her fierce loyalty.

'You're not badly hurt,' she told him. 'You'll be alright soon.'

'Yes,' he said. 'I hope so.'

'You will, because you've got to be.'

'Then I will,' he said, smiling.

'When I'm older,' she told him, whispering, 'I'm going to marry you.'

She had never dared say it before. Now she dared anything.

'Are you, Pinskin?'

This was his special name for her. She liked it that he had a special name for her, but at the same time she knew he didn't think of her as a grown-up person like himself.

'You'll marry me, won't you?'

'You'll not be marrying anybody for a long, long time.'

'If anyone else tries to marry you, I'll kill them. Even Kess. Especially Kess.'

She felt him pull away from her, but she held on tightly.

'Don't talk like that. You know you don't mean it.'

'I do! I'd kill Kess myself, I'd stab her with a knife until she was dead!'

Mumpo pushed her off him, angered.

'What do you know of killing? I've just come from a place of killing. Never, never talk like that again.'

Pinto found she couldn't stop herself.

'I would! I'd kill her! I'd stab her and cut her and make her bleed –'

Mumpo took her by the shoulders and shook her to stop the stream of wild talk.

'You say you love me, Pinto. If you love me, you love Kestrel. Do you understand? Say another unkind word about Kestrel, and I'll never be your friend again.'

Pinto stared back at him, churning with hot prickly feelings all through her insides. She wanted with a fierce yearning to pour out all her hatred for Kestrel, but she was terrified of losing Mumpo's love. The two passions fought within her with such violence that she felt faint and sick. Tears began to well up in her stinging eyes.

'It's not fair! It's not fair!'

She turned and ran and ran and ran.

No one noticed her absence. The return of the captured girls occupied the attention of all. As the winter sun rose, the Manth people gathered round the wagon, and there was meat to eat and water to drink, and the whole story to tell. By the time Pinto came creeping back, miserable and shivering, she found everyone listening as Kestrel told about Rufy Blesh, and how he had helped them escape.

'Whatever wrong he's done to us,' she said, 'he's paid for it now.'

Pinto looked from Kestrel to Mumpo, and shivered and felt ill and sad, and thought how no one cared for her at all and perhaps she'd die and then they'd be sorry.

Ira Hath heard what Kestrel had said with compassion.

'Poor boy. These are cruel times.'

Kestrel was remembering how, back in the long ago days of Aramanth, Rufy Blesh had written a poem, and it had won a prize. Now, rather than the bitter young man who had run away from the Mastery, or the bandit with the bleeding and disfigured face, she remembered the boy who had written the poem.

> *No, I'm not sad*
> *And though I say nothing*
> *I want to talk.*
> *I'm waiting for you to smile*
> *Then I'll smile too*
> *And we can begin.*
> *Are you like me?*
> *Does it go on for ever*
> *Waiting to smile?*

7

The dying of the last fire

When the march began again, Mumpo insisted on taking his place at the head, alongside Bowman. His wounds were healing, and he walked with his usual loping stride, but Bowman could tell that he was in pain.

'Why not ride in the wagon for a while, with Rollo?'

'Rollo can't walk without limping. I can.'

'The pain's stealing your strength, Mumpo. I can feel it.'

'So long as I can march, I'll march.'

A cry went up from the group by the wagon.

'Bowman! Get Bowman!'

Bowman turned and ran back. He raced past Creoth, who was trudging along behind his cows. One of the cows, startled by Bowman's pounding feet, shied and bolted across his path, narrowly missing him.

'Whoa, Tawny!' cried Creoth. 'What's got into you, girl?'

Bowman found his father holding Pinto tight in his arms. She was screaming and twisting. Her face was bleeding.

'Go away! Leave me alone! I hate you all! I'll kill you, I'll cut off your head, I love you, don't look at me, I'll claw out your eyes, Come closer, Hold me, Hurt me, Hurt you, Love you, aah! Aaahh! Kill me! Murderer! Monster! Aah! Aaahh!'

'She's scratching herself,' said Kestrel, with tears in her eyes. 'Really badly.'

'Get out!' shrieked Pinto, trying to free her hands. 'I hate you! I'll kill you!'

Bowman needed only one glance at those bleeding scratches.

'It's in her,' he said. 'It's the stinging fly.'

Mumpo now caught up with them. The sight of him sent Pinto into a further passion of violent screaming.

'I want Mumpo! Make him love me! He's not to love Kess! Don't look at me, I'll kill you, kill Kess, cut off her head, tear out her eyes! Mumpo – aah! Aaahhh!'

'Don't listen to her, Kess! Move back, Mumpo! It's not her talking.'

Kestrel and Mumpo both moved back, out of Pinto's line of sight, avoiding each other's eyes. Bowman was forming a rapid plan, ignoring Pinto's delirious shrieks.

'Creoth!' he called. 'Rope one of your cows! Get help. Hold it tight.'

To his father, who was struggling to keep hold of Pinto as she thrashed in his arms, he said,

'If there's only one fly, I think I can make it so it never returns.'

Creoth understood Bowman's command, though not the reason for it. He and Bek Shim got a rope round one of the cows' horns, and braced themselves to hold the animal still between them.

'There, Star, my Star, my beauty,' said Creoth, trying to

soothe the terrified cow. But the cow became increasingly agitated, and tried to escape.

'Hold it still!' called Bowman.

Sisi, who like everyone else had gathered to watch the bewildering events, saw what was needed to be done. She went to the blanket pile, pulled out a blanket, and threw it over the frightened cow's head. The cow became still at once, turning its blinded head this way and that, unsure what had happened.

Bowman and Hanno, meanwhile, holding Pinto between them, carried her towards the cow. Pinto fought, struggled and shrieked every inch of the way.

'Get away from me! Kill me! Save me! Aaaahh! Hurt me!'

Her screams were terrible, but Bowman paid no attention. Holding her locked in his arms, while Hanno gripped her jerking legs, he carried her close to the blanket-covered cow. The scene would have been comical had it not been so pitiful, to see Pinto so deranged and the cow so helpless.

'Everyone move back!' ordered Bowman.

'Murderer! Monster! Let me go! Aaahh!'

Creoth and Bek Shim braced themselves on the ropes that held the cow's horns, as Bowman forced his struggling sister close up to the cow's covered head. There, once in position, he pressed his cheek to Pinto's bloody cheek, and pushed his way into her mind. This time he went straight for the invader, and found it, huge and fat, swelling within her. He grasped it tight, and squeezed it, and pulled. Little by little he felt its grasp give way, for though plumper than before, it was not as strong. As he dragged it out from within her he sensed that it was shrinking, dwindling from the fat grub back to the tiny buzzing fly. Then with one last tug he had it out, and hurled it directly into the head of the terrified cow. For a moment he heard the high faint whine. He saw the cow's head shudder beneath the blanket. He felt his sister go still in his arms.

'Alright, pa. You can let go now.'

Hanno lowered Pinto's legs to the ground. Bowman kept her folded safe in his arms. He kissed her cheek, his lips tasting the sweat and blood already drying on her skin. To his father and mother, anxiously watching, he said,

'She'll be alright now.'

Kestrel came forward and lightly stroked Pinto's hair, as she lay in her sleep of exhaustion. Bowman felt her distress.

It wasn't her talking, Kess.

Wasn't it?

She gave him a look of such sadness that he didn't know what more to say.

The cow, still tethered by the horns, let out a low bellow.

'Let the cow go,' said Bowman. 'Keep away from her.'

Creoth pulled away the blanket, and the cow rolled its eyes. He untied the ropes from its horns.

'There, my Star. It's all over now.'

The cow bellowed again, a great mournful heart-breaking sound.

'There now, Star! There, my Star!'

Creoth stroked the animal's neck and flank with his

big soothing hands. The cow shifted from hoof to hoof, splaying out its legs, and started to shiver violently. Its whole hide shivered.

'What is it, Star? Bowman, what have you done?'

'I'm sorry,' said Bowman. 'I had to do it. Don't stay too close to her. The thing is in her.'

'Oh, my poor girl! My poor girl!'

He hadn't left the cow's side.

Pinto now reopened her eyes and started to gulp in air as if she had been suffocated.

'You're alright now. It's come out of you now.'

'Oh, Bo! It was horrible! I wanted – I wanted – I wanted to tear my own face off! It was there, just beneath my face! I had to tear – to dig –'

'No more. Hush now. It's gone now.'

She was crying, great sobbing tears of relief. Bowman handed her into their mother's arms.

Creoth tugged at Bowman.

'You must take it out of my poor Star, Bowman. You must save my Star.'

'No, Creoth. I won't do that. So long as the thing stays in Star, the rest of us are safe.'

'But she doesn't understand. See how she rolls her eyes! She knows something's wrong, but she doesn't know what.' The cow moaned again, even more piteously. 'Take it out of her, and put it in me.'

'No,' said Bowman. 'It's best this way.'

'Why must Star suffer? She never did any harm to any living creature. I've led a life of idleness. Let me be driven mad.'

'No,' said Bowman.

'You'd bring torment on an innocent beast?'

'Yes, Creoth. I do it, not you. I'm the one who must live with that. You are free to love and to grieve.'

Bowman's sad wisdom awed Creoth.

'Beard of my ancestors!' he exclaimed. 'You're growing up fast.'

The cow began to swing its head from side to side. Then it let out a new sound, a bellow of rage, and lunged with its horns at Creoth's body. Creoth jumped back, caught by surprise.

'Star! It's me!'

'It's not Star any more,' said Bowman. 'Let her go.'

The cow veered about and cantered away, snorting and bellowing, to come to a stop a hundred paces distant.

'I can't just leave her,' said Creoth.

'No,' said Bowman. 'We can't leave her.'

'What can I do?'

'I think you know.'

The cowman who had once been an emperor turned his bearded face to meet Bowman's steady gaze.

'Please,' he said. 'Anything but that.'

'I'll do it.'

'Oh, Bowman! How you've changed.'

'I've seen what it does to my sister, and my father, and Sisi. I won't let it follow us any further.'

Creoth turned and looked towards the tormented cow, and then back to Bowman.

'How is it to be done?'

Bowman laid one hand on his short sword.

'And if we do it, what then?'

'Then the thing is trapped in the cow's body, and we

bury the body, and we hope it is never released again.'

The cow bent her forelegs and slumped to the ground. There she lay, her hide shivering, rolling her eyes.

'Will her suffering ever end?'

'No,' said Bowman. 'The thing will grow inside her until she's driven mad, and will do anything to be free of it. You saw the man we buried by the roadside.'

'Yes. I saw him.'

Creoth bowed his head, and did not speak for a few moments. When he looked up again, his expression had changed. He had aged.

'She knows me,' he said. 'I won't leave her now to the mercy of strangers.' He held out his hand. 'Give me your sword.'

'Are you sure you can do this?'

'If she'll let me,' he replied.

Bowman gave him his sword. Creoth went alone to where the cow lay, and sat down beside her. The cow let out a long moan. Creoth laid an arm over the animal's neck.

'The long prison of the years unlocks its iron door,' he said softly. 'Go free now, into the beautiful land.'

His quiet voice seemed to calm the cow. She turned her sorrowful eyes to meet his.

'Forgive us who suffer in this clouded world.'

He raised the sword in his right hand, and turned the point of the blade downwards, above the back of the cow's head, where the skull joins the neck.

'Guide us and wait for us, as we wait for you.'

The cow uttered a quiet murmuring sound, as if in answer.

'We will meet again. We will, my Star. We will meet again.'

He struck quickly and hard, knowing his kindness depended on the power of the blow. The sword drove true. The cow's head dropped to the hard ground. For a moment, before the blood flowed, he stroked the dead face. Then he rose and walked back to Bowman, and gave him back his sword.

Bowman said, 'That was well done.'

'Don't talk to me!' Creoth's voice cracked like a whip. 'Not one word!'

He turned to his cows, of which only three now remained, and sought comfort among their slow movements.

The days were colder now, and shorter. Each morning there was a hard frost, and the sun rose dazzling bright into an ice-clear sky. The wagon-wheels locked to the axles, and had to be clubbed loose with blows from a sledge hammer. Meals were carefully rationed, so that the meat and the sourgum would last many days. The urgent shortage now was of firewood. One modest fire was no longer enough. A big fire must be built, morning and evening, to thaw out people and animals, and boil water, and soften the frost-stiffened leather harness. Already the bare boards of the wagon bed could be seen through the wood stack. Without fire, as the winter hardened around them, the Manth people knew they had no hope of reaching the distant mountains.

All that day and into dusk the Manth people trudged on, and clouds formed in the sky to the north. That night snow fell while they slept, and they woke to a white world. Snow had drifted through the gaps in the wind-covers beneath which they lay, and formed a frozen crust on their hair and clothing. The firewood too was deep under snow, and had to be knocked log against log before it would burn. While they waited for the fire to catch they jumped up and down, banging their arms by their sides, to send the chilled blood flowing through their veins.

The ice in the water barrels had to be broken with hammers, and stirred with sticks to stop it freezing over again. The cows no longer gave milk. Their feed was too meagre, and the cold too hard. Such energy as was left in their bony frames was needed to keep them alive.

Bek Shim came to Hanno Hath to ask how much firewood he was to break out for the fire. It was not an easy question to answer.

'As little as possible,' said Hanno. But after a moment's thought he changed his mind. A small fire that failed to warm them was a waste of fuel.

'The same as yesterday,' he said.

Bek Shim shook his head.

'That will leave enough for one more day,' he said.

'I know,' said Hanno. 'We must hope for kinder weather.'

The sun stayed hidden by clouds all that day, but no more snow fell as the marchers plodded on across the endless plain. In front, the smooth untouched whiteness stretched as far as the eye could see. Behind, the deep ruts of the wagon wheels, and the beaten snow where horses and cows and people had passed. The pace of the march was slowing down. The horses found it heavy going, hauling the wagon through the snow; and the people, their boots sinking to the ankles with each step, were soon wearied.

Late that afternoon, unable to go further, they drew the wagon to a stop and tethered the horses and the cows beside it. Then they pulled the weather covers outwards from the high hoops, spreading them over the beasts like the skirts of a dress, and laced tight all the slits. The Manth people then crowded in with the beasts: men, women and children together, to share warmth as they slept.

Creoth slept between two of his cows. They seemed to understand that such closeness was necessary; or perhaps they were just too weak to protest; but they settled down quietly among the unfamiliar crowd.

'Squeeze close to each other,' said Hanno. 'That way we'll hold our heat.'

A pale silver light filtered between the cracks, reflected from the surrounding snow into the shadowy shelter. Pinto, still weak from her illness, crept close to her mother. Kestrel lay down on her other side, and timidly laid one arm over her. When Pinto didn't object, she huddled up close. Bowman lay with his arms round his father, and behind him, Mumpo and Mrs Chirish pressed against him. The Mimilith family, all five of them, had drawn Scooch into their heap, and half across Scooch lay Tanner Amos and his sister Sarel. Sarel Amos held Ashar in her arms. The two had become close since the terrors of their captivity. The big Shim boys slept with Miller Marish and his two little girls. And so it went on, every one of them twined up with others, burrowing for warmth as the day ended outside, and the hard winter night set in.

The last to join the great huddle was Mist the cat. The

moon was already in the sky when he found his way under the canopy and between the wheels. He stalked delicately over the sleeping people to where Bowman lay. There in the crook of Bowman's legs he found a snug hole in which to curl up. He scratched at Bowman's clothing to arrange it in more comfortable folds, and settled himself too down to sleep.

Some time in the night snow began to fall once again, more heavily and more steadily than before. When the Manth people woke, early and chilled, they saw the covers sagging low above them, and knew they were heavy with snow. Mo Mimilith, who was the first to venture out, found that the snow was lying two feet up the sloping canopy, and he had to beat a path through the drifts. Outside it was snowing still, the visible world shrunk to a curtain of swirling white flakes.

Rollo Shim was next out, limping on his hurt leg; then Bowman, and Mumpo. Even a bare few paces away, the wagon with its tented covering and all the people and beasts within disappeared, lost in the engulfing whiteness. The young men trudged off through the snow, needing to empty their bladders, but they dared not go far. Even where the snow had not drifted, it lay knee-deep on the ground.

'The wagon'll never move in this,' said Rollo Shim.

Bowman nodded, brushing off the snow that was settling on his head.

'We'll have to wait,' he said.

They built their last fire beside the wagon shelter, and with difficulty managed to get it to light even as the snow went on falling. The people were quiet, subdued by the gravity of their plight. Everyone understood that there was no point in struggling on in such conditions. They must wait for the skies to clear, and the snow on the ground to freeze, so that it would bear the weight of the wagon. No one asked how long they would have to wait, or what they were to do when the fuel ran out. Their eyes, however, turned again and again towards Hanno and Ira Hath, as if to say, You led us here. You must save us.

When the fire was hot they boiled a pot of water and melted the last of the sourgum in it. This made a sweet tangy drink that warmed their stomachs. As they drank, their spirits revived; and with new strength came a new willingness to face their predicament.

'So tell us, Hanno,' said Miko Mimilith. 'How bad is it?'

'You know all that I know,' said Hanno.

'Well then, what I know is that we can't stay here, or we'll freeze and starve. And we can't go on, because the snow's too deep. So I say it's bad.'

'Yes, Miko. It's bad.'

It was necessary to feed the fire with logs all the time, to keep the core of heat strong enough to melt the falling snow. Each time Bek Shim went to the wagon bed and returned with another log, the people round the fire asked him,

'How much more, Bek?'

'Not so much,' he said.

Still the snow fell. Almost the worst of it for the Manth people was not being on the move, not going anywhere, not being able to see more than a few yards in any one direction. Fearful and helpless, their spirits sank as the day wore on. Tempers began to fray. There were mutterings in corners, and some were heard to say it was all the fault of the Haths.

Then Bek Shim brought the very last log from the wagon, and put it on the fire, and straightening himself up, said to those near enough to hear.

'That's all.'

The word rippled through the people.

'No more firewood! No more firewood!'

As if hypnotised, they stared at the glowing fire, which already, it seemed to their frightened eyes, was dwindling and dying before them.

'Hanno Hath,' said a grave old voice. 'What is to become of us?'

It was Seldom Erth. He was a man who had always prided himself on seeing clearly, and facing hard facts. He had no wish to blame Hanno. What use was blame now?

'I don't know,' said Hanno.

'I make no complaint,' said the old man. 'But if I'm to die, I want to know, so that I can prepare my mind.'

'It may come to that,' said Hanno. 'I hope not.'

'You hope not?' This was Cheer Warmish, speaking with bitterness. 'I hoped my husband wouldn't die, but he's dead. What use is your hope to me? Don't tell me any more of your dreams. We all know it's over for us, so why pretend otherwise?'

Hanno looked from Cheer Warmish to all the other pale faces watching him.

'If I've failed you,' he said quietly, 'I ask for your forgiveness. I have believed that one day we Manth people, few as we are, will reach our homeland, and our wanderings will be over. I have believed that so long as we stay true to our goal, whatever the hardship, we will live to see that day. I still believe it, even now, as I watch the dying of our last fire. I will believe it after the ashes lie cold under the snow. I will believe it until the moment I die. And after I'm dead, my children will believe it.'

He fell silent. For a few moments, no one spoke. Ira Hath squeezed his hand. Bowman was filled with a fierce stinging pride that made him want to cry, which he refused to do. He felt the same feeling in Kestrel, and reached out to her with his mind.

He's the strongest of us all.

I love him so much, responded Kestrel. *So much.*

Then Scooch stood up. It was comical to see how this shy little man felt he must stand to command their attention. He had never made a speech before, and mumbled rather, but they could all hear him well enough.

'I just want to say,' he began, 'I just want to tell Mr Hath, it's not so much a case of forgiving, it's more like a case of thanking. Speaking for myself, that is. I well remember back in Aramanth how I was a floor sweeper in the brickworks, and had been all my grown life, and thought it was all I was good for. It was Mr Hath who showed me how to believe I could do more. That's how I came to biscuits, and from biscuits to pastries, and from pastries to respect. I have Mr Hath to thank for that. I was proud to follow him on this march to our homeland. And if our fate is now to die here in the snow, well, I'm proud to die with him, too.'

He gave a little bow in Hanno's direction, and abruptly

sat down. These two speeches, by Hanno and Scooch, had a paradoxical effect. Because both said in plain words that they might die, the terror of dying began to fade. Every one of them had been thinking it. Now they all thought it together, and took strength from each other.

Young Ashar Warmish whispered to her mother,

'If we die we'll see papa again, won't we? So we don't have to mind so much.'

Jet Marish, the smallest of the children, not really understanding, asked her father,

'What happens when you die? What does it feel like?'

'Like going to sleep,' Miller Marish told her.

It was Pinto who thought to put the direct question to her mother. After all, Ira Hath was a prophetess.

'Will we all die, ma?'

'I don't see how it can be otherwise,' said Ira slowly. 'And yet, even here in this snowstorm, I feel the warmth of the homeland on my face. Perhaps something will happen.'

This wasn't exactly a prophecy, but it was cheering nonetheless. Old Seldom Erth pulled out some of the dwindling store of hay for his horses. Creoth saw to the watering of his cows. The cat, annoyed by the falling snow, left the group round the fire and retreated to the shelter of the wagon.

As the heat of the fire faded, the people followed the cat under cover, and sought the warmth of each other's bodies, as they had done in the night. Here in the grey half-light they felt the surrounding cold press in on them, and steal the heat from their fingers and toes. They began to accept now that it was really going to happen, that they were living through their last few hours. The cold didn't hurt them, it made them sleepy. They knew that once they surrendered to the creeping drowsiness, they would not wake again.

In this shadowy half-light they began to tell each other things they had never said before; things that had long weighed on their minds. They were like travellers who come to a wide river, and know that they must enter the water, and one by one they lay down their belongings, and then strip off their clothes, so that they can swim unburdened to the other side.

Tanner Amos knelt before Hanno and Ira Hath, and kissed their hands, and said,

'Forgive me for hating you after my Pia died. I was wrong. But I was so unhappy.'

Sisi said to Lunki,

'I've never thanked you, Lunki, for all the years you've cared for me. I couldn't live without you.'

'Oh, my pet! As if I'd ever let you! Caring for you is as natural to me as breathing. I can't stop now.'

Pinto crept up close to Kestrel and whispered to her,

'I'm sorry I said those terrible things. I don't want to kill you at all. I'm just a hateful rat-child, like Mumpo says.'

'No, you're not,' said Kestrel, kissing her. 'You're my own sister and you can kill me as much as you want and I'll still love you.'

'Can I ask you to do something for me, Kess? For me. Not for anyone else.'

'Yes. Anything.'

'Be kind to Mumpo.'

Kestrel bit her lip to stop the tears rising to her eyes.

'I'll be as kind as I can,' she said.

Bowman was watching Sisi, who was sitting alone now, her back very straight, her eyes gazing far away. He wanted to speak to her, but was not sure what he wanted to say. Then she turned and met his eyes, and inclined her head, in the manner of a princess who says, You may approach me. So he went to her.

'Well, Bowman,' she said. 'Where is the one who was to come for you?'

'I don't know. Perhaps I was wrong.'

'How can you be wrong? Aren't you the chosen one?'

'Are you laughing at me, Sisi?'

'Only a little. Do you mind?'

'No. I don't mind.'

'You can laugh at me, too. Do you know what I wish?'

'What do you wish, Sisi?'

'I wish the stinging fly would come again.'

But Bowman didn't laugh. He took her slender hand in his, and kissed it gently. Her skin was very cold against his lips.

Kestrel sought out Mumpo, as she had promised. She found him in a far corner, and they put their arms round each other, because time was running out and they were so cold.

'Do your wounds still hurt you very much, Mumpo?'

'Not the wounds,' he replied. 'Only thinking that I'm no use any more.'

'But that's not true!'

'Before, I knew that even if I was slow and stupid, I was a good fighter. So I thought, I'll always have that for Kess. I'll fight for her. That's how I'll show her I love her. But now, I don't even have that any more.'

He spoke without self pity, as if he was saying no more than the simple truth. Kestrel knew she could only respond in the same way, out of respect for him.

'I know you love me,' she said, 'and I'm proud that you do. I wish I could feel the same way. But that's not how I am.'

'It doesn't matter now,' said Mumpo, holding her close.

'It's not you, Mumpo, it's me. I can't love anybody the way you love me. If I could, I'd love you back. You're good and you're strong, and there's no one I'd like to love more. But I'm wrong inside, Mumpo. Please forgive me.'

'Nothing to forgive,' said Mumpo, happier now than he'd been for a long time. 'You're my friend, Kess. You changed my life. The day you became my friend, my life became worth something. Friends love each other, don't they? If we're truly going to die here, I don't mind so much, because I know we love each other a little.'

'More than a little. As much as I can.'

'Well, then. I'm not alone, am I? It's not so hard to die when you're not alone.'

'Oh, Mumpo. You're so very, very dear.'

She kissed his face, many times. Then, quickly, she slipped out of his arms, and between the flaps of the cover, into the falling snow.

She walked and walked, plunging her legs into the deep snow, moving fast, weak and cold as she was, needing to get away from everyone, needing to be on her own. When the veil of snow surrounded her on all sides and she could no longer see the encampment, she came to a stop. Unable to help herself, she started to sob aloud.

Tears rolled down her cheeks, warm on her chilled skin. She wrapped her arms round her chest and felt her body being wracked with a terrible wrenching sadness.

It had started when she was with Mumpo. She had felt it so clearly, his simple goodness, his power of love, his feeling that he was worth something: and with it had come a mounting despair about herself. She was neither simple nor good. She had no love in her, apart from for Bowman, and that was as much the life force in her as anything that could be called love. She was worth nothing. She took without giving, let herself be loved without loving, and was not, not at all, content to die. She felt in Mumpo a generosity that accepted death as gladly as he accepted life. There was no generosity in her. There was bitterness and rage at this slow freezing of the blood.

I won't die! I refuse to die!

She felt the furious will in herself, and hated herself for it, because she knew she fought so passionately only for her own survival. Why don't I care for anyone else? Am I a wild animal? Why can't I love?

Sobbing, shaking, weeping, she turned round and round as if trapped in an invisible cage; and all the time the snow was falling. She began to walk, not knowing which direction she took, not having a goal other than to escape her misery. Far off, where the wagon stood, they were calling her name, but she didn't hear their voices. She walked on, plunging through ever deeper snow, blinded by tears; until at last she could walk no further.

The snow covered her legs up to her knees. She was so

tired, and so sad. She hugged her chest, and let herself fall, sinking downwards into the snow, until her numb knees struck the hard ground beneath. There she stayed, kneeling, the snow now up to her waist, the bitter cold piercing her to the core.

'Kestrel! Kess! Where are you?'

She heard the voices now, but had no strength to answer. It was as if all the strength had come out of her with those great heaving sobs, with those endless tears.

'Kestrel! Kestrel!'

She got up, wanting to get away. Staggering, seeing nothing, she lurched onwards, dragging her legs through the deep snow. Then her feet became lighter, and it seemed to her she was entering a cloud. The snow stopped falling. The bitter cold receded. Have I died? she thought. Is this the place you go when you die? Confused and frightened, she walked on into ever deeper cloud, and stopped once more. Here, as she had done before, she sank to her knees – and found the ground was bare of snow.

She felt giddy. She put out her hands to support herself, just in time, as she toppled forward. Her palms pressed down onto bare rock. A tingle ran up her arms. She shuddered, and her bewildered brain stirred, recognising a strange sensation. She felt the rocky ground with her hands. What am I feeling? The cold had made her senses sluggish. She shook herself again. What am I feeling?

Hardness. Smoothness.

Warmth.

Kestrel! Kestrel, answer me!

It was Bowman, coming directly towards her through

the cloud. A great surge of excitement rose up in Kestrel, and all her body awoke. The ground was warm!

'Here!' she cried. 'Here! We're not going to die after all!'

8

Fatness is happiness

The Manth people, with their wagon and their horses, their cows and their cat, marched out of the snow-bound land, down a long slope into the cloud, entirely ignorant as to where they were going, seeking only escape from the cold. The further they went, the warmer became the ground beneath their feet. From it rose a fine mist, that gathered in the cold air and formed the cloud that now engulfed them. Who knew what dangers lay in that mist? The marchers cared nothing. They had come face to face with death. Life was worth the gamble, whatever the risk.

Here and there they passed clumps of rough vegetation. The starved cows tore eagerly at all they could find; but none of it looked fit for human consumption, until they came upon a region of thorny bushes. Among the bushes were brambles, bearing ripe blackberries. The first marchers to see them through the mist stopped and stared, as if at a mirage. The blackberries hung heavy on the bramble, glistening with droplets of moisture, each one a jewel-like cluster of deep purple beads. Bek Shim put out a hand and picked one. It fell almost gratefully off its stalk. He looked at it, lying so shiny and juicy in his palm. Then quickly, guiltily, he popped it in his mouth and ate it.

'Sweet,' he announced. 'Delicious.'

At once the others started to scrabble after the fruit. The first to pick took all the near berries, and the later marchers emerging from the mist had to push further into the bushes to get their share. Soon enough every one of them had purple lips and tongues. Heedless of the thorns, pricked and bleeding, they stripped the brambles of all their fruit, the taller ones reaching down their spoils to the eager children beneath; until all had eaten their fill.

'What kind of place is this?' asked Hanno wonderingly.

They went on, aware now that they were descending steeply now into a valley. The mist grew thinner all the time, though when they looked up they saw that it had formed a dense layer above their heads. The sides of the valley began to appear: at first stony slopes, broken by patches of bramble and coarse grass; then greener plants became more frequent, and sweeter grasses. The cows and the horses kept stopping to graze, and would no doubt have stopped entirely, had they not seen the ever richer pastures further down the valley.

Now they came to a stream, that bubbled up from a wayside spring. They stopped to drink, and found that the water was warm, like the ground. It was this warmth more than anything else that filled them with joy. Where the cold had made them heavy, drowsy and sad, the warmth brought a sudden lightness of spirit.

'I never want to be cold again!' said Kestrel aloud. The misery had dropped away from her. She almost danced as she marched along.

All the time the plants and the trees on either side became more luxuriant. They were entirely past the region of thorns. Now they saw dense curling ferns, and trees with glossy green spear-shaped leaves, that dripped moisture from their spiny tips. On the ground there grew big purple-petalled flowers that held water, like bowls; and in and out of the flowers darted dragonflies, with bright red and blue bodies. They marched on, following a broad leaf-strewn path that ran beside the stream, and now when they gazed up they saw the canopies of great trees spreading like umbrellas in the mist.

They came upon a grove of banana palms, and here and there among the clusters of young green fruit they found enough ripe bananas for all. Stopping briefly to hunt out and eat the bananas, Pinto discovered a column of ants marching down the valley floor. They were big, their bodies almost half-an-inch long, and they marched in a column ten ants wide and more, each one carrying a piece of leaf. Pinto followed their march a little way, until she saw a small red frog squatting beside the column, watching the ants march by. The frog sat motionless, then suddenly it flicked out its tongue and pulled an ant into its mouth. Pinto was fascinated. She ran off to find her brother.

'Bo! Come and see what I've found!'

She tugged him by the sleeve, and led him back to the marching ants. She and Bowman squatted in silence and watched the frog take ant after ant. The marching column never stopped. The other ants seemed not to notice that some of their number were disappearing.

'Why don't they mind?' asked Pinto.

'Maybe they do, only we can't see.'

'Do you think they're marching to their homeland?'

She gave her brother a mischievous look.

'Definitely,' said Bowman.

They both laughed. There was something comical about the way the ants paid no attention at all to the scarlet frog, as if it was just too big to be visible to them, at their low antish level of concerns. At the same time it was scary, and too like their own circumstances for comfort.

The march continued. The valley floor was level now, the misty cloud high above. Tiny birds flashed by, sudden zigzags of bright colour. The heavy air throbbed with the hum of bees and the buzz of mosquitoes. They pulled off their winter coats and found they were sweating. No sunshine pierced the lid of cloud, but the valley grew warmer all the time.

Fin Marish said wonderingly,

'Is this the homeland, pa?'

'No, darling. Not yet.'

Hanno Hath kept the lookouts in place as they marched. He looked everywhere for signs of cultivation, or dwellings. So fertile a valley must have its masters. But all he saw was the lush green growth on either side of the stream, and the occasional swoop and cry of a bright bird.

Kree-kree! Kree-kree!

It was Mist the cat who found the first signs that there were, or had been, people in the valley. Mist found the swooping flight of the pretty birds an intolerable provocation, and kept leaping at them as they passed. With each high leap, he gauged his strike more accurately, until at last his snapping jaws caught a bird in mid-flight. Bowman, who had never thought he would do it, saw this with dismay. Mist was already bounding away with the bird in his mouth, its blue and gold wings still twitching.

'Mist!' called Bowman. 'Come back!'

Bowman went after the cat, pushing a path between the drenching leaves of palm trees. He found Mist in a clearing a little way off. The bird lay dead at his feet. Now that it was no longer moving, he seemed to have lost interest.

'You're not to hunt here,' scolded Bowman. 'We don't know what sort of place this is.'

'I'm not hungry anyway,' said Mist.

Bowman picked up the dead bird with gentle fingers, and spread out one shining golden wing.

'If you're not hungry, why kill?'

'Have you ever killed a bird in flight, boy? If you had, you wouldn't be asking such a fool question.'

'You do it for pleasure?'

'Pleasure is too small a word. Call it glory.'

Bowman had stopped listening. Looking round the clearing, he realised that the carpet of dead leaves had been raked back. Some branches of trees showed clean-cut edges. And the ground was ridged.

He took a few steps to examine the ridges at closer range. Not exactly ridges: more like long humps. There were five of them, one beside another, in a row. Beyond, a second longer row, of eight. Beyond that, a third row, longer still. He counted thirteen mounds.

No animal would form earth into such regular patterns. This was the work of men.

Of course! he thought, suddenly seeing what was staring him in the face. Graves! This was a graveyard. He turned and ran back.

'Pa!' he shouted. 'Come and see this!'

They all came, and they all looked. As Branco Such pointed out, some of the graves looked recent. The near row of five were only lightly covered in grasses, and the mounds of earth hadn't yet had time to settle. All five were the same height. That suggested the bodies had been buried at the same time. What could have killed five people simultaneously? And who had buried them?

In a more sober and wary mood, the Manth people resumed their journey. Hanno doubled the lookouts ahead and behind, and every one of the marchers kept their eyes on the dense woodland to either side.

The stream that ran with them was wider now, and its water was hotter. Steam rose up from its surface here and there. The air of the valley was becoming stickier, and the marchers were sweating freely. The bitter cold that had so nearly killed them now seemed a distant memory.

A sudden crash and scuffle in the undergrowth, followed by a honking grunting noise, and out from a clump of umbrella-leafed plants there lumbered a large and very fat pig. Paying them no attention, it lurched slowly into the stream, trod steadily down it for a while, and then lay on its belly in a sandy-bottomed pool. The stream water flowed around and over the pig's pink and bristly back, while it held its snout pointed upwards so that it could breathe.

Soon after this a second even fatter pig waddled out of the vegetation and made its way to the same pool. As the column of marchers and their wagon tramped past, the pigs followed them with their eyes, but did not move. They appeared to be familiar with people; at any rate, they showed no fear.

'Those aren't wild,' said Creoth. 'Those pigs are tame.'

The umbrella-leafed trees grew closer to the track as they went on, and on the stream-side also big fleshy green plants formed an ever-denser wall, so that soon they only knew the water was flowing onward at their left side by the rising billows of steam. Big wet leaves slapped their faces as they walked, soaking their clothing, cooling the sweat now constantly prickling their skin. Pushing onwards, they heard the gush and crash of falling water ahead, but were now unable to see beyond the reach of their own arms. The track had disappeared, been overgrown by the jungle greenery. Lolo Mimilith and Bek Shim went in front of the horses, slicing at the soft branches with swords to make a way for the team to pull the wagon through. The wheels lurched over tangled roots that had crawled across the pathway, and the high hoops of the wagon's cover pushed back the overhead branches, to release them with a jerk that showered water over those that marched behind.

Then through the ceaseless gurgle of falling water came a quite different sound: the sound of a man singing. A fine tenor voice was carolling away, unaccompanied by any other voices or musical instruments, somewhere not far from their leaf-shrouded path.

> *Who is as happy as me-ee-ee?* sang the voice.
> *Who is as happy as I?*
> *Happy as happy can be-ee-ee*
> *Oh, hippy-de-happy-de-hi!*

As the astonished Manth marchers listened to the simple words of this song, which was repeated over and over again, they realised they were coming ever closer to the source of the falling water: until the last curtain of leaves parted before the leaders, to reveal the margins of a steep-sided circular pool, into which the stream fell. They stopped, crowding close up behind each other, and stared.

The water of the pool seethed and bubbled, the bubbles venting plumes of steam high up into the air. To the watchers' left, the stream they had followed rushed cascading over the smooth rock lip, to tumble down into the churning water below. All round, but for the far shore, the jungle trees leaned over the pool, trailing long parasite creepers from their branches down into the green scum. Wherever the underwater jets burst up into the air there formed a bright froth of water, but between the jets the pool's surface stewed and thickened like vegetable soup.

In one such calmer region lay the owner of the tenor voice. He had stopped singing, and was gazing back at the Manth people with an astonishment that mirrored their own. He lay floating on his back, half-immersed in the water, his vast stomach rising up from the ring of green slime in a perfect dome. His cheeks and chins seemed to run on without interruption into his bosomy chest, in rolls of flesh that spilled down his belly, down cushiony thighs, to terminate in plump, pink edible toes. He was a very, very fat man.

As they watched, a gush of rising steam beneath his right buttock exploded in a storm of bubbles, and set him wildly rocking from side to side. The sensation pleased him.

'Aaah!' he cried, seeming in his delight to forget the intruders. 'That was a brave bucker, Jacko!'

This remark was addressed to a pig that was wallowing in the pool close beside him. Strange as it was to look upon this vastly fat and naked man floating in greenish scum, it was stranger still to see him in the company of three large pink pigs. They seemed to be wallowing together as equals. There was something about their splayed forelegs and their raised snouts that echoed the fat man's posture, in the most relaxed and intimate way.

The pigs too were now looking at the newcomers. There was no fear apparent in their gaze, more that reproachful crease of the brow that greets an unwelcome intrusion.

As the fat man's floating body settled back into a gentler bobbing motion, one pudgy hand emerged from the green water to perform a slow wave. He was greeting them. Hanno Hath raised his own hand in an answering gesture.

'Shipwrecked, are you?' said the fat man.

'We're travellers,' said Hanno. 'Outside this valley the winter is hard. We need rest, and food, and warmth.'

'Rest?' The fat man repeated Hanno's words in his deep, rich, almost creamy voice. 'Food? Warmth? We have all three here. Lucky for you, eh?'

He chuckled, as if he had made a joke. Then with slow steady motions of his hands, he propelled himself to the far side of the pool, and with much floundering effort heaved his great body out of the water. There he stood, sagging and dripping, naked but for a length of cloth wound between his legs and round his bottom, like an immense and baggy baby's nappy. By way of drying himself, he patted his body all over, with a rapid rhythmic motion of both palms, beating a tattoo on his flesh.

The Manth marchers stood and watched. It was a mesmerising sight.

'So,' said the fat man, as he completed his patting, 'let's take a look at you. Quite a crowd, I must say.'

'There are thirty-one of us,' said Hanno. 'And our animals.'

'Thirty-one mouths! And all wanting food. What do you say to that, Queenie?' He addressed this remark to the pig that had just hauled itself out of the water to stand by his side. 'Look closely, Queenie. You'll see there's not just menfolk there, but womenfolk also. And where you get menfolk in the company of womenfolk, what's the result? Babies! More mouths! And they grow up, and they have babies of their own. Mouths coming out of mouths!'

Hanno could make little sense of this curious speech, but he did understand that the fat man was worried about how much they would eat.

'We have no plans to stay here,' he said. 'Once we've rested, and with your permission filled our wagon with provisions for our journey, we'll continue on our way.'

'On your way?'

'We're headed north, to the mountains.'

'Ah, that's what they all say. But it's not so easy to leave the island, you'll find. Still, time enough, time enough.' He beamed at them. 'Captain Canobius at your service. You are all cordially invited to join me as my guests, on the Stella Marie.'

With these words he turned and set off at a stately waddle, accompanied by the companionable pigs. The Manth people made their way round the pool after him.

'He's mad,' said Branco Such. 'What's all this about being shipwrecked?'

'I expect it comes from living alone,' said Gale Such, his wife.

'He's a fine figure of a man,' said Mrs Chirish. 'And a Captain, too.'

'He thinks he's on an island,' said Mo Mimilith. 'He must be potty.'

'Fatty and potty,' said Mo's friend Spek Such.

The boys broke out into giggles.

'Hush!' said Lea Mimilith. 'Don't upset him. We need him to help us.'

The overgrown path now led them down a broad and beautiful glade. Here they could see the fat man waddling along a little way ahead, and beyond him a realm of brightness that seemed to promise a break in the over-hanging trees. From this white distance there came a strange sound, a deep soft gurgling.

The glade became a wide clearing. Three sides were walled by dense jungle greenery. The last side, furthest away from them, vanished into white mist. Here on the edge of the clearing stood a curious long structure. Three tall posts rose from a raised timber floor to support a series of hanging canopies that bore a distant resemblance to sails. The fat man clambered up onto the deck and busied himself opening up various chests, that formed the only furniture. Out came a voluminous cloth wrapper, which he draped about his ample form, and a stack of bowls cut from gourds.

The Manth people approached. Closer now, they could see that the far side of the clearing, where Canobius's structure stood, was the shore of a much larger pool or lake. The water churned and bubbled, making the deep gurgling sound that filled the air, and from its surface rose a dense white steam. The whole pool was boiling.

'Come aboard, travellers!' called Canobius.

Hanno led his people up onto the wide deck. The captain filled a bowl with liquor drawn out of a large wooden barrel, and offered it to him.

'Cane juice. Mildly stimulating, no more. Welcome to the Stella Marie.'

Hanno drank. The drink was delicious.

'This is more than cane juice.'

'I flavour it with orange rind.'

'It's very good.'

Canobius handed out full bowls to all. Shortly a new and more relaxed mood began to prevail.

'So this is a hot spring, is it?' asked Hanno, indicating the bubbling steaming water.

'It's certainly hot,' replied Canobius. 'I call it my kitchen. It's a giant kettle, or cauldron. See?'

He swung round a beam fixed to a tripod stand. At the end of the beam, tied by a cord, was a metal bucket. In demonstration, he lowered the bucket into the water.

'Cook your dinner in moments.'

'Wonderful!' said Hanno.

'I'll tell you what,' said Miller Marish. 'You have a little paradise here.'

'So I have,' agreed Canobius. 'All that men struggle to win by the sweat of their brow I have here for the asking.'

'My goodness me!' exclaimed Silman Pillish. 'You don't have to work to grow your food?'

'Work?' The captain emitted his rich laugh. 'I have to get up on my legs, if you call that work. I have to walk a little way, and reach out my hand, and pluck the fruit, if you call that work. No, sir, there's no work here. There's ease, and plenty.'

'It seems wrong,' said little Scooch, his brows furrowing. 'Not to have to work.'

'So I thought also, sir, when I came here first. I fretted up and down the island, clearing and cultivating. But then I found the good things grew whether I planted them or not, and that was the end of my career as a farmer. Now I live as the birds live, on the bounty of nature, and do no work at all. You'd be astonished how quickly the habit fades.'

'Work only a habit!' Silman Pillish was even more struck by this. 'Well, well, well. But surely you get bored?'

'Bored? Why would I get bored? It's having to work that's boring. Slog, slog, slog, just to stay alive. Take away the slog, and you have the time and the energy to develop your interests.'

'And what are your interests, Captain?'

Canobius smiled and patted his great stomach.

'I have two interests, my friend. One is cooking, and

the other is eating. I have made myself a master of both.' He drew the bucket back out of the boiling pool. 'You shall judge for yourself. I shall make you a feast, to welcome you to the island.'

'We have to fit our wagon for the winter outside,' said Hanno, 'and store as much food as we can. We would be glad to stay two nights.'

'Two nights, you think? Never mind, never mind. I shall cook you a feast.' His eye fell on Mrs Chirish. 'Now that's what I call a proper woman.'

'Are you the only inhabitant of this valley?'

'The only one, yes.' The captain's attention was now concentrated on Mrs Chirish. 'I say, madam, may I refill your bowl?'

Hanno looked round for his wife. She had settled down at the side of the clearing, where she could sit with her back supported by the trunk of a tree. He joined her.

'Well?' he said, sinking down by her side.

'We're lucky to have found this place.'

'We'd be dead if we hadn't.'

'We won't stay long, will we?' she said.

'No. We'll move on as soon as we can.'

Hanno took her hand and stroked it. She spoke so softly these days. He remembered her great rages, her shouts and curses. Where had they gone?

'Hanno, my dear,' she said, 'I don't know why it is, but I can't find my direction here. Maybe the air is too warm.'

'You'll find it again once we're on our way. All we have to do is get our strength back. Then we'll go.'

Canobius's liquor made them all sleepy after their long ordeal in the snow, and as the unseen sun faded in the misty sky, the Manth people laid themselves down in their various huddles, and slept.

The next morning when they woke, refreshed by a good night's sleep, the terrors of the winter seemed far away. The morning temperature was pleasant, not yet too warm. The mist lay thick and white over the bubbling lake, but elsewhere shafts of lights from the invisible sun pierced the lid of clouds. Bees were out, humming in the air, and bright birds darted through the high green tree caverns above.

The Manth people rose, each in their own time, and washed themselves at one of the many gurgling brooks that came tumbling out of the hillside. Then they ventured into the groves of trees in search of fruit for breakfast. Miller Marish brought back a plump orange melon for his girls, which they ate so eagerly that the sweet juice ran all down their chins, and their father had to dangle them upside down in a small waterfall.

Little Fin Marish said to her father,

'I think this must be the homeland. Everyone's so happy.'

'It might as well be,' said Miller Marish. 'I don't see how any place could make a better home than this.'

At Ira Hath's suggestion, Mumpo and Rollo Shim stripped off their clothes and waded into the green pool where the marchers had first met Captain Canobius. Lying here, wrapped in warm water and rocked by bubbles rising from the depths, their wounds were soothed. Some of the others, seeing how comfortable they looked, joined them in the pool. Relaxing in the water they spread their limbs, and gently jostled each other, gazing up at the green canopy above.

Scooch passed by the pool and stopped to watch.

'You look like an uncooked sausage,' he said to Lunki, one of the bathers.

'Well, then,' said Lunki, 'I shall be cooked by and by.'

'Pleasant, is it?'

'Try it for yourself.'

So little Scooch stripped to his underwear and plopped himself in by her side.

Hanno Hath, Bowman, and Tanner Amos headed away into the trees with axes, to cut timbers for the onward journey.

One by one the others came drifting back to the wagon in the clearing, their arms laden with fruit, all with tales to tell of the fertility of the valley.

'Where is the good captain?' said Branco Such, laying two large coconuts on the ground. 'Where is our strange but amiable host?'

'He's gone off with Mrs Chirish,' said Creoth, scowling.

Branco Such attacked the coconuts with his knife. The outer rind proved to be tougher than he had expected. Also his mind was on other things.

'There's space for us all here,' he said. 'For all and to spare. And I doubt if I've ventured into the smallest part of the valley.'

'There's space all right,' muttered Creoth. 'If space is what you want.'

'Space for homes,' pursued Branco Such. 'Land for homes.' He hacked unavailingly at the coconut.

'If that's what you want,' said Creoth.

'It's what we all want, isn't it? Land for homes. A homeland.'

'Ah!' said Silman Pillish. 'I was wondering who would be the first to say that.'

'Well, Pillish. What do you say?'

'I say we should see what Hanno Hath says.'

'Hanno Hath is a good man, but he's only one man. Isn't your say as good as his? Or mine?'

Captain Canobius and Mrs Chirish now appeared, walking arm in arm with every appearance of satisfaction.

'Been showing the good lady the sights of the island,' he said.

'Such a place!' exclaimed Mrs Chirish. 'Everything a body could wish for, hanging on the trees!'

'Now you don't want to do it like that.'

Canobius had seen how Branco Such was attacking the coconut.

'You find the two dimples – here, you see? – and you prick them through – like this, you see? – and you drink off the milk.'

He demonstrated, holding the coconut above his fleshy mouth, so that the thin jet of milk spurted into it. Then he laid the coconut down on a hard section of ground.

'Then you hit it with a rock.'

He picked up a rock, and with a quick neat blow, split the coconut in two.

'And there's the meat.'

'I'm most grateful,' said Branco Such, handing the sections of nut to his children. 'I take it there are plenty more where that came from.'

'As many as you could ever want.'

'So would you say, Captain, that a group of sensible people such as us would be able to keep ourselves alive on this – er – island?'

'Why, there's a coincidence!' cried Mrs Chirish. 'The

captain has been proposing the very same thing.'

'There is a certain sort of person that does very well here,' said Canobius cautiously. 'And the good lady is that sort of person.'

'He means fat,' said Mrs Chirish, blushing and dimpling.

'Well, and if I do, where's the shame in that?' Canobius slapped his immense belly with both hands, making it quake. 'The fatter I get, the happier I become. Who would choose to be thin? Thinness is misery. Thinness can never be satisfied. Fatness is generous. Fatness is kind. Hurrah for bulging bellies! Hurrah for broad behinds! Fatness is happiness!'

'Hurrah!' cried Mrs Chirish.

The Manth people smiled as they looked on.

'You're a fine advertisement for this life,' said Branco Such. 'Clearly you eat well here.'

'And so shall you! I am preparing such a feast for all of you! I think of marinating some palm hearts. The marinade is a time-consuming business. I must get on.'

He bustled off to his deck, where he kept a store of large pots. Branco Such turned to speak to the others.

'Friends,' he said. 'I have a proposal to put to you all. Why don't we stay and make our homes right where we are?'

As he spoke, he turned to look towards Ira Hath. She sat with her daughters and Sisi, sharing a breakfast of bananas and honey. She seemed not to have heard him.

Kestrel too was watching her mother closely.

'You don't like it here, do you, Ma?'

'No,' said Ira. 'This isn't a good place.'

'What is it you feel?'

'I've been trying to find it, but I can't.' She wrinkled her brow and tried to explain. 'Everything here is squashy. Even the air is squashy.'

'You mean fat,' said Pinto. 'Everything here is fat. Look at the bananas. They're enormous.'

'No, I don't mean fat,' said Ira. 'I mean squashy. It's not the same. Fat can be sturdy and reliable. But squashy – you can't rely on squashy. Squashy will let you down.'

She looked across at the group round Branco Such. They were deep into an animated discussion. Ira Hath did not need to hear their voices to know what they were saying. She reached out to clasp Kestrel's hand, and her voice suddenly sounded urgent.

'Promise me,' she said, 'whatever the others do, and however weak I get, you'll take me away from this place.'

'I promise, ma,' said Kestrel, frightened.

9

Talking with pigs

While Hanno Hath and Bowman and Tanner Amos worked away with their axes, felling and stripping a tree for long straight timbers, Mist the cat went in search of his own breakfast. Mist was no fruit eater, but he soon found that the birds here flew too high and too fast for him to track. Simply watching them darting about gave him an ache in his neck. So after a while he went hunting for small creatures in the undergrowth. His keen sense of smell led him to a small plant concealed under larger plants, which he had never encountered before. It had fat soft dark-green leaves that curled around small yellow fruits, a little like tomatoes. The fruits he ignored. It was the leaves that interested him. They smelled ripe, rotten even, in an excitingly gamey way. He nibbled the end of one leaf, but found the taste too sharp, and ate no more.

By the time he had returned to the others, he was feeling light-headed.

'Oh, there you are, Mist,' said Bowman. 'We're ready to go back.'

'That's wonderful,' said Mist. 'You're wonderful. Everything's wonderful.'

He curled up at Bowman's feet and fell asleep. Bowman poked him.

'Don't go to sleep now. At least get back to the wagon.'

But the cat could not be woken. So Bowman picked him up and carried him in his arms, leaving his father and Tanner Amos to haul the cut timber between them.

'Poor Mist,' he said. 'He's exhausted.'

On their return to the clearing, he laid the sleeping cat gently on the blanket pile in the wagon. Mumpo was standing by the wagon, semi-naked and dripping, having just come back from the pool. He was drying himself with a blanket, patting carefully round his wounds.

'Better for your soak?' said Bowman.

Mumpo nodded. 'Much better.'

Bowman examined his wounds, to see how they were healing.

'Soon be good as new.'

Looking up, he met Mumpo's eyes and blushed. They both knew that the stomach wound was serious, and that Mumpo would never again have the strength and agility that had made him a champion fighter.

'I'll soon be good enough,' said Mumpo with a shrug. 'And good enough is good enough for me.'

The main body of the Manth people were sitting in a big circle near the Stella Marie, deep in discussion. The talking had stopped when Hanno and the others came out of the trees; and although conversation had started up again, it was not as animated as it had been, and many of them glanced across at Hanno with nervous guilty expressions. Hanno saw this, but decided to make no comment.

He joined them, speaking as if nothing had changed.

'Everything we need for our journey is close at hand,' he said. 'We cut these timbers about ten minutes walk that way. There's a grove of straight-trunked trees that will split beautifully. We need to make snow-runners for the wagon, and we need to build a second sled, too, for extra provisions. Tanner will take charge of the splitting and trimming. The rest of us must gather food. There's wild maize ripening on the far side of one of the glades.'

'Wait a moment, Hanno,' said Branco Such. 'Aren't you making rather a lot of assumptions here? Before we start on building snow-sleds, maybe we should ask ourselves a question. Do we want to go?'

'Of course we want to go,' said Hanno. 'We can't stay here.'

'Why not?'

'Because this isn't the homeland.'

'Ah. But what or where is the homeland?'

All eyes turned to Ira Hath. She replied in the words that were now familiar to all.

'I'll know it when I see it.'

'In the meantime,' said Branco Such, 'can you tell us anything about the conditions there? The fertility of the land? The comfort of the climate? The hardness of the winters?'

'I can tell you nothing,' said Ira.

'I have the greatest respect for you, ma'am. And Hanno, you know I want to see our people settled in our homeland as keenly as you do. But please, I beg you to consider.

If we leave this valley, we face the bitter hard winter that almost killed us. We must drag ourselves and our belongings through deep snow for an unknown distance, to an unknown destination. We have no certainty of reaching it alive. Whereas here we have a fertile valley, warmed and watered, virtually uninhabited, provided with everything we could ever want. Why go further? What more could any other place offer us? Are we so greedy that this richness and beauty can't satisfy us?'

Branco's words were listened to in silence by the Manth people, but from the nodding heads Hanno could see that many agreed with him. Kestrel came to his side and took his hand. The nodding heads angered her.

'What are you talking about?' she said. 'We have to go on. This isn't our homeland.'

'Our homeland is the place where we make our home,' said Branco Such. 'Why not here?'

'Because this isn't it.'

He shrugged and looked at her in a pitying sort of a way, that made Kestrel want to smack his face. Hanno too knew that he had no real answer beyond his own very strong conviction.

'This isn't it, Branco. I know it isn't. I can only ask you to trust me.'

'I think each one of us must make that decision for ourselves,' said Branco.

Heads nodded in agreement once more. Branco began to feel that he should have taken on this role earlier. After all, in the old days, in Aramanth, he had been a magistrate, whereas Hanno had only been a librarian. Hanno was a good man, but he lacked the authority of a true leader.

'I think we should take a vote.'

Hanno looked down.

'As you wish,' he said. 'I and my family will leave in the morning.'

He walked away, with Kestrel at his side. Everyone sensed that he was hurt, and because they loved and respected him, they were dismayed.

'You know, Branco,' said Miko Mimilith, 'its all very well what you say, but we owe everything to Hanno.'

'If the Haths say this isn't the homeland,' said Scooch, 'then I believe them.'

'No sky,' said old Seldom Erth. 'Can't have a homeland without a sky.'

Hanno Hath, greatly troubled, said to Kestrel,

'What else can I say?'

'Tell them what ma says,' said Kestrel. 'There's something wrong about this place.'

'The trouble is, she doesn't know what.'

It was Miller Marish who came up with a compromise solution.

'Let's wait till spring!' he said. 'Then in the spring we decide again, whether to stay, or move on with Hanno.'

This pleased everybody. It seemed like plain sense, and made it possible for them all to stay together. But when they suggested it to Hanno, he would have none of it.

'We leave in the morning,' he said. 'We have very little time left. You've heard my wife. The wind is rising.'

'Oh, yes. The wind.'

They looked at each other uncomfortably. They had never really understood what this rising wind was supposed to do.

'No wind down here,' pointed out Silman Pillish.

'Principal Pillish,' said Branco, using his old title, glad of the support, 'you have a wise head on your shoulders. Do you think we should wait here at least until the snow melts, and the road becomes passable again?'

'Of all the available options,' replied Pillish, 'it would appear to be the option that keeps open the greatest number of ... of options.'

He realised this didn't sound as wise as he had hoped, so he added slowly and with emphasis, to show he really meant it,

'That is my view. I stand by it.'

'In the light of that view,' said Branco, 'I suggest that we hold a vote on whether we should stay till spring. All in favour of a vote, raise your hands.'

The people looked at him uncertainly. Branco understood that they hesitated to take so big a step.

'All we need to decide now is whether or not to vote. Those who are happy to let others decide their future for them, need not take part. All in favour of deciding your own future, raise your hands.'

At that, they all raised their hands except the Haths, and those who were most closely associated with them: Mumpo, Scooch, and Creoth. Seldom Erth did not raise his hand; nor did Sisi and Lunki, who felt it was not right for them to vote on the location of the Manth homeland, not being Manth themselves.

Captain Canobius saw all the raised hands, and came stumping over to be told what was going on. When he understood the debate, he chuckled and said,

'You can vote all you like. You're on the island now.'

Branco Such fancied he had an ally in the fat captain.

'Captain, you believe we would find it difficult to leave this – er – place, I think?'

'You may say difficult,' said the captain. 'You may say impossible, if you like.'

'Because of the hard winter outside.'

'Winter? What do I know about winter? No, no, the hard part is the wanting to go. But I must get back to my pots. I'm preparing you such a feast!'

He left them once more.

'He's mad,' said Creoth.

'That's not true!' Mrs Chirish was grieved that her good friend Creoth should speak so harshly. 'He's eccentric, that's all. It comes from living so long among pigs, who don't answer him back.'

Bowman heard this, and it gave him an idea. He slipped quietly away.

'I think I may claim that a majority have expressed a wish to vote,' said Branco Such. 'Before we take the vote, does anyone have anything to say?'

Cheer Warmish stepped forward, her mouth pursed in bitter lines.

'We must think of the children. I've lost my husband. I nearly lost my daughter. Now I have her back, I'll not go into the snow to watch her die.'

'We must all think of the children,' said Lea Mimilith, reaching out to her three. Red Mimilith turned away crossly. She was fourteen years old, and felt she was no longer a child.

Miller Marish added his agreement.

'My girls are the youngest of all the children,' he said.

'Whatever homeland we seek, it's for them more than for us. They will pass the rest of their lives there. We must keep the children safe. What sort of homeland would it be without children?'

'Beard of my ancestors!' boomed Creoth. 'The only one among you with any sense is the old man!' He pointed to Seldom Erth. 'No sky, he says. Can't have a homeland without a sky. I call that a plain fact! You want to live the rest of your lives, and never see the dawn again? Not me! I'm sitting here sweating, and it's not yet mid-morning. I'll not finish my days in a kettle! I'd rather freeze to death on the open plains, beneath an open sky!'

'Not the rest of our lives,' said Miller Marish. 'Only till spring.'

'And then we vote again,' said Branco Such.

'And then what?' This was the cool clear voice of Sisi. She had tried to keep out of the debate. She tried now to speak in an unassuming way. But it was no good, her feelings were strong and her voice was commanding. 'Don't you understand? The Hath family will leave in the morning. If you stay here, then when the spring comes, where will you go?'

This was a new aspect to the matter. Young Ashar Warmish, who had learned to respect Sisi during their captivity, asked her timidly,

'What will you do?'

'What I do is of no importance. I'm not Manth. I shouldn't even speak in your debate.'

'On the contrary,' said Silman Pillish. 'Our debate is about our survival. It's about how we live, and how we die. You too must make that choice.'

'For me there's no choice,' said Sisi. 'I was raised as a princess in another place where I never had to work. A paradise, provided with everything I could ever want. To me, it was a prison. A kind fate has released me from that prison. I will not go back.'

'Prison?' exclaimed Cheer Warmish. 'This valley isn't a prison! We can leave any time we want.'

Sisi said no more. She had caught Kestrel watching her, and had seen the admiration in her eyes. She looked for Bowman, but he was gone. Sensing her own flicker of disappointment, she told herself, I didn't speak to please Bowman. I spoke to say what I know to be true. Nevertheless, she wished he had been there to hear.

Bowman was a little way up the valley, by the side of the smaller green pool, talking to the pigs. There were two of them wallowing in the warm slime, their snouts poking up out of the water, their little eyes fixed on Bowman as he squatted on a pool-side rock. It took him some time to make a connection with the pigs. They were cleverer than the cows he had talked to before, but this made it harder rather than easier. No man had understood the pigs before, and so they refused to believe he understood them now.

'Please,' he said to them. 'I need your help.'

Talking to himself, said the big pig. *Don't listen.*

I'm not listening, replied the smaller pig. *You're the one who's listening. Don't listen yourself.*

Both pigs fell silent, trying hard not to listen.

He's stopped talking.

Then we can start listening again.

A short silence.

'I can hear you,' said Bowman.

The pigs looked at each other.

He said he can hear us.

But we're not saying anything.

We are now.

We weren't when he spoke.

Perhaps he meant we can hear him.

I can't hear him. I'm not listening to him.

Nor am I.

There followed another short silence.

What if he's listening to us?

Listening to us not saying anything?

Listening to us not listening.

'I can hear your thoughts,' said Bowman.

He says he can hear our thoughts.

We don't have any thoughts.

I suppose that could be called a thought.

Do you think he heard it?

If he did, he'll have heard nothing.

If he heard nothing, he'll say nothing.

If he says nothing, it means he's heard our thoughts.

They swung their snouts round to gaze at Bowman.

'You're talking about not having any thoughts,' said Bowman.

He didn't hear us! He can't hear a thing! If he'd really heard us, he'd not have heard us.

There followed a longish pause. Then one pig said to the other,

I think we've gone wrong somewhere.

Bowman took this opportunity to move the dialogue forward.

'I want your advice,' he said.

He says he wants our advice.

We don't have any advice.

So let's not give it him.

'Why does Canobius think he lives on an island?'

The pigs pondered this question. They found it interesting, and forgot that they were supposed not to be listening.

An island is a place you can't leave. The captain can't leave this place. Therefore it's an island.

The big pig grunted with satisfaction. The point was neatly made.

'It's not really an island. He could leave it if he wanted to.'

Then he doesn't want to.

'Why not?'

Because it's an island.

'You mean,' said Bowman, struggling to make some sense of this, 'he wants it to be an island?'

Of course.

'Why?'

So he can't leave.

Bowman was silenced. The smaller pig turned to the larger pig with a reproachful look.

You're talking to him.

It doesn't matter. He's very stupid. He doesn't understand a word I say.

Bowman decided to try for some more practical information.

'There are some graves near here,' he said. 'Do you
know who lies buried there?'

Dead people.

'How did they die?'

From not wanting to live.

'Why didn't they want to live?'

Too much happiness.

'They died of happiness?'

Before he could learn more, there came a crashing of
running feet, and Kestrel appeared.

'Bo! You must come back! They're having a vote, and
pa's so angry about it he won't speak.'

Bowman jumped up at once and went with Kestrel
back to the big glade by the hot spring. The two pigs
watched him go with some relief.

*I'm glad he's gone. Talking to stupid people is such hard
work. Let's not do it again.*

Bowman and Kestrel found that the vote had just taken
place, and the majority had voted not to continue the
journey. The marchers were already dividing into two
groups. The larger number by far were clustering round
the Stella Marie, where Canobius was busily preparing
his feast, uninterested in the great schism. The smaller
group, the Hath group, stayed by the wagon. Here were
Hanno and Ira, Pinto and Mumpo, Creoth and Scooch,
and old Seldom Erth.

Hanno looked up at Bowman as he joined them. His
face was drawn with weariness and disappointment.

'I don't know what else I can do.'

'The graves,' said Bowman. 'Ask Canobius about the

graves.'

'Oh, he'll have some harmless explanation,' said Hanno.

Bowman saw Mist, still curled up on the blanket pile, dead to the world.

'What! Is that idle cat still sleeping?'

Sisi and Lunki appeared, laden with cobs of ripe corn for the wagon. They had removed themselves during the vote.

'Are you coming with us?' asked Hanno.

'We'll join you if we may,' said Sisi.

'Of course you can,' said Kestrel quickly. Sisi flashed her a grateful smile, and putting the palms of her hands together, interlocked her fingers. Kestrel made the same sign in return.

'We'll get more corn,' said Sisi. She and Lunki departed again.

'What was that, Kess?' said Bowman.

'Our secret friends sign.'

'They set us a good example,' said Hanno. 'There's work to do.'

While the men of their little group set about trimming split timbers into snow runners, and the women packed the wagon, Bowman crossed the glade to talk to Captain Canobius. The information he had obtained from the pigs had been virtually meaningless, but he was sure that the graves held a secret that would present this paradise in some new and darker light.

The fat man was filling his large clay pots with vegetables. The main ingredient was chopped palm hearts. To the palm hearts he had added cane juice, lime leaves, ginger root, and dried sweet potato. He moved from pot to pot, stirring, tasting, adding a little more ginger here, a sprinkle of ground peppercorns there, to satisfy his palate. As he worked he sang softly to himself.

> *Who is as happy as me-ee-ee?*
> *Who is as happy as I?*
> *Happy as happy can be-ee-ee*
> *Hippy-de-happy-de-hi!*

He greeted Bowman with a wooden spoon dipped in the mixture.

'Taste that.'

Bowman licked the spoon.

'It's delicious.'

'Of course it is. And not even stewed yet. Once the pots have stood in the hot water overnight, the different tastes will soak into each other, making new tastes. But still the original tastes will remain, alongside the new combinations. Even now, you see how the nutty tang of the palm heart mellows with the ginger alongside it? I think of it as voices in song. Catch the right notes, and they make a chord, a new note altogether.'

The fat man seemed so truly happy in his work that Bowman began to wonder if there was no dark secret after all. But he pressed on.

'I wanted to ask you a question, Captain. About the graves.'

'Ah! My poor companions!'

'You know the people who lie buried there?'

'No one lies buried there, my friend. Though my companions are dead, I've no doubt. You touch on painful memories.'

'I'm sorry. Would you rather not talk about it?'

'No, no. It's good to remember. Why else did I build the graveyard? It's my memorial to them. I go there from time to time, and imagine they lie there, at rest. I say a few words. It eases the loneliness.'

This sounded convincing enough, though it was an unusual idea.

'The graves have no bodies in them?'

'You could call them markers, perhaps. I would have buried them if I could, but where they died, the ground was frozen hard as rock.'

Puzzled, Bowman reached into the fat man's mind. He found there a quiet aching sense of loss, which matched the saddened tone with which he was speaking. But then, pushing a little deeper, he was startled to find a much stronger emotion: a terrible howling desolation.

I am doomed, he heard the captain cry, deep in his heart. *I am doomed.*

Bowman was bewildered. This was the man who lived in a little paradise, who loved to eat, who sang that no one was as happy as he. What could be the cause of such anguish?

'You will be wondering what became of my companions,' said Canobius, quite unaware of Bowman's discovery. No terror sounded in his voice, and as he spoke he continued stirring and tasting and refining his marinade.

'Yes,' said Bowman.

'We were a ship's company, the crew of the Stella Marie. We went down in a storm off the Loomus coast. Our poor ship was driven onto the rocks, and pounded to matchwood. We came ashore, twenty-three of us all told, and swore never to sail the western ocean again.'

'You were the captain?'

Canobius looked round and lowered his voice.

'I was the ship's cook. Forgive a lonely man his little vanity.'

'You're certainly the captain now,' said Bowman.

'So I am. Ah, poor fellows! Our ship was gone. We set off to cross the hills, heading for the kinder waters to the east. We proposed to offer our services to shipowners there. But winter came early that year. We were poorly clothed. We suffered.'

He shook his head, and nibbled at a spoonful of stew.

'All I really miss is salt,' he murmured.

'They died in the winter?'

'They did. One by one. I thought I would die too. But even then I was a stout fellow. I've no doubt it was my fatness that kept me alive. By the time I found the island, I was the last one standing.'

'How long ago was that?'

'Oh, years ago. I've lost count. There are no seasons here.'

'And since then?'

'Since then, as you see. Loneliness, but happiness.'

He beamed at Bowman. There seemed no more to say, so Bowman returned to the wagon. There his gaze fell once more on the sleeping cat.

'I've never known Mist sleep like this,' he said to himself.

He knelt down and put his head close to the cat's head. He heard Mist's even breathing. Gently he touched the cat's ear. The ear flickered, in automatic response, but the cat didn't wake. He stroked Mist's back, running his hand all the way down from the neck to the tail. Still he didn't wake.

Concerned, he leaned his head closer still, and reached into the cat's mind. He found no thoughts there, not of the kind that can be expressed in words; but he found a feeling, or the dream of a feeling. It was the oddest combination of two quite separate sensations: one of happiness, a great happiness that filled all the cat's mind; the other a dwindling, as if the cat was growing smaller and smaller, or moving further and further away.

Bowman found he was quite unable to wake the cat, so he whispered into his ear,

'Don't leave me, Mist.'

The cat's ear flickered again in response, and he slept on.

10

Captain Canobius's feast

The two groups, made shy by their different choices for the coming day, slept apart from each other that night. Sisi and Lunki lay close by the Haths' sleep huddle. They slept without blankets, because in the steamy air of the valley the temperature dropped very little after sundown.

Bowman dreamed confused dreams, and woke in the night, and could not get back to sleep. His mind was troubled by the feeling that there was something bad in the valley, something he was missing. He wanted to warn his friends who had chosen to stay behind, but what could he tell them? Canobius was concealing some terror, he was sure of it; but he couldn't give it a name.

There was no light in the cloud-capped valley; not so much as the faintest glimmer of a star. Bowman could open his eyes, and then close them, and detect no difference. Perhaps because of this, his other senses were more acute. He could hear the steady sleep-breathing of each member of his group, and could follow each small movement they made as they slept. He could also sense how far they were from him. It was through this sense that he became aware that he was not the only one awake.

Someone had sat up. He heard the exhalation of a breath. In such a darkness, a single breath was as recognisable as a voice.

'Sisi? Are you awake?'

'Yes.'

'What is it?'

'Nothing. I often wake in the night.'

'This is more than night. I've never known darkness like it. I can't even see my own hand.'

'Do you mind?'

'No.'

They were speaking very softly, aware of the others sleeping round them. It was comforting for both of them to hear the other's voice. It gave form to the darkness.

'I like it,' said Sisi. 'I like it that you can't see me.'

'Why?'

'You know why.'

'Because of your scars?'

'Yes.'

'You're wrong, Sisi. You think your scars make you ugly. They don't.'

'You only say that to be kind. I'd rather you were truthful than kind.'

'I am telling you the truth.'

There was a silence. Then Sisi spoke very low.

'Ah, Bowman. If I was still beautiful, you'd love me as I love you.'

Bowman hardly knew how to reply. It was strange, this

darkness. It made it possible to say things that could never be said in the light.

'You're still beautiful,' he said at last. 'More beautiful.'

'But you don't love me.'

Bowman was silenced.

'It seems strange to me that you don't love me,' said Sisi after a while. 'People have always loved me. And I love you. How can there be so much love in me, and so little in you?'

She spoke with no reproach in her voice; only genuine perplexity, and sadness.

'I can't love you, Sisi. I told you. Someone will come for me soon, and take me away, and we'll never meet again.'

'Why not? Where will you go?'

'To a place called Sirene.'

'And never return?'

'I'll die there, Sisi. Before the winter is over.'

'Die?' Her voice changed. 'You can't love me, because you're going to die soon?'

'Yes.'

'But that's not right. If you're going to die soon, you should love me now, before it's too late.'

'And then leave you?'

'Yes.'

'You don't want that.'

'Yes. I do.'

'Oh, Sisi.'

'You can say "Oh Sisi" as much as you like, but when you kissed me, you liked it. Don't pretend you didn't.'

'It's true. But what's the point?'

'What's the point of kissing? It doesn't have a point. It's

just a kiss. If everything you do is in order to do something else, when do you ever get to the end of it all?'

Bowman felt himself smiling, and wondered if she could sense it.

'You make it all sound so easy.'

'It is easy. Because of what you said. You said you're going to die soon. Don't you see how easy that makes everything?'

He was impressed. Once he had thought Sisi a stupid child. The more he came to know her, the less stupid she seemed.

'Everything you might ever have done in all your life has to be done now, or you'll never do it.'

'Yes. I suppose so.'

'Now, Bowman. Do you know what now means?'

'I think so.'

'It means now.'

A silence fell: a silence that roared like thunder in the utter darkness. Bowman found himself calculating how far apart from each other they were sitting. If he were to put out a hand –

He reached out one hand. With a shock, he felt her fingertips. She was reaching out to him.

Their hands met, palm to palm. Without saying a word, their fingers interlocked, in the secret friends sign. Without saying a word, they both leaned forward, until they could feel each other's breath on their cheeks, until their brows met and touched. Without saying a word, they kissed.

For the rest of that warm night, they lay folded close in each other's arms, and made not a sound. When light began to creep into the sky, they parted, understanding that whatever had passed between them belonged to the darkness, and must slip away like a dream with the dawn.

The Manth people woke, and stretched, and washed, their usual morning chatter somewhat subdued. This was to be the day of parting. Canobius was up and about, busying himself at his pots, which now stood neck-deep in the seething waters of the lake. Beside the three big pots stood a small pot, to which he was adding ingredients from his store.

Hanno Hath set his little group to work packing the wagon and preparing everything for their departure. Bowman shook Mist. This time the cat woke. He had slept for a whole day and a night.

'Thank goodness! I thought there was something wrong with you.'

'Oh, boy!' said Mist, still half in a dream. 'I've been so far away! Must I come back?'

'We'll be on our way soon. Can't sleep for ever.'

'Yes, boy, yes. Can sleep for ever. Such a happy sleep. Want it to be for ever.'

This dreamy contentment was out of character. Bowman looked at the cat more closely.

'I think maybe you've been sick, my Mist.'

'Life is a sickness,' murmured Mist. 'Death is the cure.'

'What! You're not sick! You're drunk.'

He picked Mist up, floppy in his hands, and carried him over to the nearest stream, and dropped him in. The cat sank like a stone, and then jerked into frantic life, clawing his way back out of the pool.

'Does that feel better?'

'It feels a great deal worse,' said the cat, shaking off the water. 'And since you're neither helpful, attractive, or amusing, I'd prefer you to leave me alone now.'

'That's my Mist,' said Bowman, relieved.

At his wife's request, Hanno Hath made one last appeal to the twenty who had chosen to stay in the valley.

'You still have time to change your minds.'

'I was going to say the same thing to you,' said Branco Such. 'Give up this foolishness, Hanno. The winter will pass soon enough.'

'We leave in an hour,' Hanno replied.

'In an hour! What about the captain's feast? You can't miss the farewell feast.'

'We need all the daylight we can get,' said Hanno; and returned to the wagon.

Mrs Chirish was sent over to Captain Canobius to ask if it would be possible to have the feast right away.

'But it's not ready,' exclaimed the captain. 'I need a good hour yet. The morning herbs have only just gone into the kettle.'

'Our friends are leaving, you see,' said Mrs Chirish.

'What of that?' said Canobius. 'My feast isn't for those who go. It's for those who stay. And for you, good lady, a special dish, which I shall share with you.' He lowered his voice. 'Corn cakes, with white truffles! I've been keeping them for a special occasion. There's just enough truffles for two.'

'I've never had truffles,' said Mrs Chirish.

'Madam, your life has not yet begun.'

Mrs Chirish returned to the others, and told them why

the feast could not be eaten yet, and how she was to be given white truffles.

Now the horses were harnessed to the wagon. Creoth rounded up his three cows. Tanner Amos stacked the last of the wood he had chopped into the wagon's bed. The time was come to say goodbye.

'We'll follow in the spring,' said Miko Mimilith. 'Only a few weeks, and we'll all be together again.'

The little girls clustered round Mumpo, hugging him and weeping. Silman Pillish coughed and cleared his throat and coughed again.

'Sad day,' he said. 'Duty to the little ones. Hard winter. Sad day.'

Creoth spoke briefly to Mrs Chirish.

'Well, madam. I hope you know what you're doing.'

Mrs Chirish held Mumpo in her arms and wept.

'Oh, Mumpie! My Mumpie!'

'It won't be long, auntie. Don't cry.'

Miller Marish shook everyone's hand, saying,

'It's for the children.'

One by one they completed their goodbyes.

'When the time comes,' said Hanno, 'head north, across the river, over the mountains. We'll be waiting for you.' But the look on his grave face told another story.

So the little group set off at last, Bowman and Mumpo in the lead as usual, followed by Kestrel, Sisi, Lunki and Pinto. Behind them came Seldom Erth leading the two horses and the wagon. Hanno and Ira walked behind the wagon. Then came the three cows, Tawny, Stumper and Dreamer. Last of all, Creoth walked with little Scooch.

They retraced their steps in silence through the dense

green jungle, following the path of the hissing stream. They were filled with sadness at leaving their friends behind, and fear of the winter waiting for them outside the valley. As for Bowman, his mind was racing with unanswered questions.

Why had Canobius been filled with terror? What had the pigs meant, when they said the people in the graves died of happiness? There were no people in the graves. They were the captain's memorial to his dead shipmates. The captain wasn't a captain at all, but a cook. He had cooked them a feast, but it wasn't for the ones who were going away, it was for the ones who were staying behind. Mrs Chirish was to have white truffles. The valley was specially suited to fat people. Menfolk and womenfolk make babies. Mouths coming out of mouths.

The questions and the fragments of remembered words crowded in on him, but he could make no sense of them. Maddeningly, he was taunted by the feeling that he was somehow putting them in the wrong order, that if only he could arrange them correctly he would be able to read their message.

The luxuriant growth was giving way to hardier trees now, and the air was cooler. They were passing the place where Mist had chased the bird, and led Bowman to the three lines of graves.

Five. Eight. Thirteen.

Twenty-six graves. How many shipmates on the Stella Marie? Twenty-three, the captain had said. Why the extra three mounds?

'Stop!'

The little column halted behind him.

'Something's wrong. Mumpo, I need you.'

'What is it, Bo?' asked his father.

'I'll tell you if I'm right.'

He led Mumpo through the trees to the graveyard. There were the rows of mounds, neatly tended, as he had first seen them.

'The captain told me there's nothing under these mounds,' Bowman said to Mumpo. 'But I want to see for myself.'

They picked the mound that looked the most recent, and with their bare hands they scraped away at the earth. In that damp warm climate, the earth was soft, and came away in sticky lumps. For a while all they found was more earth. Then their scrabbling fingers hit something that was not earth. Feeling their way more carefully, they brushed away the soil, and found cloth. They followed the cloth, disturbing it as little as possible, until they found its end. Beyond it lay several ridges of earth, harder than the soil they had been brushing away. Only this too was not earth. It was skin and bone. It was the decaying soil-encrusted back of a dead man's hand.

Carefully, respectfully, trembling a little, they covered up the grave they had disturbed, and rose to their feet. Mumpo looked to Bowman for an explanation.

'Why did the captain say the graves were empty?'

Bowman was revisiting his memory of that feeling he had stumbled on, deep inside Canobius. Was it terror?

I am doomed.

Mouths coming out of mouths. The island is impossible to leave. People die of happiness. Mrs Chirish is to eat white truffles. A happy sleep, the cat had said. Want it to be for ever.

'Quick!' cried Bowman. 'We must go back!'

There was no time to explain.

'He's going to kill them all!' cried Bowman. 'I have to stop him!'

He and Mumpo set off at a run. The others turned the wagon round and followed as fast as they could.

The twenty Manth people who had chosen to stay behind had formed an orderly line, to be given their share of the feast. A mouth-watering aroma rose from the steaming mixture. Captain Canobius held the ladle above the pot with a beaming smile.

'You've never tasted anything so fine in all your lives, I promise you!'

He had just dipped the ladle into the stew when the sound of running feet surprised them all. They turned to see Bowman and Mumpo come bursting out of the trees.

'Don't eat it!' cried Bowman, panting for breath. 'It's poisoned! He wants to kill you all! He's killed other travellers before us! You've all seen their graves!'

Utter astonishment filled every face. Their eyes turned towards Canobius. He looked as surprised as any of them.

'Kill them all?' he said. 'What nonsense! I don't know what he's talking about.'

'Then eat it yourself!'

Bowman had his breath back now. He jumped up onto the deck of the Stella Marie, took the brimming ladle from Canobius's hand, and held it up to his mouth.

'Eat it yourself!'

Canobius took the ladle. He looked from Bowman to the stew, and then, with great dignity, back to Bowman.

'I will eat it myself,' he said. 'It would make me happy to do so.'

He sat down on the deck, tipped the ladle towards his lips, took in a mouthful of the palm-heart stew, and ate it.

Bowman watched, confused.

'Am I wrong?' he said. 'I thought you'd found a poisonous plant that put people to sleep for ever. I thought you were giving Mrs Chirish her own special food because you wanted her alone to stay alive.'

'What nonsense!' cried Mrs Chirish. 'Why ever would he do that?'

'Mouths coming out of mouths,' said Bowman. 'He thinks too many mouths will eat up his paradise.'

'Look at him!' said Branco Such. 'He's eating it himself! How can it be poisoned?'

They all watched the fat man as he scooped up another ladleful of the stew. But then, as he ate, he began to weep. The tears streamed down his fat cheeks. He ate another ladleful of the stew. The Manth people looked on in consternation.

'Can it be true?'

Those nearest to the pot stepped back, suddenly afraid.

'If this is true,' said Branco Such, his anger mounting, 'then he deserves to die!'

In silent answer, Canobius ate more of the stew, sobbing as he ate.

'He'll die,' said Bowman.

The Manth people watched him with a horrified fascination. Only good Mrs Chirish was moved to pity him.

'The poor man!' she cried. 'Can nothing be done?'

Her warm heart roused the fat man from his sobs.

'Good lady,' he said. 'It will be an act of mercy. I've been so afraid, for so long.'

As he spoke, a peculiar smile began to crease his plump cheeks. Then he gave a rich chuckle. The tears still rolled down his face. If anything this smile and this chuckle were even more unnerving that the earlier mute grief.

'But Captain,' said Mrs Chirish, 'how could you do it?'

'They would have died anyway, dear lady.' With that, he burst into outright laughter. 'What is life but one long agony, ended by death?' He roared with laughter, rocking from side to side. 'At least I spare them that. Those that I kill die happy.'

'They die of happiness,' said Bowman.

'Yes! He's so right! They die of happiness!' He laughed and laughed, and wept and wept.

'It's the poison,' said Bowman to the others. 'Whatever it is, it makes you so happy you die.'

'He's right! He's the clever one! Look at me – doomed, but happy! Give me a bowlful! Best stew I ever made in my life! Just a few leaves from one special little plant to give it that extra something. Who is as happy as me, eh? Eat it myself? Makes me happy to do so!'

He rocked with laughter.

'All I ever wanted was my own chance of happiness.' He reached out one hand towards Mrs Chirish. 'You, good lady, would have made me happy. Fatness is happiness! Hurrah!'

His great body shuddered as if he had been hit. Then he recovered, and his rich laugh boomed out once more.

Who is as happy as me-ee-ee? he sang.

Who is as happy as I?
Happy as happy can be-ee-ee
Hippy-de ... happy-de ... hi ...

His voice trailed away into silence. His eyes closed. The smile on his face spread wider and wider. He drew a long last breath of deep contentment, and fell into a profound sleep.

An hour later, he was dead.

It took nine of them to lift that great body, and lay it out on the deck of his ship. They covered him with sail-cloths, and weighed the cloths down with stones. They could do no more.

When the air grew cold, and the first flakes of snow could be felt on the wind, the Manth marchers drew to a stop and put on their warmest clothing. The lush valley lay below them now. None had wanted to stay behind after the shock of Canobius's death. The fertility and plenty that had so entranced them now terrified them: the ripe fruits, the seething water, the very air itself, seeming to their fearful senses to be heavy with hidden poisons. All thirty-one men, women and children, together with the two horses, three cows and a cat, had left together. None spoke of the disagreement that had divided them. Those that had wanted to stay felt ashamed, and those that had determined to go were happy that their little band was together again.

The wagon was packed tight with food and firewood. Bek Shim and Lolo Mimilith dragged behind them an improvised sled that carried a second load of supplies.

They had enough food and water and firewood to last them several days, long enough, surely, to reach the river; so long as they were able to keep moving.

When they reached the valley's mouth, and emerged onto snowy ground, they stopped again, and eased the runners beneath the wagon's wheels. They locked the wheels and pegged the runners in place with wooden pegs and hammered them until they were secure. After that, when they set off again, the wagon rode on the surface of the snow, and the horses were able to make steady progress.

Little by little the mist cleared, and the snow fell more heavily, obscuring their view.

'Well?' said Hanno Hath to his wife.

'Well enough,' she replied.

'You feel it?'

'I feel it, Hannoka.'

She felt the distant warmth of the homeland on her face once more. They were getting nearer with each step.

Around noon the snow clouds broke. All at once, they could see for miles. The white land undulated away on either side, glinting in the pale sun. And there ahead, beyond the snow-clad plains, lay the dark belt of the forest. Above the forest rose the mountains.

11

Winter dawn

Kestrel trudged along over the white land, following in the footsteps of the leaders, Bowman and Mumpo. She walked alone. Behind her, marching for the most part in silence, came the rest of the Manth people, their steady tread crunching in the crisp snow. She could hear the plod of the horses' hooves, and the grind and hiss of the wagon's runners, and the occasional shout of a child. But none wasted precious strength on talk. The cold was bitter, and they all knew they must cover as much ground as possible, in the hope of reaching the shelter of the distant forest before the next snowfall.

Ira Hath rode in the wagon now. She had protested that she was strong enough to march with the rest, but Hanno had ordered her to ride. All of them could see how thin she was getting, though none spoke of it aloud. When Kestrel thought of her mother becoming weaker by the day, it gave her a feeling of such desolation that she couldn't bear it. At such times she felt for the silver voice hanging on its string round her neck, next to her skin. She had no superstition that this simple pendant, made so long ago by Singer people, possessed any power that could help her. It was more a reminder that somehow, hard though it was to believe, she and her brother were part of a greater plan, and her mother had foreseen it, and her weakness was necessary.

Her eyes were on Bowman as she walked: on that slight figure, so familiar to her, with whom she had shared everything. He was striding along ahead of her now, quite a long way ahead. Despite the physical distance between them, she could sense his mood. He had said nothing to her, but she knew, as directly as if he had told her, that a change had taken place in him, and that it was to do with Sisi. Kestrel had half-expected it for some time, had even half-wanted it, but now that it was come she felt afraid.

We go together, my brother. Always together.

Even as she framed the words, she knew the time was coming when they would part. When that time came, it would be good for Bowman to have a friend.

Kestrel looked away, and drew in a long breath of the icy air. These were not good thoughts. Better to feel the chill on her cheeks and the weariness in her legs. Follow those thoughts and at the far end lay the aloneness that was waiting for her, the aloneness that could not be endured.

Suddenly she was seized with fear, and with the fear came an overpowering desire to speak to him, to feel his familiar voice warm in her mind.

Bo! she called. *Need you.*

Here I am, he answered. *Always here.*

The terrors receded. Kestrel felt ashamed of herself, and full of love and gratitude to her brother.

Love you, she said.

Love you, Kess, he replied.

They tramped on past a marker post. These posts had been placed along the road in years gone by, to guide winter travellers when all the land was under snow. Only the road was safe. On either side there were cracks in the land, of varying depths, into which the snow had drifted, and now lay level with the surface. A traveller who strayed too far could find the snow give way beneath his feet, and within moments he would disappear into a white tomb.

For Creoth, leading his cows, this was a constant worry. At present the beasts were calm, and plodded along after the wagon in single file, keeping to the safety of the road. But any loud noise or sudden movement could startle them, and send them careering off into the open spaces on either side, towards the treacherous hidden pitfalls. He considered roping them, but to what? He couldn't tie them to the wagon, for fear they might drag it too off the road. And he himself was not strong enough to restrain a panicking cow.

So he walked quietly behind them, speaking to them, hoping to keep them calm.

'On and on, my Dreamer. Not long till we reach the trees. Then we'll rest, won't we? On and on, my Tawny. On the far side of the mountains, that's where the sweet grass grows and the days roll by, one just like the last. On and on, my Stumper. On and on.'

As he walked, talking aloud, Mrs Chirish came up alongside him, and matched her pace to his. For a while he gave no sign that he had noticed her, keeping all his attention for the cows. So at last she spoke to him herself.

'How you do drone! On and on, indeed! If your cows had any sense at all, they'd stand stock still just to spite you.'

'My cows have more sense than some,' said Creoth.

They tramped on in a silence of mutual irritation, each determined not to be the first to give ground. In the end it was Creoth who could contain his feelings no longer.

'The fellow was so fat!' he exclaimed.

'I am on the larger side myself,' said Mrs Chirish coldly.

'No, ma'am. Allow me to disagree. You I would describe as comfortable. He was fat.'

'Comfortable, is it?'

'You have the look about you of a woman who has a tendency towards comfort.'

'I believe I do,' said Mrs Chirish, her voice softening. 'A tendency towards comfort and foolishness. I've been a foolish woman since I grew too big to be a foolish girl, and one day I'll be a foolish old biddy. And that's all there is to be said about that.'

After this they were friends again, and Mrs Chirish helped Creoth watch over the cows with as much care as if they had been her own.

Snow clouds threatened overhead, but the snow did not fall, and the Manth people made good progress. The road ahead was clear to see, trampled by other travellers since the last snowfall; and now, as they came closer to the forest, they could make out the white stripe of the road where it plunged into the dark trees.

Hanno Hath walked beside the wagon, where his wife could see him.

'We'll be at the river by nightfall,' he told her.

'Not long now.'

'You feel it still?'

'Stronger than ever.'

The closer they came to the homeland, and the warmer she felt its air on her face, the weaker Ira Hath grew. For hours at a time now, she lay still in her wagon bed, neither moving nor speaking, letting her mind drift back over her life. She was remembering the births of her children, and their babyhood; and before that, her time of betrothal to Hanno, when she had been a young woman; and before that, her own childhood, in the handsome old house in Scarlet District, in Aramanth. All that was gone now. Aramanth was destroyed. The time of cruelty was come. Now she, like her father before her, must prophesy for her people.

In the late afternoon the snow that had threatened all day began to fall. The Manth people plodded on, feeling the heavy flakes settling on their hoods and arms, and drifting onto their cheeks. They had been through far harder times than these, and the forest was not far off now, so they followed the road in good spirits.

The short winter day was ending when at last they reached the trees. The snow did not let up, but as they followed the road into the forest, a strange peace descended. The high dark branches formed a sheltering roof over their head. The whiteness that had enveloped them for so long gave way to shadows, and the crunch-crunch of the horses' hooves, and their own boots, sounded closer and clearer, as did the hiss of the wagon's runners. They could hear their own breathing, and the rustling of their garments as they strode along. But beyond their little realm of movement, just a few yards away on either side, where the darkness was gathering between the trees, they could hear nothing.

From the plains, the forest had appeared as a narrow strip lying at the feet of the mountains. Now that they were in it, they found that it was far bigger than they had supposed. They would not reach the river by nightfall.

Dusk was advancing rapidly, here where so little light penetrated, even at noon. Hanno Hath decided to call a halt.

'Let's make camp before we lose light altogether.'

So they stopped on the forest road where they were, and built a fire, and stretched out the wagon canopy for a night shelter. As soon as the fire began to blaze, its brilliant orange glare chased away the last of the twilight, and all around them was utter darkness. Hanno charged the young men with keeping watch in turns through the night, for who knew what bandits or beasts might come creeping out of the trees while they slept? There was no shortage of firewood now, and the watchers' task was to keep the fire burning brightly till the dawn.

Under the canopy, where the Manth people huddled together to sleep, the light of the fire outside made glowing patterns on the stretched canvas, but left the interior space in deepest shadow. Here Ira Hath slept, her hands enclosed in her husband's hands; and Pinto slept by her mother, with one foot thrown out where it nudged gently against Mumpo's sleeping back.

When it was Bowman's turn to wake and watch, he took up his place by the glowing fire, sitting cross-legged on a ground-blanket, a second blanket over his shoulders. He watched the red crumbling tunnels in the fire, and felt the stirring of his mind's power within him. To pass the time, he picked on a burning fragment of wood, and holding it with his mind, pulled it into the heart of the fire. Amused by the trick, he found another fragment, and nudged and pushed it down a little fiery ravine between two red-hot logs, until it caught fire itself, all of a sudden, and exploded in a puff of blue flame.

'What are you doing?'

It was Sisi, standing between the tented wagon and the fire, watching him. How long had she been watching?

'Looking at the fire.'

She came to him and sat down beside him. He opened the blanket so that it covered her as well.

'I don't want to know any more than you want to tell me,' she said.

So he showed her his little tricks. He picked up a pine cone that lay on the snow-flecked roadway, and using only his mind, he carried it into her open hand. She took the pine cone, closed her slender fingers over it.

'How do you do that?'

'I don't know.'

'What else can you do?'

'I can tell what you're thinking. At least, I can feel it.'

'I don't mind if you know what I'm thinking. I have no secrets from you.'

'I can only feel it when I go looking. Most of the time I've no idea. It's quite hard work.'

'Look now.'

She closed her eyes to show she was thinking a special

thought, and he was to discover it. He looked at her, sitting so close to him in the firelight, and thought how beautiful she was, and how much more beautiful because of her scars. He leaned his face close to hers, kissed her scarred cheek with gentle lips, and slipped into her mind.

When he found it he laughed: quietly, so as not to wake the others.

'You're thinking of you and me dressed up like your mother and father.'

The picture he had found was comical: the ornate gold crown and stiff jewelled robes of the Johanna and Johdi of Gang, arranged like outsize fancy dress around the forms of himself and Sisi, sitting side by side on gilded thrones.

'We look ridiculous. We're not emperors.'

'You see emperors. I see a husband and wife. A father and mother. The only kind I've ever known.'

'I'm sorry, Sisi. I shouldn't laugh.'

'Even ridiculous people can love each other.'

'Of course they can.'

'I pray they're both safe.'

'I think so. I think they've been banished from the city, and they're living very quietly, in a small house far away, with no servants. But my mother will have my father, and my father will have his dogs.'

'How do you know this?'

'I don't know it. I hope it. I did a terrible thing when I chose you, and left my family. I tell myself, one day I'll go back and find them, and ask their forgiveness. So you see, they must be alive, and well. So I can find them again.'

'So they are, I'm sure.'

'Perhaps you'll come with me.' Then she remembered, or pretended to remember. 'Oh, no. You have to go away. You're the chosen one. Will you be going soon?'

'I think so, yes.'

'I wish you would go, Bowman. It's hard, waiting for you to go.'

'It's hard for me, too.'

Sisi was sleepy, and shortly she laid herself down beside Bowman, with her head in his lap, and he stroked her to sleep. He himself must wake and watch.

A little before sunrise, the sleepers beneath the canopy began to stir. Bowman wondered whether he should wake Sisi and send her away, but decided against it. These things couldn't be hidden for ever.

Little Scooch emerged from beneath the canvas, and nodded his greeting to Bowman, before setting about his morning business. Bowman watched him putting a pot of water on the fire, and he heard the sounds of other sleepers waking, and the swishing back and forth of the canvas flaps.

He looked round, and there was Kestrel staring at him, blinking. She looked at him sleepily for a moment longer, and saw Sisi on his lap. Then she smiled, and turned and padded away through the trees.

Kestrel had slept well, and had woken refreshed. The frosty air filled her lungs with vigour. She felt young, and strong, and full of hope. And now, with a sudden overwhelming intensity, she wanted to be alone.

Treading lightly over the thin coating of snow that lay between the trees, she made her way to a point where the fire was no longer visible. Her unguided footsteps led her far from the road, down paths made by forest animals, between tall trees whose shade permitted little else to grow. She was not distressed, she told herself. Bowman was growing close to Sisi, that was no surprise, she had sensed it already. And yet the sight of them together under the same blanket, his hand moving over her hair as she slept, had changed everything.

A glimmer of brighter light ahead drew her attention. She pressed on, deeper into the forest, glad to be further and further away from her people. She could see now that it was a ray of sunlight, falling in a long slant through a gap in the trees. Where it struck the snowy ground, it glittered, in a pool of dazzling brightness. She went on, wanting to bathe in that pool of light.

In a little while she emerged from the close-pillared cloisters of the trees into a sudden space, a long open glade, into which streamed the golden light of the rising sun. She stopped, to look and to wonder. The low rays of the sun, passing between the branches of the surrounding trees, threw bars of sharp brightness and velvet dark over the white floor of the glade. Between the trees to the east glowed a radiant sky, while on the trees to the west fell a light that rimmed each trunk with gold. The glade shimmered in the sunrise like a hall of enchantment, and Kestrel, seeing it in its brief moment of glory, knew that here was a promise made to her, an assurance that somehow all that was dark to her would one day be made light.

She stepped out, moving slowly, into the middle of the glade. All the time the light was changing round her. She found the heart of the light, and felt the sun's rays falling on her cheek, lighting her hands as she held them out before her. On an impulse she closed her eyes and reached her hands high above her head, and looking up, turned herself round and round, feeling now the dazzle and now the darkness on her face.

Why should it ever end? Why shouldn't I live for ever?

The sound of footsteps brought her to a stop. She dropped her hands and opened her eyes and felt him, felt him coming as she had known he would, felt his beloved nearness. He walked out of the trees and into the sun-lit space, over the white earth and into her out-stretched arms.

They held each other tight and shared the warmth of the rising sun and heard the rush of the wind in the surrounding trees.

Why should it ever end? Why shouldn't we love each other for ever?

We do, came her brother's answer. *We will.*

Hand in hand, they left the bright glade together, and returned through the trees to their people. They said nothing to each other about what had changed, for what was there to say that they didn't already know?

Sisi was another matter. Later, as the Manth marchers tramped onward through the forest, Kestrel walked by her side, and speaking softly so only she would hear, wished her joy with Bowman. Sisi looked guilty but relieved.

'You always said he'd love you, right from the start,' said Kestrel.

'I don't know that he loves me. But he's stopped avoiding me.'

'Oh, he loves you.'

'You think I'm not good enough for him, don't you, Kess?'

'Sisi, look at me.'

They stopped for a moment, and Kestrel gazed deep into Sisi's big beautiful amber eyes.

'You have to believe this. If you make my brother happy, you make me happy. If he loves you, I love you. If you love him, you love me.'

'I do love you, Kess. You're my first friend.'

'But all this love doesn't mean we won't be hurt.'

'That's what Bowman says. He says soon he'll have to go away.'

'It may be so.'

'You have your feelings about what will happen to us all. And I have mine.'

With this, they rejoined the march.

By late afternoon the trees were thinning on either side of the road, and the sun was shining on the snow. Ahead they could see open land, and a scatter of houses. Another half hour's march, and they saw the high pillars of the bridge, and knew that they would be at the river's side by the end of the day.

12

All my loves

As the Manth people and their wagon and their cows approached the village ahead, there came sounds on the breeze, the cry of voices and the jangle of bands. It seemed a large number of people were gathered round the bridge and along the river. The river itself, its dark water gleaming, now lay clear before them; and on the far side, a white ribbon in the dusk, they could make out the road winding away up the hillside, towards the mountains. Here was the last stage of their journey, the steepest, but also the shortest. In the morning, at first light, they would cross the river and begin their ascent.

Hanno Hath chose not to lead his people into the crowds and bustle of the village, so instead he looked out a quiet spot by the river where a grove of trees offered some shelter from the winter wind. Here Seldom Erth drew up the wagon and tethered the horses, and Creoth set his cows to graze on the tufts of grass that poked up through the snow. The rest set about building a fire and laying out the blanket bags for the coming night.

Scooch was one of the many who stood gazing in awe

at the mountains. So close now, after so long a journey, they seemed almost to be an illusion, a picture of mountains, painted onto the fading evening sky. He nudged Branco Such, who stood beside him, and pointed.

'You wouldn't believe it, would you? You were all for giving up. But look!'

'Not there yet,' said Branco Such; but his beaming face showed that he too felt the worst was over.

'Now, madam,' said Creoth to Mrs Chirish, 'now that our journey is nearing an end, you and I must understand each other.'

'I don't see how,' said Mrs Chirish, 'any more than we understand each other at present, which is well enough.'

'Then I ask you straight. Are we to go home by the same door?'

'Home by the same door, and sleep in the same bed, if it pleases you.'

'It pleases me mightily.'

'Only, when you rise of a morning from this same bed, you're to leave me sleeping.'

'It shall be so, madam. Beard of my ancestors! I have a powerful wish to dance!'

'Then dance, sir.'

Smiling broadly, Creoth performed a little jig round Mrs Chirish's stout body, while she watched, clapping her plump hands in time with his steps.

As fires began to be lit, the Manth people realised that there were crowds of other travellers encamped along the river. The bridge was the only crossing point for many miles, and it soon became clear that a great migration was under way. Hanno Hath sent Bowman to the nearest group to ask them what had caused them to leave their homes.

'Fire in the sky!' they answered. 'Signs and wonders! The end days are coming!'

'People fleeing the cities! Houses standing empty –'

'Silver plate in the dressers –'

'Grain in the barns –'

'Never need to work again! A poor man can live like an emperor!'

'No more emperors! They've all run away!'

'Why?' asked Bowman.

'Fire in the sky! The end days are coming!'

He could get no more sense out of them, and so returned to his father.

'They feel the coming crisis,' said Hanno. 'Aramanth is burned. The Mastery has fallen. This is a time of signs and wonders.'

The rumours of abandoned cities to the south drew so many people to the bridge that the tiny riverside village had swollen into the size of a town. At its heart, right by the bridge itself, a bustling market had grown up, to cater to the needs of the travellers. Here makeshift stalls sold vegetables and dried meat, kitchen implements, blankets and harness, books of prophecies and maps. There were booths where sausages were roasting and hot spiced wine could be drunk. And everywhere, it seemed, roaring bonfires ringed by excited faces.

The Manth people were now in need of provisions for the journey. They had no money, and so needed to sell before they could buy. They decided to sell the wagon. Their way ahead lay up steep mountain roads; there was no certainty that the horses would be able to haul the wagon all the way. So Hanno Hath, with the agreement of all, decided that it could be sold, and the proceeds used to buy food. The horses and the cows they resolved to keep, for use in the homeland itself.

Hanno and Bowman walked the short distance from their camp to the market place, to find a buyer for the wagon. The scene by the bridge was chaotic. Stall-holders shouted on all sides, banging pans that glinted in the light of the roaring fires. Succulent smells rose up from sizzling roasts turning on spits, beside which grease-covered cooks stood plying their carving knives. A baker had built an oven out of stones and clay, and from its orange mouth he was drawing trays of plump white buns, that smoked as they emerged into the frosty air. Traders in mysteries touted their books, showing pictures of the days of fear and wonder to come: showers of fire from the sky, and great lights, and ghosts as tall as trees.

'Wonders! Terrors!' they cried. 'Be ready for the last days! Maps of the mysteries! Lists of the cities that will perish! The last days explained!'

Bowman was looking at one of the pictures of doom when he felt a touch on his shoulder. Turning, he found there was no one there. His father was at another stall, talking to a trader whose business was tents and harness and wheels for wagons. Bowman joined them. The trader was a small wiry man, with bright eyes and quick movements, like a bird.

'A whole wagon?' he said suspiciously, in answer to their enquiry. 'You want to sell all of it? Why? What's wrong with it?'

'We don't need it any more. We're going north, over the mountains.'

'Over the mountains? What for? There's nothing there.' He stuck his head into the small canvas cubicle behind his stall. 'Some people here going over the mountains.'

'More fools them,' came back a woman's voice.

The trader looked at Hanno in a sideways fashion, as if Hanno was trying to get the better of him.

'Where're you from, then?'

'We've come from the Mastery.'

'From the Mastery? The wagon'll be well used, then. Badly well used.'

'It's in good enough condition.'

'I'll be the judge of that.' His head disappeared back into the cubicle. 'I'm going after some business. Mind the stall.'

'Don't you go paying a fool price!' said the woman inside.

'Did I ever pay a fool price for anything?'

'You were born a fool and you'll die a fool,' came the reply.

The trader gave Hanno a shrug.

'Marriage,' he said.

He then returned with Hanno and Bowman to the camp by the river, to view the wagon. By now, Ira Hath had been lifted out of her bed in the wagon, and was lying well covered with blankets, by the trees, her head propped up by bundles of tent-cloth. Kestrel sat by her side.

The trader examined the wagon thoroughly. Then he joined Hanno and Bowman, and sighed, and sucked his teeth, and shook his head.

'Needs work,' he said. 'I can fix it. But I'm looking at,

oh, five days work. That's five days away from the stall. And who knows how soon we'll all be dead? The day after tomorrow, according to the fellow in the stall next to mine.'

'How much will you give for it?' asked Hanno.

'I couldn't go higher than five crowns.'

'Five? Is that all?'

'Imperial crowns. None of your home-made rubbish.'

'Well –'

Bowman laid a hand on his father's arm, and spoke to the trader himself.

'How much do you think you can sell the wagon for, when you've repaired it?'

The trader frowned, and carried out a mental calculation. Bowman reached carefully into his mind, and followed his thoughts with ease.

New buckboard, new cover, coat of paint, the trader was thinking. *It'll go in a day for a hundred crowns. That's the crazy times we're living in.*

'Ten crowns if I'm lucky,' he said aloud. 'Hardly pays me for my labour. Needs new wheels, of course. Four of them.'

'You can have it for eighty crowns,' said Bowman.

'Eighty!' exclaimed the trader. Even Hanno looked surprised. 'This boy of yours.' The trader addressed Hanno as if in confidence. 'Bit of a dreamer, is he? Not quite learned which way up his boots go on?'

'That's the crazy times we're living in,' said Bowman.

The trader shot him a surprised look.

'Eighty crowns!' he said. 'Now, if you'd said twenty.'

'I said eighty.'

The trader shook his head and turned again to Hanno. 'What do you say, sir?'

'We'd better find another buyer, pa,' said Bowman.

'Another buyer it is,' said Hanno, smiling; and to the trader, 'Thank you for your time.'

Hanno and Bowman set off back towards the market place. The trader followed after them, bubbling with indignation.

'Slow down, sirs, slow down. Did I say I wouldn't buy? I have to think of my reputation, that's all. Would you have me the laughing stock of the market place? I can give you an excellent price, but' – he lowered his voice – 'you must swear to keep it to yourselves, or you'll shame me before my own people. And good sirs' – he dropped his voice to a whisper – 'I wouldn't have my wife know it, she does so love a hard bargain. Let's say fifty crowns, and here's my hand on it.'

'Eighty,' said Bowman.

'Ah, youth is cruel. What does he care, sir? What does he know of married life? You have a married look, sir. You know how a man must keep his respect before his wife or he's done for, and might as well live in the dog kennel and eat scraps. Sixty crowns.'

This with a sidelong glance at Bowman.

'Eighty,' said Bowman. 'It's a fair price.'

'A fair price, but not a manly price. There's nothing about fairness lets a man walk tall. Is there victory in fairness? Is there the envy of men and the love of women? No, sir, no. Fairness is for boys and bachelors. Seventy crowns.'

'Eighty,' said Bowman.

'Eighty, then!' cried the trader with real tears in his eyes. 'Eighty crowns, and may the Morah rot your pockets. So take your money, and if you meet my wife, it's eighteen, you hear me? Eighteen I gave you, and if you say more, I'm a ruined man. So I'll send my boy for the wagon right away, shall I?'

Hanno and Bowman returned with the money, greatly amused. Scooch and Lunki undertook to go provisioning. The others unloaded the wagon and divided the goods into packs of varying sizes, to be carried on their backs over the mountains. The firewood was tied up in bundles, and the bundles were strung together to be hung over the horses' flanks. Miko Mimilith and Tanner Amos set about constructing a litter in the shape of a long triangle, on which Ira Hath could be drawn up the mountain paths behind one of the horses.

The excitement of the market place infected the Manth people too, and as they huddled round their own fire they exchanged theories on what form the coming crisis would take. The talk of fire in the sky became confused in their minds with the Manth prophecy of the wind on fire, and shortly they began to predict that they would all be burned alive, quite possibly that very night. At this the little Marish girls burst into tears, and Ira Hath had to be called, to promise them they would wake unharmed in the morning.

Bowman and Kestrel stayed away from the main group, each for their own reasons. Kestrel had discovered that for all the chill of the night, the silver pendant she wore round her neck was warm, warmer than her own body. When she held it and pressed it to her chest, it hummed softly, and gave her feelings she didn't know how to name. She tried to explain it to Bowman.

'It's like there's something moving just behind me, but when I turn to look, I see nothing. Or I hear a sound, only when I listen, I can't hear it any more.'

'Like nothing's happening, but something's about to happen.'

'Yes. Exactly that.'

'Kess, I think he's here.'

'The one who's coming for you?'

'Yes.'

'Can you feel him?'

'Ever since I went with pa to sell the wagon. Like a touch on my shoulder.'

They reached out their hands and clasped them together, as if some outside force was threatening to part them. The press of palm to palm calmed them both.

'I think maybe I have to go and look for him.'

'No, Bo. Don't.' She gripped his hand very tight. 'I don't want everything to be over.'

As Kestrel said this, Bowman felt a sudden cold wash of memories splash over him, and knew they were her memories. Memories of the two of them in the days before they could speak or walk, sitting side by side on the kitchen floor in Aramanth, rocking at the same pace. Memories of being curled up in the same bed, smelling the same smells, dreaming the same dream. Memories of their first day in school, when they had held hands from the moment they went in to the moment they came out. Memories of the feel of a soft face on your own face, and not knowing where one ends and the other begins.

My other my self.

He jumped up, breaking the contact between them. So long as he was so close to Kestrel, he would never go, and he knew he must go. However much it hurt his sister, however much it hurt himself, this was what he was born to do.

'I have to find him, Kess.'

Without waiting for an answer, he hurried away.

Late though it was, he found the market place still thronging with people, and bright with the lights of their lanterns and fires. The traders had mostly closed their stalls for the night, but in their place had come another sort of salesman, each of whom had taken a pitch standing on a box or a chair or a ladder, from which vantage point they shouted their wares to the crowd.

'You, young man! Yes, you!'

The speaker pointed directly at Bowman.

'Are you lost? Are you bewildered? Do you find you can't make sense of half the things people say to you?'

Bowman paused, wondering for a fleeting moment if this could be a coded message addressed to him.

'Rejoice!' cried the preacher, encouraged. 'The day of the stupid people is coming! The stupid will inherit the earth!'

Bowman moved on, and so fell into the ambit of another speaker, who also attempted to engage his attention.

'Love! Love! The joys of love!' boomed this second preacher, pointing directly at Bowman. 'You who walk alone! I know you, sir! You are a man in want of a woman! In that tent are women in want of men! You need never be alone again! The end times are coming, sell all you have, and fill your final days with the joys of love!'

Bowman looked round at the jostling foolish crowds, and decided that the one who was coming for him would not wait for him here. So he left the market place and made for the riverside beyond the village, and walked along it in quietness and solitude. The river was broad and fast-moving, its dark waters eddying round mooring posts, setting tethered boats banging against each other. A moon had risen in the sky, and by its light he could see the line of mountain peaks, high above. It would be a hard climb, but not too long a climb, he calculated; only, he would not be taking part. All this crying about the last days had made him all the surer that soon now he would join the Singer people, and complete his own journey.

Let them live in the stillness and know the flame. They will lose all and give all.

He turned back to retrace his steps. There, approaching him along the river path, between him and the flickering fires of the village, he saw a figure in a hooded robe. Bowman's heart suddenly began to beat fast.

He directed his steps so they would meet. He could see nothing of the stranger's face, because the light of the fires and the light of the moon were alike shining from behind. He stopped when they were close, and the stranger came to him.

'Eighty crowns!' shrieked a shrill woman's voice he had heard before. 'Robbery! I won't stand for it!'

Bowman was too surprised to respond. The woman shook back her hood to reveal her furious face.

'No use looking round! There's no one here but you and me, and I'm here for my money. I knew my man was a fool, but I never knew he was that big a fool.'

By now, Bowman had grasped that this was the wife of the wagon dealer. She was holding out one hand in a menacing way.

'Take your pox-stained wagon, and give me back my eighty crowns, or I'll set the dogs on you. Eighty crowns! Am I your mother?'

'I don't have the money,' said Bowman. 'And it was a fair price.'

He set off back across the village towards the place where the Manth people were camped. He felt angry and cheated. He had come looking for his destiny, not for some petty quarrel over money. The woman followed him, shrieking.

'Thief! Give me my money back!'

'Go home, woman! You'll make your profit.'

'We'll see who makes a profit!'

She put her fingers in her mouth and let out a shrill whistle. Distracted by her whistle, Bowman almost bumped into a little round-faced person, coming the other way.

'I'm so sorry,' said Bowman, stepping to one side.

Suddenly two very large dogs came hurtling across the snow, heading straight for him.

'Get him, Slasher! Bite him, Ripper!' screamed the woman. 'Thief! Thief!'

Bowman came to a dead stop, concentrated all the powers of his mind, and prepared to withstand the dogs' attack. Their fangs were showing as they raced towards him, and they were snarling low vicious snarls. But all at once, they turned aside. They trotted over to the little round person, and lay on their backs, panting, and he tickled their tummies.

The trader's wife was apoplectic.

'Slasher! Ripper!'

The dogs wriggled on the ground, their jaws lolling open in happy grins. Bowman looked with rather more attention at the unlikely figure patting the dogs.

'Who are you?'

'Who would you like me to be?' he replied.

The trader's wife came stamping over to her dogs and kicked and beat them to their feet.

'Up, Slasher! Up, Ripper!' She shrieked at the round person. 'What have you done to them? You – you – thing!'

In answer, he looked up and met her eyes. Somehow, without anything seeming to change, he became older. In a deep gentle voice, he said,

'Lady, what do you want with me?'

'Oh – oh,' croaked the trader's wife, trembling and blushing.

'Be calm. Be still. Be content.'

He put out one hand and touched her cheek. Then he turned back to Bowman and said in his more usual light high voice, 'Shall we go?'

The trader's wife had fallen completely silent, her eyes fixed on the strange figure who had touched her cheek. Bowman for his part realised now that this small, soft creature must be the messenger for whom he had been waiting.

'The Singer people sent you to find me?'

'Of course.'

'Are we to go tonight?'

'We're to go now. We have very little time.'

'May I say goodbye to my people?'

'Of course. Then we must go.' He added softly to himself, 'Bounce on, Jumper.'

Bowman and Jumper walked back to the Manth camp in silence. Bowman's mind was racing with a confusion of thoughts. The moment had come, but without grandeur or certainty. This messenger who hopped along beside him had no aura of power, no dignity. Even Dogface the one-eyed hermit had inspired more respect. This little creature's voice slithered, so that one moment he sounded like a boy, the next like a girl.

As they reached the encampment, Bowman said to Jumper,

'Wait here. I'll be with you soon.'

The truth was, he was ashamed of Jumper. Now at this heart-wrenching moment, when he was to bid farewell to all who loved him, he did not want a small round-faced man-woman making his departure look ludicrous.

Jumper stopped obediently, and waited in the shadows. Bowman went on to the group beneath the dark trees, where his mother was sitting. His father was here, and both his sisters.

He knelt by his mother's side. She looked up, and saw his intention clearly in his face.

'So it has come then, my Bo.'

'It's come,' he said.

'They wait for you?'

'Yes.'

She nodded, unsurprised. Pinto started to cry.

'Don't leave us, Bo. Let them take someone else.'

Bowman kissed her and whispered to her,

'You have to look after ma and pa. You have to be strong. Don't cry.'

So Pinto tried her best to stop crying. She hugged him very tight.

'You'll come back to us again, won't you? I'll see you again?'

'I don't know,' he said gently. 'The thing I have to do may take a long time.'

'You've always been there, Bo. You have to always be there.'

'Love Pinpin.'

'Love Bo.'

They hugged the way they used to when she was little, and for once she didn't mind that he used her baby name. Then he let her go, and she went into Hanno's waiting arms.

Bowman knelt before his father and kissed his cheek.

'You understand, pa.'

Hanno stroked Pinto and looked at Bowman with a sad smile.

'Yes. I understand.'

Bowman saw Kestrel watching him, her eyes burning. He would say goodbye to her last of all.

He kissed his mother, feeling how thin she had become.

'I may never–'

'Yes, yes,' she cut in, impatient. 'We do what we have to do. Time for you to go, so go.'

It was a flash of the old Ira Hath, who had shouted at laughing crowds, 'O unhappy people!' He hugged her, grateful for her brisk spirit.

'Goodbye, ma.'

She smiled for him again, and he knew she was proud of him. He rose, and sought out Mumpo. An awkward silence was settling over the marchers, as they realised a solemn moment of parting was upon them.

'Dear friend. We've been through hard times together.'

'Let me come with you, Bo. I'm much stronger now.'

'That's why you must stay. Be a son to my parents, a brother to my sisters. Look after them for me.'

'For as long as I live.'

They embraced, and Bowman turned at last, with a heavy heart, to find Kestrel. This was one farewell he did not know how to make. She had taken herself off to the river's edge.

'Kess –'

'No! Don't say it!' She turned and flung the words at him, in a fury of passionate feeling. 'I don't want your goodbyes! I won't listen!'

'But Kess –'

'Where is this Singer who's come for you? Take me to him!'

'But Kess –'

'If you go, I go too!'

'You don't understand. Where I'm going – what I have to do – Kess, there's no coming back.'

'Where is he?'

Her sharp eyes now discerned Jumper, standing waiting quietly where Bowman had left him. She ran to him. Bowman followed.

'Is it you?' Kestrel demanded of Jumper, looking him up and down. 'Have you come from the Singer people?'

'Yes,' said Jumper.

'Well, look at this!'

She pulled out the silver voice that she had rescued from the wind singer, that had hung on a string round her neck ever since.

'Feel it! Feel its warmth! That's more than my warmth! That's more than the heat of my body!'

Jumper felt the silver voice with his soft plump fingers.

'It is warm,' he said.

'I come too! We go together!'

Jumper wrinkled his soft pink brow.

'I was sent to bring the child of the prophet,' he murmured. 'Not the children.'

'We are the child of the prophet,' said Kestrel.

Jumper looked deep into her eyes and pondered.

'Kess,' said Bowman gently. 'I don't want to leave you. More than my life, I want to stay with you. But if I die and you live, then we both live. Don't let us both die. That would be death indeed.'

Kestrel seemed not to hear him. Her fierce eyes were fixed on Jumper. She still held the silver voice in her hands.

'You felt it,' she said. 'It was warm.'

'Of course it's warm,' said Bowman. 'You wear it against your skin.'

'He knows what I mean.'

To Bowman's surprise, Jumper bowed his head.

'Perhaps it's best so.'

'I can come?'

'You can come.'

Before Bowman could make further objection, Kestrel ran back to her mother and father.

'You should have made her stay with the others,' he said to Jumper.

'She wants to be with you.'

'The parting must come. If not now, then soon.'

'True enough, true enough.'

He sighed, but made no attempt to change his decision. Bowman felt relieved and dismayed at the same time. He had dreaded parting from Kestrel. Now he was spared the pain, but since it must come, one day soon, he was not spared the dread.

'Bowman!'

He looked round. It was Sisi.

'Is it true you're going?'

'Yes.'

She turned her great eyes onto Jumper.

'Have you come to take him away?'

'Yes,' said Jumper.

'Keep him safe.'

Jumper bowed his round head.

'Bowman, you always told me one day you'd leave me, so I don't complain. But I want you to know that I'll wait for your return.'

'No, Sisi. You mustn't do that.'

'You know the things you know, and I know the things I know. Now kiss me.'

He kissed her.

'See? I don't cry.'

'I cry, Sisi.'

There were tears in his eyes as he held her hands and spoke to her.

'You're to marry, and have children, and live a long happy life.'

'I will, Bowman. Oh, I will.'

Ira Hath held Kestrel silently in her frail arms and rocked her back and forth, as she'd rocked her when she was a baby. Neither spoke. Kestrel was crying, but making no noise.

'We will meet again,' said Ira at last, speaking the words said by the Manth people at the time of a death.

Word spread through the marchers that both Bowman and Kestrel were leaving them. They began to crowd round, asking questions, growing afraid.

'Why must you go? Where are you going? Will you be with us in the homeland?'

'We don't know. Perhaps not.'

'Then we must say goodbye. You can't go without saying goodbye.'

All the marchers felt the same way. They pushed close, clamouring for their turn. In the darkness it was hard to tell who was who, so little Ashar Warmish, squeezed to the edge of the gathering, drew a burning stick from the fire and held it before her, to light her face.

'Kestrel! Say goodbye to me before you go!'

Tanner Amos saw her face shining in the dark, and took a burning stick of his own, so that he too could be seen. After that, they all did the same, each holding a brand from the fire, from which a blue-yellow flame, or a red glow of embers, gave out a little gleam of light. As they came back from the fire they took up positions standing side by side, in an ever-lengthening line. When Kestrel and Bowman saw the line, they knew there was no question of slipping quietly away. They must make their farewells to each and every one of their people.

'Ashar.'

'Come back soon, Kestrel.'

'Tanner.'

'Miss you.'

'Bek. Rollo.'

'Bowman.'

So it went on, down the line, the farewells distilled from all that could be said into a simple litany of names. Silman Pillish, Sarel Amos, Cheer Warmish whose husband was dead. Little Scooch and big Creoth. Miller Marish and his girls, Fin and Jet. Miko Mimilith and his wife Lea, and Red Mimilith, and the boys Lolo and Mo. Old Seldom Erth and plump Lunki, and Mrs Chirish holding Mumpo's hand. The Such family, with Seer Such in tears. And Pinto, there at the end of the line that had begun with her mother and father: Pinto, the last flame-lit face in that line of faces, watching like ghosts over the parting.

'You must be all of us now, Pinto.'

'I will.'

Kestrel leaned close to kiss her little sister's face. As she did so she whispered to her,

'Love him for me too.'

Now Bowman and Kestrel were at the end of the line, and there was Jumper waiting. Kestrel turned back one last time to look on her people, their faces glowing in the dark.

'Goodbye,' she said quietly. 'All my loves.'

13

The egg's song

Jumper moved surprisingly fast, heading across an open stretch of land in the moonlight. Bowman and Kestrel had to run to keep up.

'Are we going to run all the way to Sirene?' asked Bowman.

'No, no,' said Jumper, slowing down. 'We're going by boat.'

They now saw that he had taken them across a spit of land that lay within a bend of the river, for here was the river once again before them. Moored by the bank lay a long low barge, with the light of a lantern glowing in its cabin windows.

'Climb aboard, and I'll cast off.'

Bowman and Kestrel scrambled onto the barge's deck, while Jumper, following behind, unlooped the mooring rope from its post. Had they been looking they would have seen that he achieved this without touching the rope: just a little nod of his head, and it unwound itself, and snaked back aboard the barge.

Almost at once the barge began to move, carried downstream by the currents of the river. Bowman could see the wheel that controlled the rudder, through the cabin window.

'Shouldn't there be somebody at the wheel?'

'There is,' said Jumper.

He gestured for them to go on through the low cabin door, and so down three steps into the cabin itself. Here they found a snug well-appointed room, with a table and two padded benches, several cupboards, and a door through to the forward section; this main cabin, with its raised housing, being in the stern.

On one of the padded benches there lay a man asleep, covered by a blanket, snoring loudly.

'That's Albard,' said Jumper. 'You'll meet him in the morning.'

The sleeping man's face was turned away, towards the bench's back, but something about his bulky body seemed familiar to Bowman.

'Who is he?' he asked.

'He's the one who will teach you,' said Jumper. 'It won't be easy. It takes years to make a Singer, in the usual course of things. Albard has two days.'

To make a Singer! Bowman felt a thrill of excitement at the words.

'I'm to be a Singer.'

'Of course.'

Kestrel watched and listened, and said nothing.

'But first, I advise you to sleep. The teaching will begin at dawn. There'll be little sleeping once you've begun.' He indicated the second bench, on the far side of the table from the sleeping man. 'Do you think the two of you can squeeze onto the bench?'

'Yes,' said Bowman. 'But where will you sleep?'

'On the floor. I'm used to it.'

So Bowman and Kestrel twined themselves up together on the bench, glad of the familiar closeness. Pressing their brows together, so that they would share dreams, they let themselves drift into a much-needed sleep.

Jumper laid himself down on the boards, easing his plump little body into the most comfortable position he could manage. They were not awake to see, but had Bowman or Kestrel looked, they would have seen that he was lying an inch or so above the floor, as if resting on an invisible mattress.

The barge cruised on down the wide river, sometimes out in mid-stream, sometimes carried by the currents to the snow-covered banks, but never quite striking the trees that grew there. The wheel in the wheel-housing jerked this way and that in the lantern-light, as if a ghost was in command of the rudder; but in reality it was the rudder that turned the wheel. The river had taken charge of the barge, and was guiding it on its way. Jumper had found the river's song, and tuned the barge to its notes, and now he slept at his ease.

What not even Jumper knew was that as the barge was carried down the river, a lean grey cat was running along the river bank, waiting for his moment. When at last a bend in the river brought the barge gliding almost alongside the bank, the cat jumped, and landed safely on the shallow-pitched roof of the hold. From there, he found a place of refuge inside a coil of rope, where he turned round and round, scratching a comfortable bed, and so lay down to wait for morning.

* * *

'Wake UP!'

The last word came out in a furious bellow, as if the sleeper addressed obstinately refused to do as he was told.

'You slug! You lard-cake! You clod of dung! Up! Up! On your feet!'

Bowman and Kestrel, ripped from dreams, confused as to where they were, blinked and struggled to wake. Albard stood over them, prodding at Bowman with a stick, himself only just up, to judge from his wild hair.

'You empty snake-skin! I should have crushed you when I had the chance! Pity, that's my vice. Too much damned womanish pity. Look at you! A wet-eyed child!'

Bowman was now sufficiently awake to see the man called Albard clearly, and to recognise that booming bullying voice.

'You're the Master!'

'What of that? The past is past, thanks to you. Please inform me' – pointing his stick at Kestrel – 'what is that?'

'My sister Kestrel.'

'Throw her in the river! Don't want her.'

Kestrel was as astonished to see the Master as her brother.

Bo! What's he doing here?

I don't know. I thought he was dead.

'You died,' said Bowman aloud. 'I felt it.'

'Oh? And do you feel this?'

He hit Bowman with his stick, across his shins.

'Ow!'

'Not as dead as all that, eh?'

Jumper now joined them, from the door into the forward section. He was carrying a tray of breakfast. Albard turned on him with a snarl.

'Can't do it,' he said. 'The boy's a lump.'

'You can,' said Jumper mildly. 'You're the best.'

'Grease, grease, grease. You think I don't know what you're up to, you little grease ball?'

'Breakfast,' said Jumper.

The tray sailed gently from his hands to land on the cabin table. Once there, the mugs and plates and knives, the basket of eggs, the loaf of bread and jug of milk, the butter and the honey jar, all shuffled about until they were arranged for a sitting of four people. Albard watched this miniature display of mind power and let out a groan.

'Once I ruled a nation. Now I can't even move a plate.'

Sighing, he sat down to eat. The others joined him. They ate and drank in silence, until they were done. Then Jumper said to Bowman,

'Albard will teach you.'

'But not her!' said Albard, stabbing a butter-smeared knife in the direction of Kestrel.

'You will do everything he says.'

'Throw her in the river!' added Albard.

'You'll find it hard. You must not give up. Do you understand? Whatever you feel, however great your distress, don't give up.'

'I understand that,' said Bowman. 'But I don't understand why he is to be my teacher.'

'Nor I, boy,' echoed Albard.

'Surely the Master is the enemy of the Singer people.'

'Not at all,' said Jumper brightly. 'Albard is our brother. We love him and embrace him.'

'Please!' groaned Albard. 'Spare me your embraces!' Then turning to Bowman, 'You remind me of a boy I knew, long ago. A boy who believed he was different from all other boys, and lived to prove it.'

'Your son?'

'Not my son, you earthworm! I have no son! I'm talking about myself. Did I not tell you, you will become me?'

'Time is passing,' murmured Jumper.

'Oh, passing, is it? Well, well, well! There's a surprise.'

But Albard accepted the implied instruction, and led Bowman out on deck. Kestrel followed, unasked. It was a cold clear morning. Bowman felt invigorated by the winter air, and by the prospect of the teaching that was about to begin.

Kestrel was still bewildered by the presence of the man she had known as the Master.

How can he teach you? He's the one who made slaves of us all.

I don't know.

Don't you want to know?

I want to learn how to be a Singer. Then I'll know.

'None of that!' bellowed Albard. 'I can't tell what you're saying, but I know you're twittering to each other.'

'You don't need to shout all the time,' said Kestrel. 'We're not your servants.'

Albard glared at her.

'You'd shout if you'd been through what I've been through,' he grumbled. 'He should have left me to die.' This with a glowering look at Jumper.

'Time is passing,' said Jumper softly.

'Yes, yes, yes.' Albard turned on Bowman. 'So, boy, vessel of my destruction – for it wasn't you, don't flatter yourself it was you, you were the channel for powers greater than either of us –'

'I know that.'

'You'd better know it, and more too. You're to know you have no special abilities. No special powers. No special destiny. You're nothing but the tool, the plaything of others. Do you know all that?'

'No –'

Smack! Albard struck him across the face with the flat of his hand. Not hard, but it brought tears to Bowman's eyes.

'I say yes!'

His hand was raised to strike again. Bowman rallied the powers of his mind to resist the blow, but found his powers were gone.

Smack! The second blow stung far more. Involuntary tears trickled down his cheeks.

'Aren't you going to stop me? Are you going to sit there like a whimpering puppy and let me hit you?'

Smack! Bowman found he could do nothing, not even raise his arm, or move aside to escape the blow.

Smack! Smack! Smack! Albard struck him and struck him, until the tears streamed down Bowman's red and smarting cheeks.

Kestrel watched in mounting anger. But just as she had determined to intervene, a voice spoke in her mind.

Let him alone. Let him learn.

Very surprised, she looked round and saw Jumper

gazing at her. The look in his eyes had as powerful an effect on her as the voice in her head. She saw deep understanding there; and more, she saw that he knew why she was here, which neither Bowman nor Albard knew. So she remained still, and followed the teaching.

'Beg my forgiveness!'

Bowman stared back at Albard, wounded in body and spirit, but still defiant.

'Kiss my hand!'

Bowman did not move.

'Still proud? What have you to be proud of? You have no power! You can't resist me! You think because you're the child of the prophet you have some great part to play in the world?'

'Yes,' said Bowman.

'Ha!' Albard snorted with contemptuous laughter, his big belly heaving. 'Ha! Don't you see it? What a joke! You think because you're the child of the prophet you're someone special? Precisely the opposite is the truth! You're nobody! You're anybody! All that matters about you is that you have certain ancestors. You could be a cross-eyed cripple and still play your part. Don't you see how that makes you so much less than everyone else? What are you, but a postman with a letter from the past? You think because what you carry in your pouch has power that you are powerful?'

He struck Bowman again, much harder. Bowman shook with the hurt of it.

'Now kiss my hand!'

'Is this necessary for my teaching?'

'I give you no reasons! Only orders!'

Bowman hesitated a moment more, then leant forward and kissed Albard's hand. Kestrel's heart ached for him as she watched. She felt his misery. Albard's words had been well chosen, and were taking effect.

'Ask my forgiveness!'

'Forgive me.'

'You stink of the Morah! What business have you in Sirene?'

'I don't know.'

'Take off your clothes.'

Again Bowman hesitated, but this time he didn't ask again if it was necessary. With trembling fingers he untied his belt, and drew off his clothes. When he was naked, shivering in the cold air, he looked so frail that Kestrel had to bite her lip to stop herself from crying.

'Look at yourself! Look at your body! Do you like your body?'

Bowman stood tensed against the cold, not sure how he was meant to answer.

'Does your body like you? I don't think so.'

A sudden cramp seized Bowman's leg. He cried out, and bent down to soothe the pain. A second stab went through him, this time in one arm. Then his neck, his gut, his other leg, all began to scream with pain, as if knives were being thrust into his flesh. His throat began to burn and his bowels to melt. Frantically, he fell to the deck and tried to rub his agonised flesh, but all the time more pains burst forth, in his ears, in his wrist joints, in his lungs, even as he pulled in terrified gulps of air.

'Your body hates you!' cried Albard. 'Your body is your enemy! Your body wants to hurt you!'

Bowman started to scream. He couldn't help himself. He writhed screaming on the deck. Kestrel could bear no more.

'Stop!'

But even as she moved forward, some unseen force met her like a soft impenetrable wall, and forced her back.

Bowman fought the pain as long as he could, which was not long at all; and then he lost consciousness. It happened slowly, like a walking away from himself, and as he went he cried and reached out his arms and didn't want to go, but there was too much pain.

He woke in utter darkness. He moved one hand, to feel where he was, and met timber walls on either side, and a timber roof close above his head. He was lying down, wrapped in blankets, in what felt like a long box. He could hear only a low rushing sound all round him, a sound that absorbed all other sounds, and never ceased. The pain was gone: so far gone that with it had gone almost all sensation. He was naked, but for the covering blanket.

No light, not even a crack. No sound, but for the one sound. No feeling.

He tried to speak aloud.

'Help!'

His voice sounded strange, as if it belonged to someone else.

Kess! Where are you?

No answer. Was she no longer on the barge? Had she been sent back?

Suddenly he felt very frightened.

'Help!' he cried. 'Help me!'

There was no answer. Nobody had heard him. He felt it himself, he was so completely sealed up that no one would hear him however loud he cried. So he must wait.

'How long will you leave him?' said Kestrel.

'Until he gives up.'

'But you told him not to give up.'

'Yes, I did, didn't I?' Jumper spoke in an absent-minded voice, as he gazed out over the passing riverbank.

'He'll feel he's failed.'

'Yes, I suppose he will.'

'Do you want him to fail?'

'I think you know the answer to that.'

'All I know is you're doing this to teach him. But I don't see what you're teaching him by leaving him alone in that hole.'

'The teaching is still to come. This is the unteaching.'

Bowman had no way of gauging how long he lay in the darkness. It might have been hours, it might have been days. After a while he thought perhaps he was dead. After a little while more, he thought nothing.

Kestrel ate her supper with Albard and Jumper. Jumper had cooked them a dish of eggs with butter. She kept silent and listened as they bickered and grumbled. She too was learning, in her own way.

'Why you, eh, Jumper? Why did they send me a dull blob like you?'

'I'm sorry you find me dull. I'll try to be more amusing.'

'Please! Spare me!'

Then after a few moments,

'I'll tell you why they sent you. Because they hate me. Sirene has always hated me.'

He turned on Kestrel, as if glad for once to have a neutral audience.

'Did you ever see my Mastery, girl?'

'Yes,' said Kestrel.

She remembered all too well how close she had come to death. It was this man, this Master, who had driven Ortiz's blade to kill. But Albard seemed only to recall the glories of his rule.

'Ah! My Mastery was something! That's what the powers of the Singer people can do in the world! But they won't do it. They'd rather stand aside, while the world burns.'

'We conserve our powers for the one great task,' said Jumper.

'One great task!' Albard appealed again to Kestrel. 'These Singer people, you know what they wait for? You know what they train for, and give their lives for? Death! That's their one great task! Death!'

'You took the vow also, Albard.'

'So I did. But why wait a lifetime, with such powers, when all around us the people are suffering?'

Again, to Kestrel,

'That was my crime! To use the powers I was given, to build a better world. For this they turned the might of Sirene against me. For this I was brought to what you see now. See?'

He tossed a fragment of bread into the air. It fell to the table.

'I can't even command a piece of bread! He can.' He

stabbed a finger at Jumper. 'This blob-faced man-woman can.' He threw another piece of bread at Jumper. It stopped in mid-air, turned about, and floated back onto Albard's plate. 'See? But I, I who created the noblest city man has ever known, I can do nothing!'

'Why must the Singer people die?' asked Kestrel.

'You're the child of the prophet,' said Albard. 'You should know.'

'I know Ira Manth began it all. I know the Singer people are the only power that can stop the Morah. But I don't know why they have to die.'

'Vanity!' grunted Albard. 'Makes them feel important.'

Kestrel had addressed her question to Jumper. He ignored Albard, and responded with his own question.

'What is the mor?'

'It's the desire for power, I think,' answered Kestrel. 'And wanting things only for yourself. And hurting other people to get what you want. And being afraid. And hating.'

'The prophet understood that to control the mor, he and his followers must take the opposite path. Seek no power. Want nothing. Possess nothing. Take nothing. Give. Let go.'

Kestrel quoted from the Lost Testament.

'They will lose all and give all.'

Jumper nodded.

'There's no end to it, once you've started down that path.' His eyes held her very still. 'The giving has no limits. Even life itself.'

Kestrel understood. She understood the look in his eyes, the feeling in him, more than the sense of his words.

'You ask why Singer people have to die. Why should they not? Why hold on to such a little thing as life?'

'Ha!' snorted Albard. 'Vanity! Sheer vanity!'

'You think death is the end? No. Lose your life, and find everything. The firesong is the sweetest song of all.'

'You still end up dead,' said Albard.

'So do all living creatures. But very few know the wind on fire.'

'The wind on fire.' Kestrel felt she understood more than before, but hadn't yet fitted the pieces together. 'It destroys the Morah?'

'It's the only power greater than the Morah. The power of all the Singer people combined.'

'And then the mor rises again,' said Albard. 'The Morah returns.'

'As do the Singer people.'

'Round and round,' said Albard. 'Makes you giddy. Makes you sick.'

'There's always the boy,' said Jumper.

'Yes, yes. There's always the boy.' Albard became a little less irritable as he thought of Bowman. 'I wonder if he's got what it takes.'

'You're the teacher, Albard.'

Bowman heard him before he saw him. He heard a door open and close. Then footsteps. Then a voice.

'Boy?'

He tried to speak, but he found to his surprise that he had forgotten how.

'Close your eyes, boy. The light will hurt you.'

Bowman closed his eyes. He heard a rattling above

him. Then faint light touched his eyelids. Hands reached down, and tied a scarf round his head, so that he was blindfolded. All this was done to him without his own help or hindrance. He had lost control over his own body.

Now he felt the hands reaching round and under him. A sudden lurch, and he was lifted up in strong arms. He was carried over creaking timbers, and came out into light. He saw the light through the tiny triangular gaps where the blindfold was raised by the bridge of his nose. He smelt the sharpness of fresh air. He sensed other people round him, but he had no strength to wonder who they were, nor any desire to do so. In that dark hole he had lost more than his body. He had lost all sense of himself.

Now he was being put down, on a makeshift bed. He lay there thankfully. There were sounds all round him: the river, the wind in the trees, the breathing of the people close by. He felt his hand lifted up, and a small object placed in it, and left there for him to hold.

It was an egg.

He felt the egg, heavy in his hand, and a surge of joy flowed through him. The egg was so smooth, and yet its smoothness was pitted with tiny grains. It was so beautifully curved, curved to perfection, and yet not a sphere. It formed its own shape, that obeyed no rules. He could feel now that the cool surface of the shell was absorbing the heat of his hand. He closed his fingers round the egg, sensing the space it occupied, and the way it resisted his grasp. He tightened his grip, delighting in the shell's strength. He squeezed more tightly still, and *kakakash!*, the egg broke, and all was transformed. The smooth curves turned to spiky fragments, the full firm form vanished, and a cool balm spread over his hand.

That moment of breaking astounded him. He relived the sensation, seeking the exact point at which resistance had given way, the instant of transformation, *kakakash!* From firm to yielding, from solid to liquid, from egg to not-egg. He sensed it then: that if he could enter that instant, and hold it in suspension, he would be in the very heart of – of what? He hunted down the thought. Of life? Of reality?

'We call it the song.'

The voice shocked him. That it spoke in answer to his thought shocked him. But the sense of it was no surprise. At the heart of the egg lay that which made it egg, lay its eggness. Why not call it the egg's song?

Albard and Jumper looked down on Bowman as he lay blindfolded on blankets, with egg-yolk dribbling between the fingers of one hand, and a smile on his face. Jumper nodded, satisfied.

'He's going to be alright,' he said.

'Alright?' exclaimed Albard. 'He's going to be a master!'

14

Pinto grows up

The Manth people crossed the bridge early that day, and struck the mountain road. The loss of Bowman and Kestrel lay heavy on each one of them, but none spoke of it. Their task lay clear before them: they were to climb the high snow-covered mountains, and so at last reach the homeland on the far side. Bowman and Kestrel were engaged on some other task, which they did not understand, but which was somehow necessary, somehow part of their own journey. So in sombre mood, they followed in a long line, up the track that climbed the tree-lined slopes.

Mumpo took the lead. No longer paying any attention to his wounds, he carried a heavy pack, and strode forward with as steady a step as if he was unburdened, and close to home. It was a bright morning, the sky clear blue above the white mountain peaks. He felt that he must take Bowman's place: Bowman who was always alert to all that was happening, who sensed what others were thinking. He felt strong enough for the tasks ahead, and needed, and full of anticipation. The last stage of the journey was begun.

Hanno Hath walked beside the litter onto which Ira Hath had been strapped. Seldom Erth led the horse that drew the litter over the stony ground, doing his best to find an even way between the frozen wheel-ruts; but inevitably Ira was jolted as they went.

'This is how they used to put babies to sleep in the old days,' said Hanno. 'When the Manth people were still a wandering tribe.'

Ira smiled from her bundle of blankets and straps.

'I feel like a baby,' she said.

Pinto walked on her other side, carrying a pack of her own. Her pack was small, and she felt ashamed, but her father had refused to let her carry more. He had also refused to let her lead the second horse, saying she was too young. Pinto knew she was young if you counted in years. But inside herself she felt she wasn't at all young, she was as good as any of them, better even. And now that Bowman and Kestrel were gone, she was the oldest child in her family, the only child. That made a difference.

As they marched, they passed travellers going the other way.

'You don't want to go into the mountains!' they told them. 'Not in deep winter. Not when there's fire in the sky.'

Others were even more insistent.

'Turn back! There's no way over the mountains. Head for the coast and take the sea route, if you must.'

But Ira Hath could feel the warmth on her cheek, and she grew more certain with every step they took.

'We go north. Follow the road into the mountains. We'll find a way.'

They came to a stream, fast-flowing and ice-cold, and stopped to water the cows and horses, and fill their bottles. Rollo Shim was still limping, but he was able to keep up. The one in difficulty was Mrs Chirish. When they stopped by the stream she sat down quite suddenly, and didn't move again, even to fetch water.

Creoth spoke discreetly to Hanno Hath.

'We have to do something. She's a good woman, but she has more to bear than the rest of us.'

Hanno saw that he was right. The road began to climb steeply ahead. Mrs Chirish would slow them down.

'We'll make a second litter. She can keep my wife company.'

Tanner Amos and Miko Mimilith set off into the trees to cut the side rails for a second litter, while Cheer Warmish went through her bundle to find a length of tent-cloth. Hanno took Mrs Chirish aside and explained what he wanted to do.

'My wife finds it hard,' he said, 'to be lying at her ease while the rest of us have all the labour of marching. I'd like her to know she's not the only one. We're making a second litter, to carry whoever needs a break from the march, and I'd like to ask you to be the first to use it.'

'Oh, I couldn't be carried along like a queen! Don't you worry about me. I shall manage. Let poor Rollo take the second litter.'

'Rollo Shim must keep moving, or his leg will stiffen up. And it's not you that I worry about.' Hanno lowered his voice. 'I worry about Creoth. You remember how he helped carry you, on the long march to the Mastery? He swears he'll carry you again. But look at the road ahead. It'll kill him.'

'He shan't carry me! I won't allow it!'

'He's so very determined. And my wife feels so guilty. If you could just ride in the second litter, you'd be doing us all a kindness.'

'Well, well. Since you put it that way. I must say, your family have always been good to me. I'll do what I can to help.'

So when the column set off again, Mrs Chirish bumped along in a litter alongside Ira Hath, and the two of them pulled faces at each other every time there came an unusually violent jolt.

All morning, as the winter sun travelled across the sky behind them, they tramped up the winding road. By noon, the way was running between trees, and doubling back on itself in ever sharper bends, to control the gradient on the steep mountainside. As they trod onwards, here and there through breaks in the trees they could see, not far above them, the next loop in the road, and knew it would be a long time coming. They had no choice. The mountain goats that stood still as statues, staring at them through slotted eyes, could bound up the tracks between the trees; but they were not goats, nor were their horses and cows. They must take the long winding road.

Mumpo kept the lead, now with Bek Shim at his side. Their keen eyes scanned the dense forest on either side, as well as the way ahead. They no longer expected to meet bandits in this little-travelled region; now the fear was of wild beasts. In the village by the bridge there had been talk of mountain cats that crouched on overhanging branches and dropped onto their prey; and of wolves. Mumpo remembered the wolves from the long-ago journey with Bowman and Kestrel. Bowman had talked to the wolves, and they had understood him. But Bowman was gone.

Mumpo felt a shiver of fear, which he controlled at once. Bowman was gone: he must take his place. Kestrel was gone: he must find a reason for living without her. The enormity of his new responsibilities helped Mumpo more than he knew. He was no longer the friend, the follower, the last in line. He was now one of the leaders.

Even Sisi sensed this. Since Bowman and Kestrel's departure, she had taken to seeking Mumpo out and talking to him, which she'd never done before. She asked him about Bowman, wanting to hear the story of the search for the voice of the wind singer. In particular, she questioned him about what had happened in the halls of the Morah. Mumpo did his best to answer her questions, but the details had grown confused in his memory.

'So Bowman came close to the Morah?'

'Yes. We all did.'

'Did he touch the Morah?'

Mumpo remembered with shame how he had been flooded with a terrible joy, and had marched with the Zars. But what had happened to Bowman?

'I don't know. Maybe he did.'

He saw again the white and gold uniforms to left and right, and the beautiful smiling faces of the young Zars. He heard the band, and the voices that sang the song of the Zars, that had only one word –

'Kill, kill, kill, kill! Kill, kill, kill!'

He saw Kestrel ahead, standing still, looking at him – Yes, of course. Bowman too was in the marching ranks, his drawn sword in his hand.

'Yes, he was touched by the Morah. Bowman was our leader.'

'Whose leader?'

'The beautiful people. The soldiers of the Morah. The Zars.'

Sisi said nothing more. She became very thoughtful.

'Then we ran away,' said Mumpo.

The details remained unclear. It was all years ago.

'And now,' said Sisi slowly, 'he's gone to join the Singer people, to destroy the Morah.'

'Yes. I think so. I wonder if we'll ever see him again.'

'I'm sure of it,' said Sisi. 'If I weren't, I'd lie down here by the road and die.'

'You love him so much?'

'My future is with Bowman. Until he returns, time stands still.'

Mumpo was amazed that she could say it so simply, and be so sure. He wanted to speak of Kestrel, but then he didn't. I'm a fool for Kestrel, he thought, and I expect I always will be. But there's no call for others to know.

Out of the corner of his eye he glimpsed a shape moving through the trees. He searched the deep shadows, but it was gone. Then as soon as he directed his gaze up the sloping road ahead, he caught the movement in the trees once more. It was a wolf, he was sure of it. One of the great grey wolves that made no sound as they tracked their prey through the mountains, waiting for night.

Quietly, he fell back until he was level with Hanno,

and told him of his fears. Quietly, Hanno briefed Tanner Amos and Bek Shim and Miller Marish, and they all spread themselves out down the length of the line, and watched the trees.

By general agreement, the marchers did not stop for a midday meal. The winter days were short. They would eat when they camped for the night. They all carried water bottles to quench their thirst, and the little children were given cakes to eat as they walked. Lolo Mimilith refused his cake, on the grounds that he was no longer a child, being twelve, like Ashar Warmish. His brother Mo, two years younger, refused his cake too, but a little later his mother gave it back to him when no one was looking, and he ate it gratefully. Pinto accepted her cake, too proud to copy Mo Mimilith, but she gave it to Mrs Chirish to eat. Mrs Chirish's arms were under the blanket, strapped onto the litter, so when Pinto held the cake to her mouth, she was unable to push it away. She opened her mouth to say no thank you, but somehow she took a bite of the cake instead. Having started, and so lost any respect she might have won by a refusal, there seemed nothing to be gained by shutting her mouth against the rest. So she ate the sweet cake, with tears in her eyes.

In the middle of the afternoon, the winding climbing road suddenly emerged from the trees, and came to an end. Before them lay a long flat mountain plateau, stretching for miles to the east and the west, but no more than half a mile wide ahead. The snow lay untouched on this plain. No footsteps or wheel-tracks led across it to the northern side, where the last range of peaks began.

The Manth people gathered at the road's end, and

rested their packs, and puzzled over what to do next. This sudden expanse of virgin snow made no sense at all. Why did no trees grow here? Why were there no tracks?

Old Seldom Erth provided the answer, in all its obviousness.

'Water,' he said. 'It's a frozen lake.'

Mumpo investigated, moving forward carefully, striking the ground ahead with a stick. Shortly he struck ice. He brushed away the snow on the surface, and tried to break the ice, but it was too thick. He stood on it, close to the shore, ready to jump: but it held his weight.

Hanno had Ira Hath's litter turned round, so that she was facing north. Her eyes were closed. The jolting of the litter had weakened her.

'Do you feel it still?' asked Hanno.

Ira nodded. She raised one finger, and pointed north, directly across the ice. This was all Hanno needed to know.

'We cross the lake,' he said.

The smaller children cheered, and at once ran onto the snow-covered ice, and lost their footing, and went flying.

'Fin! Come back at once! Jet!'

The ice held. The children returned, snow-stained, laughing. But Silman Pillish was concerned.

'How do we know the ice will hold us all the way across? How do we know it'll bear the weight of the cattle and the horses? If it gives way out there in the middle of the lake, and we fall into the water, we'll freeze to death.'

'We must take that risk,' said Hanno. 'We have no choice.'

'On the contrary,' persisted the teacher. 'We could follow the lake shore to the west until we came to a crossing place.'

Hanno turned to his wife. She had been listening. Now she shook her head.

'No time,' she murmured.

'It would take another day at least,' said Hanno. 'We must cross the ice.'

After that, no one questioned his decision, but there were many concerned glances. Hanno worked out a plan for the crossing that he hoped would give them the best chance of reaching the other side in safety.

'Mumpo, you and Tanner go first. Sound the ice as you go. Keep a little way apart. If you feel the ice move, or crack, call back.'

Mumpo nodded. Tanner Amos went to cut himself a stout stick.

'The rest of us will follow in groups of three or four, spread out from each other. Creoth, you wait on the shore with the cows. Seldom, you wait with the horses. When we're all on the other side, follow us with the beasts. If the ice breaks under their weight, you must abandon them. Move away from them as fast as you can.'

Seldom Erth had been testing the ice for himself.

'It'll hold,' he declared. 'So long as they go quiet, it'll hold.'

'Now remember,' said Hanno to them all, 'if you feel the ice crack beneath you, spread your weight. Move slowly. The ice is thick. It will carry you even if it cracks.'

He looked up at the declining sun.

'We have an hour of daylight left. No time to lose.'

His plan was that he would pull Ira Hath's litter himself, strapping the horses' harness to his own shoulders. As soon as Mumpo saw this, he stepped forward.

'I'll take that. I'm stronger than you.'

'No, Mumpo. I need you in front.'

'Let Bek Shim go in my place.'

Hanno looked at Mumpo and understood that he needed to show he was strong again, so he let him take over the harness, and placed himself behind the litter, where he could watch over his wife. Mrs Chirish had been released from her litter, to cross the frozen lake on her own legs.

'Go quietly, he said,' she murmured to herself. 'That'll do me just right. Going quietly is how I like it.'

Just as they were lined up and ready to begin, Cheer Warmish burst into bitter sobs.

'We're all going to die!' she sobbed. 'The ice will break and we'll all die!'

Her crying set off a small panic among all those who had been struggling to control their fears.

'What if she's right?' said Gale Such.

'Shouldn't we take the safe way round, even if it is longer?' said Miko Mimilith.

'Don't let me drown!' cried Lunki, and began to howl.

'Be quiet, Lunki!' said Sisi sharply. And turning to the others, she chided them.

'Why should we be safe? Did we leave the Mastery to be safe? We did it because we believed Ira Hath would lead us to the homeland. If you no longer believe, turn back and follow some other prophet. If you do believe, then believe all the way. Believe the ice will hold you. Believe that nothing can stop us now. Not the end days, not the destruction of cities, not fire in the sky. So hold your heads high, and be proud, and fear nothing and no one!'

Her words electrified them all. Creoth said out loud,
'Beard of my ancestors! There's a girl!'

'Let's go,' cried Hanno Hath. 'The sun is setting.'

As he passed Sisi, he pressed her arm in silent gratitude.

Tanner Amos and Bek Shim stepped out onto the frozen
lake, tapping their sticks before them as they went. Hanno
waited until they were well out from shore, then he signed
for the next group to follow, and the next. The little figures
moved cautiously over the coating of snow, sliding their
feet forward step by step, learning how to stay upright,
sensing the strength of the ice beneath them. Mumpo
now followed, drawing Ira Hath in her litter behind him,
and Hanno and Pinto came too, not too close, to spread
the weight of the group.

Miller Marish held his two girls' hands, one on each
side, controlling their urge to run and slide.

'Slowly, girls. Slow and even.'

Mrs Chirish stumped along, breathing heavily, with
Scooch to one side, and Lunki and Sisi to the other. The
girls who had come so close after their capture by the
Barra klin stayed together on the ice, all holding hands:
Red Mimilith and Sarel Amos, Seer Such and little Ashar
Warmish. Creoth waited by his cows, and Seldom Erth
waited by his horses, on the snowy shore.

On they went, feeling the soft crunch of the snow
beneath their feet, and the slight skid that was the ice, as
they took the next step. Little by little, the shore receded
behind them. The girls who were holding hands gripped
each other more tightly. Miller Marish raised his arms, as
if to lessen his daughters' weight on the ice. Mrs Chirish
swung each foot down more carefully than before, rolling

her weight forward, fearing the first protest from the frozen lake. Now that they were out of reach of land the expanse of ice seemed much bigger than before, and they were all only too aware that if it broke, they would stand no chance.

Ahead, the leaders, Tanner Amos and Bek Shim, passed the halfway point. Hanno called to them.

'All well still?'

'All well.'

Hardly had Tanner Amos spoken the words, when he felt a shudder beneath his feet. He stopped, and braced himself. He spoke softly.

'Bek? Did you feel that?'

'Yes.' Bek Shim was a hundred yards to his right. The ice was bouncing.

Tanner took a few steps forward. The shudder came again. He looked back. The others were spread out all across the lake, black forms moving slowly over the white surface.

'Do we warn them?' said Bek Shim.

'Not yet,' said Tanner. 'It may be nothing.'

Hanno, watching them from behind, saw their nervousness, but said nothing to the others. One way or another, they must cross the lake before nightfall.

Creoth watched from the shore. He saw no reason for alarm.

'The ice'll bear the beasts.'

'So long as they go quietly,' said Seldom Erth.

'They'll be quiet enough. It's been a long climb.'

But as he spoke, one of his cows jerked up her head and shifted nervously from foot to foot.

'There, Dreamer, there! Nothing to worry about.'

Seldom Erth saw that his horses' ears were twitching.

'Don't be too sure of that.'

He looked round. The light was beginning to fade, and it was hard to make out anything in the deep shadows between the trees, but he thought he saw something moving.

'What is it?' said Creoth, now picking up more nervousness among his cows.

'I don't know. But I say we start moving.'

The nearest of the people ahead were almost at the mid-point. The others would be safe enough even if the ice did break here by the south shore.

'Come on, then. You go first.'

So Seldom Erth led his two horses onto the ice, one on a short rein, the other on a long rein, to keep them apart. The ice groaned under the horses' hooves, but it held.

'Off you go,' said Creoth. 'I'll follow in a while.'

Hanno Hath looked back and saw to his surprise that the horses were already on the lake. He frowned, asking himself why they hadn't waited as they had agreed. He looked ahead, and saw how slowly and cautiously Tanner Amos and Bek Shim were proceeding. Then there came a sound from the distant trees: a long, low howl.

Mumpo's head swung round at once.

'Wolves!'

The cows heard the wolf cry and started forward onto the ice before Creoth could stop them. He followed at once, doing his best to calm them with his voice.

'Now, Tawny! Now, Stumper! Easy, easy.'

The long howl sounded again. Mumpo looked back

towards the shore, and caught sight of movement between the trees.

'They'll stampede the cattle,' Hanno said.

Then the ice would break. He didn't need to say that.

'They were our friends once,' said Mumpo.

Hanno understood him.

'Could they be again?'

'Maybe. I can try.'

Without another word, Mumpo unbuckled the harness that drew the litter, and Hanno took it from him. Mumpo then turned and began to slide slowly and carefully back across the lake towards Creoth and the cows.

'What is it?' called the others. 'What's happening?'

'Keep moving!' cried Hanno. 'Keep on to the far shore!'

Bek Shim, who had stopped to look, turned back on hearing this. His first onward step was a little too eager. Even as his foot landed on the ice, he knew he had applied too much pressure. The ice shivered at the impact, and let out a single sharp report, like the crack of a whip.

'Bek!'

'I'm alright.'

He could feel the crack, could sense its weakness, but already he was sliding away from it, away from Tanner Amos, the other leader.

'Ice crack!' Tanner called back. 'It's holding. Keep away. Follow me.'

Mumpo paid no attention to the ice crack. He forged on, back across the lake, until he came up with Seldom Erth and Creoth. The horses were jittery, but under control. The cows looked anxious.

'Alright so far,' said Creoth. 'I think it's a wolf.'

'I've seen it,' said Mumpo.

As he spoke, the first great grey wolf stepped out of the trees, and stood on the shore, watching them. It held its head high, its great thick-pelted body tensed and alert.

'Keep the beasts moving.'

'Look at the size of the animal!' exclaimed Creoth.

'They were good to us once. They may not harm us.'

'They're wolves,' said Seldom Erth. 'Wolves must eat.'

Two more wolves now came out of the trees, and stood looking over the lake.

'Keep the beasts moving,' said Mumpo again. 'I'll wait here.'

Creoth and Seldom Erth set off again, urging their nervous beasts over the ice. Now the rest of the Manth people became very afraid. They could see the wolves behind them, and they could feel the cracked ice ahead. In their fear they stopped moving, and stood still. Hanno Hath called to them, his voice carrying clearly through the twilight air.

'Keep moving! Think of nothing but your next step! One step at a time. Every step brings you nearer the shore. Don't stop moving! Not too fast, not too slow. One step at a time.'

This simple instruction steadied their nerves, and they set off again, over the bouncing ice. Only Pinto disobeyed her father. She was small and light, she knew the ice would hold her. She turned back, towards Mumpo.

Mumpo was watching the wolves. Still they stood, sniffing the air, not venturing onto the ice. Did wolves hunt on ice? The cows and the horses were making steady progress away from him across the lake. That was good.

Beyond them, Bek Shim, the leader, was close to the far shore, despite the cracked ice. That was good.

Then one of the wolves stepped out onto the ice.

That was not good.

The wolf stood for a moment, perfectly at ease, on the snow-blanketed lake. Then it started loping forward, towards Mumpo.

Pinto increased her pace. She still had fifty yards of slithering ice to cover.

Mumpo heard the cows bellow with fear behind him, but he did not turn. He heard Creoth's urgent efforts to calm them.

'So, so, so! Easy, easy!'

He kept his eyes on the wolf. What was it Bowman had done? He had met the wolf's eyes. He had let it touch him. He had shown no fear.

The wolf kept coming towards him. Mumpo shivered, but did not look away. He felt a sudden stab of pain in his wounded stomach.

I must be very afraid, he thought; as if his fear was a separate part of himself.

Behind him, unknown to him, Pinto was running now, running and sliding, propelling herself back over the ice.

Now the wolf was close to Mumpo, within easy leaping distance. Now it was stopping and crouching, its yellow eyes fixed on him, its jaws a little open, showing its white teeth.

'I'm your friend,' said Mumpo. The words sounded meaningless in the icy air. Why should the wolf understand him? Wolves can't talk.

Two more wolves came loping up behind. Mumpo

reached out a hand, meaning to show friendship. His wound throbbed. The lead wolf's claws dug into the ice, its muscles tensed, its ears flattened. It let out a low snarl.

Pinto raced towards Mumpo as fast as she could. She had no idea what to do, she was driven solely by the need to protect him. She heard the snarl, saw the look in the wolf's eyes, and knew that it was about to attack. She drove herself faster –

'Pinto! No!'

– faster and faster, straight at the wolf as it made its spring, and she too jumped, sprang like a wolf, hurling herself off the ice and into the air. In that flashing moment, as she jumped, there in mid-air, a hot light exploded within her, and she cried out – she thought aloud, but no sound came – cried out to the wolf – *Friend of my friend! Enemy of my enemy!* – collided with the wolf in mid-air – and was knocked, sprawling, breathless, to the ice.

The wolf landed on its great paws, half-stunned, confused.

'Pinto!'

Mumpo was coming for her.

'I'm alright.'

The wolf swung round its great shaggy head, glared at Mumpo, then turned on Pinto, its mouth leering open.

'No! –'

There was nothing to fear. Pinto reached out one hand. The wolf lowered its head and licked her hand with its rasping tongue, and nuzzled her neck, and licked her face.

You heard me, wolf! You felt me!

Mumpo came to a stop, watching, silent with

astonishment. The other wolves were clustering round Pinto now, three of them, then four and five. He had seen it happen before, long ago, only this time it was little Pinto who was talking with wolves.

'You too!' he said.

She turned to look at him: a seven-year-old child with eyes that were suddenly so much older. This was how Kestrel had looked at him, before she had gone away.

'They won't hurt you,' she said. 'They're our friends.'

She stroked the wolves' shaggy necks, and rose to her feet. She waved to the others, who stood looking back over the ice, fearful in the twilight.

'I'm alright! Go on!'

The people and the cows and the horses turned and continued on their slow way over the creaking ice. Pinto left the wolves, and joined Mumpo.

'Come on, Mumpo.'

The wolves stood still, in a guardian line, watching her go.

Goodbye, my friends.

Seek shelter, little one, came the reply. *The storm is coming.*

Pinto took Mumpo's hand, and they set off after the others, Mumpo no longer sure if he was supporting Pinto or she was supporting him.

'I didn't know,' he said.

'Nor did I. Not until now.'

'What does it mean?'

'I'm growing up,' she said. 'Do you mind?'

'No. Of course not.'

They walked fast over the lake, both for different

reasons unafraid of the bouncing ice. Pinto was filled with the sensation she had had before when the passion fly had made her drunk: she felt she could do anything, that nothing could withstand her will. Let the ice crack! What did she care? She would command the ice to carry her, and it would obey. Only this time she was not drunk, her mind was sharp and clear, she understood many things. She saw her father ahead, pulling the litter that carried her mother, and she felt how much they needed her, and how strong she would now be for them.

I'll look after you, she called to them without sound. *I'll look after you all.*

She wasn't drunk, but the sensation was intoxicating. She saw her people reach the far shore, she saw them gather on the lakeside, dark figures in the growing darkness, she saw the horses and the cows stumble up onto the frozen ground, and it felt to her as if it was she, Pinto, almost the youngest of them all, who had delivered them safely to the other side.

I can do anything!

Mumpo held her eager hand in his and followed the others, his mind full of wonder at the change in her. Mumpo's nature was such that he only ever thought of one thing at a time, and thinking of Pinto left him no room to be afraid of the groans and shudders of the ice. How had she changed? She looked the same. Why then did he feel a new timidity in her presence, a sensation of unworthiness? He clasped her hand more tightly, not thinking what he was doing, and then felt ashamed, and let it go.

'It's alright, Mumpo,' she said. 'I won't leave you.'

He blushed in the dusk, glad she couldn't see.

'I'm the one who's meant to look after you.'

'We'll look after each other.'

They reached the lake shore. Hanno Hath gave his daughter one keen look, then he turned to the mountain peaks ahead.

'We'll make a fire here for tonight. The way ahead's too steep to climb by moonlight.'

Ira Hath reached up her hand and Pinto took it and clasped it tight. Her mother said nothing aloud, but Pinto felt her meaning clearly.

It's not fair, her mother was telling her. *It's too soon.*

'How old were you when it happened, ma?'

'Me?' Her mother smiled on her, and whispered soft words. 'I can't remember a time when I didn't know it. Before I could talk, or walk. I just lay in my crib, knowing.'

Pinto laughed.

'So you see. It's about time I knew, too.'

15

Bowman flies

Mist the cat lay on the deck of the barge, concealed beneath a fold of canvas, listening to the voices rising from the cabin below. In the normal run of things, Mist paid little attention to human voices. Chatter chatter chatter: so much talk, so little sense. Long ago the cat had concluded that men and women talked to ease some pressing internal need, like letting air out of an over-inflated balloon. The words themselves were of little consequence. These voices, however, were different. The loud one, the contemptuous booming voice, impressed Mist as being full of wisdom; though it would be fair to say that in the cat's world-weary eyes any strong expression of contempt sounded wise. The other voice was Bowman's. He said little, and in low tones which were sometimes hard to hear, but Mist liked the boy. He was soft, and he'd turned out to be a disappointment in many ways; but still he liked him.

'Great stars!' shouted the big voice from the cabin. 'Don't you know how to listen? Is the boy deaf as well as stupid?'

'What am I to hear?'

'Hear? Did I say hear? Did anyone say hear? You're not to hear, you're to listen! You know what that means? It means you don't know what sound is out there. It means you're waiting for the sound to come to you. Did you *hear* that? Yes? Nod your head if you understand a single word I'm saying. Good. Maybe we're getting somewhere at last.'

Mist crept forward to peep through the cabin window, curious to know what the boy was being commanded to listen to. There, gathered round the cabin table, were Albard and Bowman, Jumper and Kestrel; and in the middle of the table, the object of all their attention, making no sound that the cat could discern, was a spoon.

'The spoon has its own song,' said Albard, not so angrily now, seeing the attentive expression on Bowman's face. 'Listen to its song.'

Bowman nodded, his eyes on the spoon.

'Now tune your song to the spoon's song.'

Bowman nodded again. Kestrel, in direct contact with her brother's mind, felt a series of soft vibrations run through him.

'Now lift the spoon.'

Bowman eased the spoon off the table, using only the grip of his mind. He had done this sort of thing before. This was nothing new.

The spoon hovered in the air.

'Now,' said Albard, 'scoop a hole in the table with the spoon.'

Bowman wrinkled his brow in perplexity. The spoon dropped to the table with a clatter.

'You have a problem with that?'

'The spoon's too blunt to cut into the table.'

'But not too blunt to cut into custard?'

'Not too blunt to cut into custard. Too blunt to cut into wood?'

'Then don't cut into wood. Cut into custard.'

Bowman thought about this in silence for a long moment. Then without asking further questions, he turned his attention from the spoon to the table. Albard saw this, and met Jumper's eyes. Bowman began to listen to the table as he had listened to the spoon. It sounded deeper, duller; more – wooden.

Kestrel, watching, followed her brother's every thought. She felt the intensity of his attention to that simple timber surface. She heard the low thudding sound that it made in his mind, and probed it curiously along with him. She felt too the undercurrent of frustration in him, that he was asked to do something he didn't yet understand. Kestrel herself felt no such frustration: she was no more than an onlooker. Perhaps for this reason it was she, not Bowman, who all at once found herself tumbling, as into a woodland pool, into the ripple-grained surface of the table.

It was the oddest feeling. One moment she was looking at the table, the next moment it was all around her, and fluid, and warm. It even had its own distinctive smell, of resin and damp cloth. She knew at once that she could form this substance into any shape she wanted, she could puddle it like clay or pour it like water. The table, while still standing before her, had opened itself up to her and allowed her to find the true matter out of which it was made, matter that was only provisionally assembled in the form of a table.

Why, she thought to herself, it could just as easily be custard.

She looked up, eyes bright and laughing, and her gaze fell on an old calendar pinned to the cabin wall. With a soft hissing sound, the out-of-date numbers began to uncurl and form into wiggly lines on the faded paper. Then with a little *pop!* they burst into sparkly dust, and shivered into the air, leaving the paper blank on the wall.

Kestrel blinked, to force her eyes back into focus. But her eyes were seeing clearly: more clearly, more penetratingly than ever in her life. For now the cabin wall was disintegrating. With a curious gurgling sound that surely the others could hear, though they showed no sign, the planks were turning spongy, and separating into clumps of what looked like moss, and dropping down in floppy heaps onto the floor. Only, the floor wasn't there. Beneath her feet was water: water that gleamed and rippled, and yet was firm underfoot, and entirely translucent, for looking down, looking through the vanished bottom of the barge into the shining river below, she saw the sky – or at least, bright space – and then she realised this wasn't water at all below her, it was air – and not even air, but light –

Dizzy, frightened, she looked up, and the cabin, her brother, Albard, Jumper, all were gone. She was alone in a world of light. She held out her hand before her, and saw – nothing. She looked down at her own body and saw – nothing. She too had gone. There was only this infinity of humming light – and herself, knowing it.

So I can't be gone. I must still be here.

But where?

Everywhere, came the answer. *I'm everywhere. I've joined everything.*

With that, she stopped being afraid, and at once she was filled with joy. She understood it now. Somehow she had slipped between the walls that hold things apart from each other to enter that place where they all join up. She remembered the winter dawn, when she had stood in the dazzling light of the sun streaming through the trees and had said to herself, *Why should it ever end?* Here, now, lost in a greater light, she knew there was no end, no boundaries, no this and that, no then and now. All existence had melted, including the thing she had once known as her own body –

And my mind? My self? Is that melted away?

That was scary. She shied away from the thought, and with a lurch, found she was back in the cabin, and there was Bowman wrinkling his brow, trying to turn the table into custard.

It's easy, Bo. Like this.

She let him into her mind. He felt the light-heartedness in her, and relaxed his fierce attention. She looked with him, her eyes guiding his, at the surface of the table, and she caught its song, her ears guiding his, and spoke to him in their mind, telling him what to do.

It's hard because it's shivering so fast. Slow it down, and it'll go softer.

After she'd said this she wondered how she knew it. It was something to do with the way everything had disappeared, and yet had still been there. In that brief moment, she was sure things had moved slowly, had hardly moved at all.

Bowman tried to do as she said. He felt the shivering of the table quite clearly, but he didn't see how he could slow it down. It struck him as he listened to it that its sound was quite different to his own sound, which was sweeter and softer. Perhaps if he were to surround the table sound with his own sound, that would slow it down. So he focused his attention on the weave of sound that Albard had taught him to know as his own song, and started to fold it like a blanket around the table. Then he thought of custard.

Albard saw and approved. He had not detected Kestrel's silent intervention. He saw only that the boy, unguided, was taking control of the solid matter before him and making it serve his will.

For a few moments, nothing happened. Bowman felt foolish, staring at a table and thinking of custard. But then he felt Kestrel give him a nudge, and he tipped over, and with a quick gulp of his mind the table's buzz was overcome, was swallowed, by his own vibrations. The table was still there before him. But all its essential qualities were now inside him, and under his control.

Custard. He thought smooth. He thought creamy. A spoon could dip into that without any difficulty.

He raised the spoon, still using only his mind, and scooped up a brimming spoonful of table. It came up like custard. The surface of the table flowed back to smooth out the scoop, just as a thick creamy custard would, but what he had now in the spoon was table: that is, it was wood.

'Good boy!' bellowed Albard. 'Now he's getting it!'

The spoon dropped to the table. The piece of wood

rolled out, and lay there rocking back and forth on its curved underside.

'You see that, blob?' said Albard. 'This boy of mine is going to be alright.'

Bowman gazed at the fragment of wood. He felt a surge of power swell up within him. He turned his attention onto the spoon, and thought: water. The spoon dissolved into a silver puddle.

'Who's a clever boy?' crooned Albard. 'Who's not a cloth-eared cretin after all? Oh, blob! If I was younger, and there was any room to move in this floating coffin, I'd dance a jig!'

Jumper looked at Bowman and smiled. Then his eyes turned quietly to Kestrel, and became thoughtful.

'Great stars!' shouted Albard. 'Storm down below!'

He pounded up onto deck, and there he stood, legs planted wide apart, and urinated violently over the side into the river.

'Aah!' he cried as his bladder emptied. 'Storm passing. Fair winds. Clear skies.'

The others followed him up onto deck. The barge was running on the fast-flowing currents, some ten yards from the bank.

'You, blob! Make yourself useful! Tie us to the riverbank.'

Jumper obediently picked up one end of the mooring rope and stepped over the side of the barge, and onto the riverbank. He did this with so obliging a manner that only Mist, watching from his hiding place, noticed that he walked over the water itself.

'So, boy!' boomed Albard. 'Time you learned to fly!'

Mist heard this with a surge of excitement. Now at last his long-cherished dream would come true. Ever since he had seen the hermit Dogface, his former companion, fly down from his tree, he had dreamed of being a flying cat. Since then he had learned to fly short distances, given a good run up before take off. But real flying, he knew, required no run up. Dogface hadn't run anywhere, ever. He had just floated into the air.

Jumper drew the barge to the riverbank and moored it to a tree. An inch or so of snow covered the ground, and lay on the branches of the tall pine trees that grew almost to the river's side. The spot chosen by Jumper for mooring the barge was evidently a well-used river crossing point, for here the encroaching forest stood back a little way, forming a semi-circular glade; and on the further side of the glade, a cart-track wound away southwards through the trees.

Albard heaved his great body off the barge, and stamped about over the snow investigating the open space. Bowman and Kestrel followed. Mist remained in hiding on the barge. The cat had no reason to hide, other than a general liking for secrecy; and here, surely, secrets were about to be revealed. Mist valued information more highly when he supposed he was not meant to be learning it.

Albard discovered that the clearing was man-made, and that here and there the woodsmen who had felled the trees had left stumps standing in the snowy ground. He fixed upon one such stump, that stood some two feet high, and had been sawn clean across, like a stool.

'Stand on this, boy.'

Bowman stepped up onto the tree stump and stood there.

'You want me to fly from here?' he asked.

'Fly? How can you fly? Have you got wings?'

'But I thought you said –'

'No wings, can't fly. Not hard to grasp.'

'No.'

'Right, then. No more talk of flying. All I want you to do is take one step off the stump towards me. One step, no more. Got that?'

'Yes.'

'Off you go.'

Bowman took one step off the stump, and landed on the snowy ground.

'No, no, no!' bellowed Albard. 'Did I say fall off? No, I did not! I said take one step!'

'How am I to stop myself falling?'

'The same way you stop yourself from sitting down. You choose not to. You fall because you expect to fall. Now get back on that stump, take one step, and wait there.'

'How?'

'How? HOW?' Albard went red and stamped his feet. 'NEVER ASK HOW! How doesn't matter! How doesn't exist! How is for fools and slaves! How makes everything small! You're greater than how, you don't care how, if you will it, the how must follow! You're to be a master! A master knows nothing of how!'

After this sudden tirade, a silence fell over the snowy glade. Albard shook himself, and stared crossly at Jumper, who was looking at him with a smile.

'Well? What's so funny?'

'Nothing,' said Jumper. 'You're right, of course.'

'No, he's not,' said Kestrel. 'He's talking nonsense. It has nothing to do with masters and slaves.'

Albard stared at her in angry surprise.

'Who are you?' he demanded, as if he had never seen her before. 'Who cares what you think?'

'My brother does. So does he.' A nod at Jumper.

'No they don't. Go away. Obliterate yourself.'

'I will not.'

'Burn the brat!'

'You can't burn anyone any more.'

'I can break your scraggy little neck.'

He made a move as if to take hold of her. She showed no fear.

'Go on, then.'

'I warn you –'

Kestrel took hold of his out-reached hand and bent it back with ease. He was very weak.

'Ow! That hurts!'

Tears of pain and humiliation sprang into his eyes.

'She hurt me! It's not fair!' he cried. 'This is all your fault!' He glowered through his tears at Jumper. 'Why didn't you leave me to die?'

'Your time will come,' said Jumper gently. 'But first you must pass on your skills to the boy. Make him strong in your place.'

'Yes,' said Albard, cheering up, 'yes, he's young, he can be strong for me.' He turned to Bowman. 'When I've made you strong, you'll crush this worm-child for me, won't you? Out of respect for your teacher.'

'She's my sister,' said Bowman.

'Is she?' Albard seemed surprised. 'Ah, well. Be a good

boy, attend to what I tell you, and you'll rule the world. Then I shall go in peace.'

'I don't want to rule the world. I just want to be a Singer.'

'Hey ho. Things come as they will. I wanted to play the violin to applauding crowds, but here I am, all skin and bone, with barely strength left to draw breath. Sun and moon! I made such music once! But you took my fiddle from me, boy – no, not you, what did you know? Sirene took it from me. Sirene never forgets, and never forgives.'

He dabbed at his eyes, took a deep breath, and returned to the task in hand.

'Back on the stump. Take one step. Choose not to fall.'

Bowman got back on the tree stump.

'No doubts. No uncertainty. No *how*. The ground has power to draw you down, but you have power too. Use it.'

Bowman stepped off the stump. Then he fell. But for a fraction of a second, before he fell, he caught the sensation of what it would be like not to fall. He understood his mistake. He had supposed effort was needed not to fall. He had been straining invisible muscles. But no effort was required. He needed stillness. It was more like finding the point of perfect balance when standing on one leg. Until you find it, you wobble and wave your arms, but once you have it, perfect stillness keeps you in place.

He returned to the stump.

'Don't say anything. Let me try again.'

He stepped onto air – and stood there.

Hubba hubba Bowman!

He grinned to hear Kestrel's silent cheer, and dropped to the ground.

Albard looked at him suspiciously.

'Could you have stayed there?'

'I think so.'

There came a splash from the river. Mist had tried to float off the boat, in imitation of Bowman, with less success. He crawled soaking onto the river bank.

'Mist! Where have you come from?'

'It doesn't work,' said Mist bitterly, shivering his coat.

'Shoo! Filthy animal!' said Albard. 'Go away!'

'Let him alone,' said Bowman. 'He's a friend.' And to Mist, silently, he said, 'Don't rush at it. You have to take it gently.'

In demonstration, not knowing at all how he was doing it, he let his arms rise from his sides, and he floated slowly up into the air.

Albard eyed him critically.

'What have you got your arms out for?'

'I'm not sure. It feels right.'

'It's pretend wings, isn't it? Forget wings. You're not a bird.'

Bowman let his arms fall.

'How do you do it, boy?' cried Mist, whimpering with longing.

'I don't know. I just do it.'

Jumper understood the cat's desire. He reached out and touched Mist with the fringes of his mind. Mist started, and the hair went up on his back. Then he softened again, as he felt an unfamiliar lightness flow through him. He turned to see where it was coming from. Jumper was watching him, smiling. He looked to Mist for all the world like a comfortable purring mother cat.

Jumper nodded encouragingly. Mist stretched his long lithe body, and sprang.

'Wheee! Here I come!'

The cat bounded up into the air, turning slowly over and over as he went. Bowman, still hovering, rose higher still, and in doing so, collided with a snow-laden branch, knocking the snow off to shower down on the cat below.

'Yeow! Don't do that!'

Mist wriggled in mid-air, to shed the snow that had fallen on him. Goaded by the cold snow, he made another mid-air bound that took him past Bowman and over his head, to land lightly on a higher branch. His weight shook snow onto Bowman below.

'See how you like it, boy!'

He sprang away, moving from branch to branch, and Bowman gave chase, both forgetting that they were leaping from nothing to nothing, and landing with ease on the tips of branches that would barely sustain the weight of a bird. Albard and Jumper and Kestrel watched from the ground, all smiling the same smile, as boy and cat danced through the high branches, and the snow fell in cascading clouds between the trees.

When Bowman floated at last to the ground, pink-faced and glowing and proud, Albard strode up to him and wrapped him in his broad embrace.

'Wonderful boy! You remind me of my first time!'

He kissed him on the cheeks and on the brow, then he stood back from him and said,

'Did you hear it?'

Bowman knew Albard meant the sound within himself.

'Yes. I heard it.'

'Can you sing it?'

Bowman tried to imitate the sound with his voice. What came out was a humming burbling sound.

'Get it right.'

He made his mouth refine the song, until he was as close as he could make it to the sound he heard within himself.

'Don't try too hard. Let the song sing itself through you. Like the old wind singers.'

Like the old wind singers? He remembered the wind singer of Aramanth well. The high creaking structure of wooden struts and metal pipes had possessed no mind of its own. The wind drove it round, and made its way down its pipes, and used it for its song. Could he be as empty, as mindless, as a wind singer?

He tried again. This time he opened his mouth and let the song pass out of him of its own accord. He knew at once that it was exact: the song he sung was the song he had heard. He felt his body rise in the air.

'Yes!' cried Albard, smacking his sagging belly, well pleased. 'Learn the song. Use it at will.'

Let me hear it, Bo.

Bowman gladly opened his mind to Kestrel. He felt her enter and reach for the new sensation in him, and find the power that Albard called a song. He sensed her learning it, and taking it into herself. It was what he wished. His mind and all its power belonged to her, as hers belonged to him.

'Boy!' said Mist. 'Let's fly again!'

Mist curved up into the air, this time ostentatiously in control, arching his back and stretching as he flew, and showing his claws. Bowman followed, bounding up into the air with long strides of his legs, as if he was climbing an invisible giant's staircase. And after a moment's hesitation, Kestrel, watching them, smiling with pleasure, rose gently upwards to join them.

Kess! You can fly too!

Bowman danced through the air towards her, and took her hand. Hand in hand they floated up above the tree tops.

'Shall we go higher?'

'Higher, yes! And higher!'

Up they went into the clear winter sky, higher and higher, holding hands, until they became frightened that there was no end to their ascent. They could, it seemed, go on for ever. So they paddled to a stop, as if their limbs controlled their movements, though they knew very well it was their minds that chose to fly or not to fly. And there, treading air, up where thin clouds were passing, they looked over the forest and the land beyond.

For many miles the land was white. Snow lay on the trees of the forest, and on the rolling ground beyond. The cracks in the land showed as shadowed slits. Beyond, where the hills rose again, they could see clusters of houses, and here and there, bright flickers of flame.

As they became accustomed to being so very high and seeing so very far they began to pick out more of these points of flame. Why so many fires out of doors? Were these the camp fires of wandering people, driven from their homes by the troubled times? But as they learned to look better, they realised the fires, though small to them, were far bigger than those built for boiling kettles. These were great fires, these were whole houses burning, these were villages. All over the immense white landscape, homes were burning.

What's happening, Kess? Who's doing this?

It's the time of cruelty, Kestrel answered, knowing this was no answer.

A gust of wind carried towards them the distant smell of wood smoke, tinged with charred meat. It could be the smells of cooking, or it could be something far more grisly.

In silent consent, the twins floated back down to the snow-covered ground.

'Everything's burning,' said Bowman. 'It's as if the world has been set on fire.'

'That's what happens,' said Albard with some bitterness. 'Take away mastery, and you get chaos. I warned them. But they don't care. They just watch.'

'Our time will come,' said Jumper.

'Our time, our time. And meanwhile what? Suffering and ugliness.'

Jumper replied only, 'We should be on our way.'

They returned to the barge, this time joined by the cat as an acknowledged member of their group. Mist had half a mind to go flying after birds, but he felt tired and decided to rest first. Bowman too felt tired, heavy tired, as if he had been doing hard labour. So he and the cat curled up on the cabin bench and went to sleep.

Jumper cast off the mooring rope and remained on deck, sitting like a small fat gnome astraddle the prow, with his legs dangling down on either side. Here Kestrel found him.

'Who are you?' she said.

'Who would you like me to be?'

'I need someone to explain things to me.'

'Then I'm the explainer.'

He looked at her with a friendly smile. As he looked, his appearance altered. Nothing physical changed, but he seemed to her to grow older. He was turning into a grandfather. As she watched the transformation, she realised that she must be doing it herself. She wanted a wise old grandfather, and he was obliging her.

'What do Singer people do?'

'They live in the stillness and know the flame.'

'Please don't talk like a book. Tell me what they actually do, and why.'

'But you know that, my child. You've felt it.'

'When have I felt it?'

He smiled back at her with his owlish eyes, but said no more.

'Do you mean earlier, in the cabin?'

He inclined his head.

'When I felt I wasn't there any more?'

Again he inclined his head.

'But that was like dying.'

'Like dying, but not dying.'

'Yes.' She puzzled over her memory of that brief extraordinary moment, when the cabin had turned into bright nothingness. 'Is that what Singer people do?'

'They do many things. But that's what they're for.'

'For dying?'

'If that's what you want to call it.'

'In the wind on fire.'

'You see,' he said. 'You do know.'

'But I don't know what it is, or why.'

'Don't you?'

She said nothing. His tone of voice rather than his words told her to ask no more questions. She looked at him steadily. He was such a funny little creature, so round-bellied and short-legged, so ridiculous and yet so powerful. He started to hum quietly to himself. She found herself studying his hair, which was, like all of him, of an indeterminate colour, and wispy. It was lifting up off his mottled scalp and rippling in the river breeze, catching the light and giving off silvery glints. You would almost have thought that his hair was glowing, the way the surrounding air shimmered as he hummed. Now that she looked further, she realised that it was glowing: and more, his skin was glowing, and his coat, and his hands. All over him there was forming a layer of bright trembling air.

Kestrel stared at Jumper. He had gone very still. His humming continued, but very low. His eyes were open, and directed towards her, but she knew he didn't see her. This sheath of light that now surrounded him was familiar to her, but she couldn't recall from where. Then, looking up above his head, she saw how the bright air rose in a tall plume, through which the trees on the riverbank beyond were distorted, and seemed to wave and dance.

Of course, she thought. It's heat rising. It's like the heat that surrounds a candle flame.

Jumper was generating heat. She put out the palm of her hand and felt it clearly. He himself was not burning, there was no flame at the centre of the cowl of heated air, and yet she understood that this plump and homely body was its source. In some strange way, Jumper was aflame.

Little by little the heat died down, and the disturbance in the air was calmed. Jumper awoke, if he had ever been asleep. He smiled at her once more. He had stopped his humming.

'What would have happened if you'd gone on longer?'

'I would not have returned.'

'And that's what Singer people do, at the end?'

He inclined his head.

'It's the only thing we do. Everything else can be done in one way or another by others. Only Singers know the flame.'

'Only Singers choose to go so far and not return.'

His grandfatherly gaze showed her respect.

'If you know that, you know everything.'

'And after the wind on fire? What then?'

'The time of kindness.'

'No, I mean for the Singers.'

'Ah, child. That I don't know. That no one knows. We make that journey without maps.'

Kestrel looked out at the rushing river, and let her thoughts run with its currents. The river was wider now, and fuller, as ever more mountain streams came rushing to join it on its race to the sea. The barge moved swiftly past tree-clad banks, following the turns of the river as if commanded by an expert pilot, though there was no one at the wheel.

'When you came for my brother,' she asked after a while, 'did you know I would come too?'

'What a one you are for knowledge!' Jumper answered.

'No, I didn't know. I know very little. I have no plan.' He waved one plump hand at the river. 'It's like this river. Do I know where there are rocky shallows, or dangerous cross currents? No, I know nothing. But I stay alert, and when I meet danger, I do what I must. So when you joined us, I thought to myself, I must stay alert, and see what comes my way.'

Kestrel asked no more.

In a little while she heard people moving about in the cabin, and the hatch slid open, and Bowman came out. He stepped carefully over the sloping roof of the hold to join Kestrel and Jumper on the prow.

'Albard says we're nearly at the river's mouth.'

Jumper nodded. 'Not long now.' He looked up at the clouds massing above. 'Snow on its way.'

He had hardly spoken the words when the first flurry of snowflakes began to fall. Within moments the snow was falling steadily, powdering their heads and shoulders.

'We'd better go below,' said Kestrel.

'Stay a moment longer,' said Jumper.

Albard joined them on deck, stamping far too hard on the roof boards, cursing the snow.

'Damn winter!' he complained. 'Damn cold! Damn everything!'

'Look,' said Jumper.

The riverbanks were widening on either side, and there ahead, in a churning ridge of white foam, the fast-flowing river water crashed into the sea. The sight of so much open horizon came as a shock after the long day bound in on all sides by winter forest. The falling snow blurred the line between grey sky and grey sea, surrounding the barge with a boundless featureless immensity. Even the coast on either side lay veiled and insubstantial in the falling snow.

The barge rode on, out into the open sea. As it crossed the bar it lurched violently, forcing its human cargo to cling to the hatch-handles and straps. Once past the confluence of the waters the rocking settled down again, to a new motion, a long regular swell.

'You see that dirty smudge ahead?' said Albard, pointing with one finger. 'North-west of us, on the horizon?'

Bowman and Kestrel looked through the curtain of snow in the direction he was pointing, and just made out a low shape that was a deeper grey than the clouds above.

'That's Sirene,' said Albard. 'Damn fool place, full of damn fool people.'

Kestrel looked at Jumper and found that he too was gazing towards the island. He looked young again.

Bowman stared and stared.

'Sirene,' he murmured. 'At last.'

16

Ira sees the future

The snow fell on the column of the Manth people as they toiled up the mountainside. The track that they followed was narrow, and climbed steeply. Beneath its coating of snow the sparse earth had been scraped from the stones by the hooves of goats, and the beat of their passing had formed the ground into narrow steps, all of different sizes. It was hard going, treading up this irregular stairway, between the snow-laden trees.

As the mountainside became steeper still, the travellers faced a second hazard. Rollo Shim brushed a loose stone with his limping foot, and sent a shower of debris tumbling down on those below. One larger stone, gathering speed as it tumbled, triggered a small avalanche, a rush of snow that was heavy enough to knock Fin Marish over and send her rolling back down the track. Miller Marish and Lolo Mimilith clambered down to her aid; and the entire party was forced to wait while they carried the child back up.

Rollo Shim cursed his wounded leg, but he was glad of the enforced rest. The climb was hard: most of all for the horses, who hauled Ira Hath on one litter and Mrs Chirish on the other. They felt their way with nervous hoof-fall, plodding on up the track, their sweating coats melting the snow as it settled on them. The cows too were a matter for concern. They followed the column willingly enough, but time and again came to an exhausted standstill, their breath steaming through the falling snow. At such times Creoth waited with them, calling ahead to Hanno,

'Pause a while!'

After a few moments the cows would shiver their hides and set off again, knowing this was no place to stop. Creoth would cry out,

'On our way!'

The whole column, grateful for the rest, would set off once more up the stony staircase of the mountainside.

Hanno walked beside his wife as she was jolted along in her litter. They had covered her up with blankets against the snow, so that nothing of her could be seen except, beneath a projecting peak of cloth, her familiar eyes. Now as he watched her he saw that most of the time her eyes were closed. Whenever they stopped to rest he would kneel down so that his face was close by hers, and they would speak, but her voice was weak. He never asked her how she was feeling, it only annoyed her. He told her what was happening, and how far they were from the mountain's ridge.

'Will we reach the top before dark?' she asked.

'Perhaps,' he said. Then, 'I don't think so.'

'Not this evening, then,' she murmured. 'Tomorrow evening.'

He knew that she was thinking of the sunset, and the red sky she had seen in her dream.

'Most likely tomorrow evening,' he said.

'Help Pinto,' she told him. 'The child needs you.'

Hanno knew at once that she was right. In his anxiety over the climb, and Fin Marish's fall, and the waning day, and his wife's all too visible decline, he had forgotten about Pinto. She had struggled on with the rest, quiet and uncomplaining: too quiet, in fact. It struck Hanno now that she had barely spoken a word since they had left the frozen lake.

When the column resumed the wearying climb, he left Ira's side and tramped up the track to find Pinto. For several minutes he climbed the mountain by her side without speaking, letting her adjust to his nearness. This was one of Hanno's habits. He believed it was always a mistake to open a conversation cold; more than a mistake, a kind of assault. It took time, he felt, for two people to organise their feelings about each other, to bring them up out of store, before it was appropriate to speak the first words.

The falling snow matched his mood. A constant motion between him and his daughter, but not a distraction, it soothed them both. In a little while, he felt her turning towards him. He felt her fear and her uncertainty. He said nothing. He let her feel his love and his patience. He listened.

So it was Pinto who spoke first; and they were already in mid-conversation.

'Why us?' she asked.

'You,' said Hanno. 'Not me.'

'Do you mind?'

'No. I'm proud.'

Hanno knew well that the gifts and burdens of the prophet came through his wife's kin. He had married into the line of Ira Manth. He had no gifts himself.

'Why are some people different?' asked Pinto.

'How are you different, my darling?'

'I can do things.'

'Then I expect you're different so that you will do those things.'

'Do you think so?'

'Does it make you feel afraid?'

'Yes. I'm afraid of – of being the one who does things.'

'You don't need to be afraid. In a way, it isn't you that will do the things you'll do.'

At this point in their climb the track was running close to a mountain stream, a narrow fast-moving thread of icy water that raced down the mountainside over a shiny stream bed. Here and there the ground dropped away beneath the stream, and the water hurled itself out in a miniature waterfall, to land seething in a pool below, before tumbling on its way. Hanno Hath pointed out one such jet of sparkling water, as he tried to explain to his younger daughter how her new-found powers were hers and not hers at the same time.

'You see how the water makes a curve in the air? That arch of shining water – you see it?'

'Yes, pa.'

'You're like that waterfall. All the power, everything that makes it leap out from the stream bed and hover in mid-air like that, it all comes from the water flowing down the mountain. The water in the waterfall is changing all the time. But the waterfall stays the same. Do you see?'

'Yes, pa.'

'So you don't have to be afraid, my darling. The power doesn't come from you, or belong to you. It flows through you, and makes you the shape you are.'

She listened gravely as his soft words came to her through the falling snow, and young as she was, she understood.

'Is it like that for Bo and Kess?'

'I believe so, yes.'

'And ma?'

'Yes.'

'So we don't really do anything at all. We get done to.'

'No, darling. You can do many things. You can refuse the power you feel in you now. You can take it for yourself. You can fight it. You can throw it away. But whatever you choose to do, know that the power doesn't begin with you, or end with you.'

'I don't want to do any of those things you said. I want – I want – to make things right.'

'Then so you shall.'

'Is it so easy?'

'Not easy. Not easy at all. Think how much is wanting to make things wrong. All the fear in the world, and the violence that comes from the fear, and the hatred that comes from the violence, and the loneliness that comes from the hatred. All the unhappiness, all the cruelty, it gathers like clouds in the air, and grows dark and cold and heavy, and falls like grey snow in thick layers over the land. Then the world is all muffled and numb, and no one can hear each other or feel each other. Think how sad and lonely that must be.'

'Yes,' said Pinto, feeling it just as her father described it. 'Yes.'

They tramped on without speaking for a while. Then Pinto said,

'You know so much, pa. I think you must have the power too.'

'No, my darling. I have no powers at all. I can't prophesy, like Ira. I can't read thoughts, like Kestrel, or strike with my mind, like Bowman. I can't talk with wolves. All I can do is listen, and learn. Read, and learn. Think over what I've heard and read, and learn.'

'That's how you know so much. We don't know the things you know. Not even ma.'

'I wish knowing was enough,' said Hanno, sighing. 'I'm not even sure how useful it is. It's how I am. I like to try to puzzle things out. But all my knowledge can't help me, now that –'

He fell silent.

'Now that Bo and Kess are gone. Now that ma is dying.'

'You have changed,' he said quietly.

'We all know. We just don't talk about it.'

Hanno turned and looked back down the track, through the veil of falling snow to the horse pulling his wife on her litter.

'I don't know what I shall do without her,' he said. He spoke simply, without self-pity, and Pinto knew he was telling her a plain truth. He couldn't imagine a future without his wife. Then he added,

'But of course, when it happens, I'll find out.'

* * *

The light in the sky was dimmed by the heavy clouds, and by the falling snow, and it was not easy to tell how long they had been climbing, except by the aching in their legs. But in time it became clear that night was falling. The snow, which hadn't ceased all day, now came down more heavily than ever. With visibility shrinking by the minute, and no means of knowing how close they were to the top, the Manth marchers decided they must make camp for the night.

The first plan was to shelter under a row of pines that grew beside the track. But Creoth, leading his cows deeper into the trees in search of forage, found a better resting place.

'Hanno!' he called. 'Come and see!'

It was a single, huge old oak, an evergreen oak, its rust-brown leaves still clinging to its branches. The snow had formed a dense canopy over the upper branches, but beneath, where they reached out from the massive trunk, there lay a high-vaulted dry-floored shelter, as big as a house.

Here the Manth people gathered, grateful to be out of the falling snow, with their cows and their horses. They stamped their feet and shook the snow off their coats and hats, and propped up the two litters by the great tree trunk. They unbundled their firewood and lit a fire in the most sheltered spot, while the young men scraped up the snow outside to form a wall round their house, to shut out the night wind. As the fire caught, and the yellow flames sent dancing flickers of light up to the ribbed branches that formed the ceiling, the darkness fell all round, and suddenly it was night. The heat of the fire warmed them, as they gathered round, and the food they had brought with them filled them and gave them strength. Within a surprisingly short time the chilled and weary marchers were feeling cheerful and full of hope. The rising heat of the fire melted the snow in the branches above, so that it dripped hissing onto the burning faggots, and threatened to douse the whole fire; so Miko Mimilith fashioned a canopy out of sticks and cloth, well soaked in snow. This canopy, erected high over the fire, caught the drips from above, but also sent the rising smoke of the fire swirling down to sting their eyes. To counter this, they made a second contraption, a frame of tied sticks over which they stretched a length of cloth, which could be flapped slowly back and forth, to send the smoke away to the far side of the under-tree hall.

In these ways and others, the Manth people turned their natural shelter into a comfortable home for the night. More than comfortable: it was beautiful. The firelight on the snow walls and on the tracery of the branches arching above made their house seem somehow ancestral, as if they had built it long ago, and had lived in it for generations. Beyond the heaped-up snow, beyond the living roof beams, there was nothing. All life was here, in this red and golden light. Firelight makes faces beautiful. The travellers looked at each other in wonder that they had come so far, and were still together. As for tomorrow –

'Will it be tomorrow? Are we almost there? Will we see the homeland tomorrow?'

Only Ira Hath knew. Hanno had made her comfortable,

and she had eaten a little bread, and was sitting bundled in blankets smiling at them all.

'Maybe tomorrow,' she replied. 'Not long now.'

Hanno was happy to see her smiling, and to hear her voice. It was firmer and clearer than it had been all day.

'You're feeling better?'

'Yes. I have some strength now. I must use it.'

'No, no. Save your strength. We haven't got there yet.'

'Ah, Hannoka.' She gave him a reproachful smile. 'You know my strength is given me for getting there.'

Hanno frowned and looked down.

'What is it you want to do?'

'I must do what it's given me to do. I must prophesy.'

'No.'

Every time I touch the future I grow weaker. My gift is my disease. I shall die of prophecy.

The words of the prophet Ira Manth sounded in Hanno Hath's ears every day now, as he watched his wife become thinner and quieter.

'No,' he said again.

'Yes,' she said. 'Before it's too late.'

So Hanno bowed his head and accepted that it must be.

'I shall listen.'

'And the others. All of them.'

Hanno gathered the others round, twenty-seven of them, now that Bowman and Kestrel were gone. With Ira and himself, they made twenty-nine. Jet Marish, the youngest of them all, only six years old, was asleep in her father's arms. Seldom Erth, the oldest, had his eyes closed, but was not asleep. They were all there to hear Ira Hath prophesy. Even the cows and the horses, drawn by curiosity, loomed out of the shadows and stood watching behind the circle of people.

For a few moments, Ira Hath was silent. The only sounds were the crackle of the fire, and the pat-pat-pat of melting snow dripping on the canopy.

'I think we will see the homeland tomorrow,' she said at last, 'I think as the sun sets tomorrow, we will look down on the homeland at last. I feel its warmth on my face, stronger than the heat of the fire.'

The people listening all smiled and nodded at each other as they heard her. The end of the journey at last.

'Now that we're so close,' said Ira, 'I find that I can see a little further. If you would like, I could tell each of you the little that I see.'

Their eyes opened wide.

'You mean,' said Branco Such, 'a personal prophecy? For each of us?'

'Yes,' said Ira. 'If you would like that.'

Branco Such wasn't at all sure he would like it. He still felt troubled over the part he had played in dividing their group, in Canobius's valley. It seemed to him that his decision had been right, given what he had known at the time, and yet it had turned out to be wrong.

Ira Hath understood the source of his nervousness.

'I think,' she said gently, 'that you and your wife will do very well in the homeland. You will establish a shop.'

'A shop?'

Branco Such was extremely surprised. He turned to look at his wife.

'You don't want to have a shop, do you?'

Gale Such looked guilty.

'Well,' she said, 'I have sometimes thought how neighbourly it would be to have a little shop, just a very little shop, where people might call by and pick up a little of this and that, and pass the time of day.'

She blushed as she spoke. Branco had been a magistrate in the old days, and she knew he would think shopkeeping beneath him.

'You astonish me! A shop! Whatever next?'

But he did not reject the idea out of hand. Gale Such looked gratefully at Ira Hath. She had not dared suggest it herself.

Little Scooch heard the exchange with excitement.

'And me!' he cried. 'I'll have a shop too!'

'Of course. You will have the bakery. You and Lunki.'

Now it was Scooch's turn to blush. Lunki was at the back, sitting beside Sisi, and her face was deep in the shadows; but Sisi heard her utter a little gasp.

The others were too excited at the prospect of hearing their own futures to linger over Scooch and Lunki.

'I know my future,' said Creoth. 'And I don't care who else knows it too. This lady' – he pointed to Mrs Chirish – 'this lady and I have come to an understanding, and we are to have a farm.'

'You may have the farm,' said Mrs Chirish. 'I plan to lead a quiet life.'

'Me, me, me!' cried Fin Marish. 'Talk about me!'

'Come here, dear.'

The little girl ran forward, and Ira Hath took her little hands between her own hands.

'You will marry,' she said, 'and have five children.'

'I want to marry Spek. Can I marry Spek?'

'You will marry Spek Such.'

Spek Such scowled as he heard this.

'Do I have to?' he said.

'Not at all,' said Ira. 'But I think you will.'

Tanner Amos stepped up with a simple question.

'Will I marry again?'

'You will,' said Ira.

'Who will I marry?'

'Why ask me, Tanner? It's no prophecy to tell you what you already know.'

Tanner Amos looked round, and his gaze fell directly on Ashar Warmish. That was how he told her that he was waiting, and that in three years time he would come for her, if she was willing. Ashar said nothing, but nor did she blush. Some things felt right.

In this same manner, sometimes holding their hands, sometimes just looking into their faces, Ira Hath prophesied for each of them, telling them for the most part what they already knew, but had not yet admitted to themselves. Bek Shim was relieved to learn he would marry Sarel Amos, because it meant he wouldn't have to ask her. He could proceed now as if it was already established as a fact; which he found much easier. The teacher Silman Pillish was gratified to learn he would become a schoolteacher again, and frankly incredulous at the prophecy that he would marry the widow Cheer Warmish. Cheer Warmish too protested loudly that she had no such wish. However, they both began to look at each other in a new and curious way.

Red Mimilith was told she would marry and have two children of her own, but four children altogether. This made no sense, and she was about to ask more questions, when she saw Miller Marish staring at her. She went bright red and asked nothing. Miller Marish was a good man, but he was ten years older than her. He was a good father, too, loving and reliable. Red Mimilith began to think about the possibility.

Rollo Shim was to become a fisherman, which made him shake his head, and was to marry Seer Such, which made him laugh.

'Well, I don't want to marry you either,' said Seer Such, irritated by his laugh.

Sisi did not come forward for a prophecy.

'I shall make my own future,' she said.

Mumpo wanted to know, but didn't dare to ask. By now it was too late, anyway. Ira Hath was becoming tired. Hanno begged her to speak no more, desperately worried that she was using up the last of her strength.

'Almost done, Hannoka,' Ira murmured. She beckoned Pinto towards her, and took her in her arms.

'My baby,' she said.

'I don't want to know,' said Pinto. 'Just tell me if I'll be happy.'

'You'll have a long life,' said Ira. 'How can it all be happy?'

'Can you really see the future, ma?'

'Yes. A little. The part that's in you now.' She drew Pinto close, so that she could whisper to her without the others hearing. 'You love Mumpo. I see it in you now. There's part of your future.'

Pinto kissed her and said nothing. Her mother's words made her very happy.

'And you, my dearest.' Ira turned to Hanno and took his hands.

'I have no future,' said Hanno. 'I need no prophecy. You talk too much, woman.'

Ira smiled, and kissed his hands. He was right. She had talked too much. She was very tired.

Pinto was woken by the dawn light. It was the strangest light, filtered through the snow on the leaves above, and tinged with the faintest rose pink. She stood up, and felt the aching and the stiffness in her legs, and wondered if the snow had passed. She made her way out between the snow walls, and into a space between the surrounding trees. Here she found snow was still falling, but the flakes were light and far apart. The snow clouds were at last moving away. And where they had already cleared, the sky was glowing a light watery pink.

The sun was about to rise.

Pinto had slept well, and for all her aching bones, she felt refreshed. The glimpse of dawn sky through the trees enchanted her. Wanting a wider view of the sunrise, she made her way between the trees, up the rising slope, looking for a clearing in the forest. Shortly she came upon the mountain track they had been following from the valley, only this was an upper reach of it she had not seen before. the track led directly upwards, trodden into steps like a staircase, as before, while the mountain slopes rose higher on either side. Between these slopes was a notch of sky, in which snow clouds were giving way to the serene pink of dawn. The slopes to left and right limited Pinto's view in an annoying way, but it seemed to her that if she climbed just a little further, she should come to a place where the land levelled off.

On she went, as the last flakes of snow sailed to earth around her, and the pink in the sky deepened to red. She had come farther than she had intended, but she could not turn back now. She was so close.

She shivered in the morning cold. Stupidly, she had forgotten to put on her outer coat. She heard the crunch of the crisp snow beneath her feet. She smelt the freshness of the dawn air. She felt strong, and bold, and excited.

Faster now – up the last steps –

Still snow-covered slopes rose on either side of her. Still the flurries of snowflakes settled around her. But now the sky was red, such a deep strong red, the red of a perfect dawn. And all at once, she had reached the top, the very top of the track, and she had come to a stop, and was gazing before her, and she knew what she was seeing.

Through a V of hills, a red sky. Snow falling. A land far below, where two rivers ran to a distant sea.

It was the homeland.

In a wondering daze, Pinto walked forward, and then came to a stop once more. Just a few paces before her there was –

Nothing.

No mountains sloping down to foothills, no foothills sloping into the coastal plain. Nothing. The land just ended.

She lay down on her stomach on the snow, and inched her way forward. In this manner, she came to the edge of the land, and dared to look over.

It was a sheer cliff, that dropped thousands of feet, down to the beautiful unreachable land below. Already giddy, she made herself look to the left and to the right, and saw how the immense cliff ran away in both directions as far as she could see. In some far distant time, the mountains on this western flank had cracked and crumbled away, leaving a massive and impassable precipice.

Shaking from the vertiginous sight, Pinto crawled back to safety, and rose once more to her feet. She looked up at the red sky, which was not sunset after all, but sunrise. There was the homeland before her, just as her mother had dreamed. But there was no way they could reach it.

17

The meeting place

As the barge carrying Bowman and Kestrel to Sirene made its way into the open sea, a northerly wind began to blow, slowing their progress. Beyond the snow clouds, the horizon darkened to a leaden grey.

'Ha!' cried Albard. 'The game begins!'

A great wave, driven silently from the ocean by the rising wind, picked the barge up, and sweeping on towards shore, smacked it down again with a terrific crack. Bowman, Kestrel and Jumper, who had been in the cabin, came reeling out, half-stunned, to find Albard standing on deck, legs astraddle, arms reached up to the sky, shouting at the storm.

'Come on, then! Do your worst! See if you can get me! What do I care?'

Seeing the others, he called to them, eyes shining.

'She's trying to stop you getting to the island!'

There was no time for explanations. A second bigger wave was racing towards them. There sounded a long rumble across the sky, culminating in a mighty clap of thunder. Up went the barge once more, tossed high on the crest of the wave: as it did so, without any words passing between them, Jumper, Bowman and Kestrel all lifted themselves a few feet into the air, so that as the boat plunged down again, they remained hovering above it. Only Albard had stayed with his boots firmly planted on the deck, letting himself be tossed and rolled with the boat.

'Cowards!' he yelled at them. 'Runaways! Spectators!'

They dropped down beside him onto the heaving deck. Albard seized Bowman by the arm.

'You, boy!' he shouted at him over the rolling of the thunder. 'This is power! This is energy! Don't you want it?'

'I don't want to be smashed to pieces!'

'Afraid, are you?'

'Yes. I am.'

The barge rose once more, this time tipping to one side so far that Bowman had to grab hold of the hatch cover to stop himself being thrown into the sea.

'Use the fear!' cried Albard. 'There's power in fear! Find it, take it, use it!'

Bowman saw Jumper watching him with that odd little smile of his. Kestrel was beside him, braced against the storm, watching him too. He felt as if he was expected to do something, but he wasn't sure what. And all the time, the storm was rolling closer, and the waves were tossing with ever greater violence.

Use the fear. But how?

Crash! The sea struck from beneath like a whale, lifting the barge up until it was almost vertical, throwing Bowman out into the snow-filled darkening air –

'Aaaah!' he cried. And then louder, letting his panic terror sound all through his body –

'AYAYAYAYANNAYANNAAAA!'

He caught himself as he fell, and kicked with his legs like a swimmer rising through water. Up he shot, tingling and glowing from his shout, soaring up into the storm above, tumbling himself over and over in the electric cloud. As he spiralled and span, he called out long wordless sounds, drinking in the danger of the storm, vibrating with his own fear and fury. A slash of lightning tore across the sky, followed by a hammer-crack of thunder, whipping him and spinning him with dazzle and noise. Throwing wide his arms and legs, he let the storm toss him like a rag, a blanket, a sail, he spread himself wide, wide as the storm, and hugged it and wrapped it and bundled it. He sang to the storm as he took it in his arms and stomach and knees and feet, hooking it in close, blanketing the thunder, hugging the wind, taking the power into himself for ever and ever –

'Tha-a-at's my boy!'

Albard bawled up from the deck, watching him tumble in the storm, his voice cracking with pride. Jumper and Kestrel were watching him, rocking, smiling. Then the rage of the sky began to abate, and Bowman felt himself floating downwards, until his feet came to rest once more on the deck. The barge was riding over a calm sea towards Sirene.

'Has the storm passed?'

'Passed? No! You've eaten it! You've a belly full of thunder! You could fart a hurricane!'

Albard rocked with laughter.

'Is it true?' Bowman asked Jumper.

In reply, Jumper held out his hand, and Bowman

reached across to touch it. As his fingers came close to Jumper's hand, a vivid blue spark jumped the gap, startling him. He pulled his hand away quickly.

'You have the storm's energy in you,' said Jumper.

'Let me feel it, Bo.'

Kestrel came up close to Bowman, the same strange look in her eyes he had seen before. But everything was strange now. She reached out and touched him. A shiver of sparks rose up where her hand rested on his arm.

'Hold me.'

He put his arms round her, feeling the shivering at every point of contact. She held him close, and her body absorbed the hot-cold hurting-sweet needle-points of energy that pulsed from every part of him. The shock of it made her hold her breath, but she didn't let go until she had taken as much as he had to give. Then they parted, their eyes locked on each other still.

I can do anything, Kess.

Kestrel said nothing. For her the pain was beginning. She could feel the silver voice that hung on a string round her neck, lying against her skin. It was hot to the touch, from where she had pressed herself against her brother. Now, slowly, her body was cooling; but the silver voice was growing hotter.

The passing storm had swept away the snow clouds to reveal the light of the moon in the twilight sky. As night gathered round them, they saw Sirene ahead: the rock-strewn hill, the high roofless walls of the great hall. The barge which had neither sails nor oars passed quietly now over the rolling sea, and so nosed its way into the little cove that formed the island's harbour.

Albard was the first to step onto land.

'Sirene!' he cried. 'This is for you!'

He urinated noisily onto the stony ground.

Bowman and Kestrel followed, their eyes straining in the dusk to make out the details of this mysterious island they had dreamed of for so long. All they could see was bare rising land, and here and there the bent shape of olive trees.

Mist the cat came after them, and was unimpressed.

'What's the use of learning to fly,' he complained, 'if we come to a dull rock like this?'

'They're waiting,' said Jumper.

It was Jumper who led the way up the path, hopping and stopping, hopping and stopping, in his maddening way.

'For pity's sake!' exclaimed Albard. 'Must you jig about so?'

'Would you prefer me to creep?'

'Yes, creep.'

But Jumper's creeping was so slow and peculiar that it annoyed Albard even more.

'Alright, alright. Do as you like.'

'Bounce on, Jumper!' said Jumper cheerfully.

Shortly the little band arrived at the top of the low hill in the centre of the island. Here stood the high stone walls that formed the Singers' roofless hall. The outline of the arched windows could be made out clearly against the moonlit clouds. The space between the walls was inky black.

'I suppose they're all here,' said Albard, sounding suddenly subdued.

'All but you and I,' said Jumper.

'Who leads the song?'

'He waits for us.'

'Ah, moonface. Not for me. I left Sirene long ago.' Albard's voice sounded even lower. 'The boy is ready for the final test. My work is done.'

'Not quite all.'

'I have no power left.'

'The wind will carry you.'

'Well, then.' He squared his great shoulders and tossed his shaggy grey-haired head, as if defying his fate.

'Boy,' he said to Bowman. 'Let me hold you in my arms.'

Bowman went to him, and Albard's great arms closed round the youth's thin and bony back.

'I loved you the first time I saw you. Did you know that?'

'No,' said Bowman.

'No, nobody ever knows the big things. But so it was. I wanted to die, so you could live. Did you know that?'

'No.'

'But so it was.' He sighed, and kissed Bowman's brow and cheeks. 'Live for me, boy.'

'But I –'

'Tush, tush! Do as you're told. If not from fear, because no man fears me now, then from pity. I was a Master once. I made a world.'

'They wait for us,' said Jumper.

He hopped ahead, through the high doorless doorway, into the blackness. Albard followed. Then Bowman, and Kestrel, and the cat.

They were given no warning. One moment they were stepping over grassy ground; the next moment, nothing. Neither Jumper nor Albard made a sound. When Bowman felt himself falling, he spread his arms, in some instinct of flight, which achieved nothing at all: and only then remembered what he had been taught. Taking control of his descent, he slowed himself down, and so was able to catch Mist, who forgetting everything, was dropping like a stone.

Kestrel landed after him, as gently as if she had stepped over a threshold. Bowman was impressed. The cat wriggled, and leapt down from his arms, only to stop, back arched, bristling.

They were in a cave, through which an underground river ran. Slowly their eyes adjusted to the glimmer of moonlight that fell from above. Ghostly in the deep shadows stood the Singer people, hundreds of them, with their arms folded before them and their eyes open, but a look on their faces that showed they neither saw nor heard. They wore coarse robes, and their feet were bare, and dust had settled on their heads and shoulders. Men and women, of all ages, all shapes and sizes, they waited for the moment that would awaken them and set them on their final journey.

Albard began to tremble. He sank to his knees, and hung his head.

Bowman gazed at the Singer people. As his eyes became used to the darkness, he saw more and more of them, stretching away into the vaulted shadows of the caves. There were thousands of them.

'What are they waiting for?'

'For the child of the prophet.'

For me! thought Bowman. He understood very little of what was happening, but he felt no fear. Quite the opposite: he felt excitement. He felt, This is what I've been preparing for all my life.

Kestrel sensed the joy in Bowman and she was glad, but there was no joy in her. She felt sad, achingly sad. The sadness was linked to the silver voice, which she felt all the time, hot against her breast.

'Go to the tomb,' said Jumper softly.

There before them, surrounded by the silent unmoving throng of Singer people, rose the stone columns and the carved stone canopy of the tomb. Bowman and Kestrel threaded their way between the robed figures to the tomb's side. At first it seemed to them that there was nothing there but the stone platform. But shortly, in the faint silver glow, they made out before them the shrunken corpse, the web of dried skin stretched over bones, the hands clasped over exposed ribs, the face that was a skull.

'Your ancestor,' murmured Jumper. 'The prophet, Ira Manth.'

Bowman and Kestrel stood on either side of the tomb, and stared at the bones of the prophet, and felt nothing: not reverence, not fear. Only Kestrel felt the burning heat of the silver voice, so hot now that surely it must burn a hole in her covering shirt.

Bowman recalled the first line of the Lost Testament.

A child of my children will always be with you at the time of the consummation. In this way, I live again, and I die again.

He knew what he must do without being told. He reached out one hand. As he did so, he became aware that Kestrel was reaching out a hand, too. He was surprised, but glad.

We go together, she said to him, without breaking the silence.

Jumper had become still and grave. He watched the hands pass through the air, the fingers stretching for the touch.

Nothing, thought Bowman, as his hand came to rest on the dry skin of the prophet's arm. I feel nothing. Only the bones of a long-dead man.

Kestrel too laid her hand on the bones, and felt nothing.

Then it began. At first it was no more than a growing tiredness. Then Bowman began to feel weak. A dizziness passed through him. He tottered, and nearly fell.

What's happening, Kess?

He's taking our strength.

She could feel it clearly: her strength was being drained out of her, slowly, pitilessly, unstoppably. Soon, if she didn't remove her hand, and break the contact, the dead man would suck away all she had.

He wants our life, she said to Bowman.

I give it, replied her brother.

Too weak to stand, he sank slowly to his knees, his hand remaining on the bony arms. His head fell forward, over the dead man. After a few moments, Kestrel too crumpled, and fell.

Jumper looked on, not moving. The boy and the girl knelt motionless, their heads bowed over the skeleton as it lay on its stone bed. They were breathing, but very slowly. They were unconscious.

One by one, the Singer people nearest to the tomb began to awake. Eyes blinked, and faces turned. One reached up a hand to scratch a cheek. Another shifted his weight from leg to leg. The rustling sound of breathing filled the quiet air of the cave. More awoke, and more. Then quietly, the first wakers began to sing. They sung a low wordless song that sounded more like light rain on a lake's surface than human voices, a murmuring whisper of a song. Albard rose quietly from where he knelt, and joined in the song. As did Jumper.

Before long the Singer people were awake, all of them, in their thousands; stirring and stretching, drawing deep breaths, singing.

The sound of their singing gathered like the breath of life round Bowman and Kestrel. It pressed against their eyelids and eardrums, waking them from their sleep, pouring into them a power greater than the strength that had been taken from them, the power of the Singer people. Blinking, unsure what had happened, they stood up, on either side of the tomb, and looked round them. Thousands of faces looked back, without curiosity, without demands.

'The time has come,' said Jumper.

His voice had changed yet again, but this time all who heard him knew this was the true voice. His eyes shone as he spoke, not with youth but with certainty. Albard, watching, singing, filled with a calm he had not known for years, smiled to see it.

Ah, moonface! he thought to himself. So you are the first of us all!

Dimly, as if recollected from a long-distant past, Albard sensed his own foolishness. But he was not ashamed. He cared nothing for the mistakes he had made in his life, for he felt now that the Singer people had watched over him, and he had done his duty in his own way. He was ready

now for the release for which all Singer people train and
wait, the firesong, and the storm of bliss.

Mist the cat, all the hairs on his back bristling with fear
at the changes taking place round him, stalked between
the robed figures, seeking one he had known before. He
found him at last, arms clasped before him, face raised,
chanting the wordless song that flowed and eddied round
the great cave: Dogface, the tree hermit.

'So what's all this about?' said Mist, speaking to his
one-time friend and companion.

Dogface didn't answer, and didn't look down. As
always, thought Mist, he had failed to hear him. But
looking up at that familiar ugly head, the cat felt a sudden
wave of love. How did I fail to see it before? he thought.
My hermit is beautiful.

'Dogface,' he called. 'You're beautiful!'

The hermit did look down then, hearing the cat's
mewling cry, and without pausing in his song, he smiled.
Mist flew up before him and circled him twice, showing
off his new powers. Dogface followed him with his eyes,
smiling and singing. Mist realised as he flew that this
flying was no more than a party trick, and that something
of far greater power was happening all round him, and
Dogface was part of it. So he dropped gently to the ground,
and behaving now like a common cat, he rubbed his
body along the hermit's legs, and twined his tail round
him, and purred. It was a little demeaning to be reduced
to such an ordinary gesture of affection, but it had the
advantage that the hermit understood it. Mist was saying,
with the press of his soft grey fur and his lithe long body,
I was happy with you, all our years in the tree. And

Dogface, reaching down a hand to stroke him, was replying, I was happy with you too, my Mist.

The song of the Singer people was changing now, growing louder, the rhythm a little faster. Now as Bowman and Kestrel stood stiff and silent, side by side before Jumper, the Singer people began to rise up. First one, then two more, then a dozen, they floated up out of the cave and into the moonlit night. Jumper had changed yet again, and now seemed to be very old, infinitely old, and wise, and full of love.

'The time has come to sing the song to the end.'

His voice was soft and sweet, as if it was part of the greater song that hummed around them. Bowman was filled with the sensation that he had heard all this before, that he knew what would be said to him, and what he must reply.

'A child of the prophet must go with you.'

'I see two children of the prophet,' said Jumper.

'I'm the one,' said Bowman. 'I've been chosen. I've been trained. Kestrel knows that.'

Then at last Kestrel spoke, with a heavy heart, as the silver voice burned her skin.

'No,' she said.

Bowman misunderstood, thinking that she didn't want to let him go.

'This thing must be done, Kess.'

'It must be done,' said Kestrel, 'but not by you.'

'Not by me?'

Bowman was shocked into a new alertness. He turned to Jumper. The little old man seemed unsurprised.

'Tell her,' said Bowman. 'Tell her it's me who has to come with you, into the wind on fire.'

'One of you must come with us,' said Jumper. 'The one in whom the prophet lives again, and will die again.'

'That's me! It must be me!'

'No,' said Kestrel sadly. 'Sorry, Bo.'

'Sorry? What do you mean, sorry?'

He spoke angrily, because he was confused and hurt. Why was Kestrel saying such things? She knew he had been preparing for this all his life. Why else had he been trained? Why else had he been given power?

'Don't stop me, Kess.'

Of course! Why hadn't he seen it before? She wasn't trying to hold on to him out of love. She was jealous. She knew this coming wind on fire, that was called the storm of bliss, was the one true reward, and she sought it for herself. But he had the power. If necessary, for the sake of this great act for which all the Singer people had assembled, he would use his power.

'Don't stop me, Kess.'

Oh my brother. Can't you see?

He caught the note of sadness, and of pity, in her mind's voice, and it angered him. All his life he had been the fearful one, and Kestrel had been the leader. He had been the one who feels, she had been the one who does. Now, at the end, she couldn't accept that he was the leader, and had the power.

All round him the Singer people were floating up and away, hundreds and hundreds of them, as gradually the great cave emptied. The song they sang went with them, to sound from the air above, rising, falling, rising. There was no time to lose.

'I must go now,' he said. 'They wait for me.'

I love you, Bo.

Her love angered him. Using the power of his mind, he reached out to push her back: not to strike her, or to hurt her, just to show her that they must be parted.

He couldn't move her.

He pushed harder. She seemed heavy, impossibly heavy. He met her eyes. He saw it there: she was using her own power, such as it was, to resist him.

Don't make me do this, Kess.

Let go, she answered him. *Be still.*

I won't hurt you, Kess. But I won't let you stop me.

He summoned up greater powers, and bore down upon her, to break her resistance. Under such an assault, he expected her to crumple to her knees, but she didn't move by so much as a shiver. Then, to his shock, she struck back. The mind-blow made him stagger.

Kess! Don't fight me! I don't want to hurt you.

You can't hurt me, Bo.

Why are you doing this?

To make you understand.

She struck him again. Again he staggered back. Tears came to his eyes, not of pain but of distress. He turned to Jumper, and saw how he watched them with a look on his face that showed he had expected this.

This must be it, Bowman thought. This must be the final test of my training. I must lose all and give all. I must even lose my sister, who is half myself. I must be free to do what I was born to do.

Armed with this new conviction, he called up all the power he possessed, and hurled a blow at Kestrel that sent her flying across the cave, rolling and tumbling to crash against the rock walls on the far side. As soon as he had done it, he made himself go still, and quietly sang his own song, to restore the power he had unleashed.

Kestrel stood up, and stepped softly back towards him.

CRACK! An explosive force struck Bowman and lifted him up into the air, hurling him twenty, thirty feet up. He struggled to slow his fall, and gained control just before his feet touched the ground.

At once he threw a mind-blow at Kestrel, and felt her meet it with a wall of power, and strike back. He brushed her strike aside, and hit again, and again, hammering at her defences. She was strong: much stronger than he had expected. He changed tactics, and focusing all his power into one narrow beam, he drilled into her mind, so that he could possess and subdue it. Instead of meeting this attack with a resisting mind, she gave way at once. He found himself tumbling into her mind, through curtains of longing and fear and ferocity and love, through the part of her that loved him, into a far place he had never known before, where there was a vast stillness.

Here his attack ended. There was nothing to strike, no enemy to subdue, no prisoners to take. Instead it was his own furious power-driven mind that was subdued, and taken prisoner. He knew he could not compete against this, any more than he could sweep away the ocean, or hurt the sky.

It has to be this way, my brother. Do you see it now?

Gently, Kestrel released him from the fortress of her stillness.

I'm the one who will go, she said. *I'm the one who will die.*

Bowman looked around him. The Singer people were

all gone, but for Jumper. He could hear their song still. They had not gone far. He tasted salt on his lips, and realised tears were streaming down his cheeks. He heard his own voice, saying, lost and afraid,

'I would have given all I have.'

So you shall.

'What am I to do?'

Go back to our people. They need you.

Bowman wanted to ask, For what? But no words came. Then Jumper spoke, in his slow kind voice.

'You're the meeting place.'

The meeting place? An odd thing to say, and yet familiar. He had never heard it before, and yet he understood it. The understanding broke through in a rush, like the shock of a suddenly-opened door that reveals an unexpected road ahead, a different road, a new vision of the future.

Of course! There must be a meeting place. Was he not a child of the prophet, trained by the Singer people? And had he not been touched by the Morah? He was the meeting place of the passions of mankind, of the hopes and the fears, the kindness and the cruelty. His destiny was not to be the saviour, but to be saved.

In that flash of revelation, he saw the simple truth of his childhood journey into the halls of the Morah. That moment of ecstatic power and shameful weakness, that knowledge that had never left him since, that willed and guilty union with the Morah's million eyes, that had been the entire and necessary purpose of his coming there. Not the saving of Aramanth, which had not been saved. Not the return of the voice to the wind singer, which had been burned. All that had endured from that perilous journey was the silver voice that Kestrel wore round her neck, and his own contamination by the Morah.

He almost laughed out loud as he saw it all.

Sirene watches over you. It was written on the old map. Oh, they were clever, these Singer people. They were hunting bigger game than an old wooden tower, built long ago. They had been preparing the next generation, that would build the world again, after the wind on fire.

First you destroy, then you rule.

'I'm the meeting place!'

Jumper watched, and saw that the boy was ready now.

'We have given you all we have to give. Use it well.'

Kestrel had followed her brother's tumble of understanding, and now she too understood. Her hand reached inside her shirt and drew out the silver voice. It burned her as she touched it, but she wasn't hurt. This is what we found the voice for, she was thinking. Not for the wind singer. For now. For this. To lead me to the wind on fire.

She looked up at her brother, and saw the gleam of tears on his cheek. She heard the song of the Singer people filling the air above.

'They wait for me.'

Jumper bowed his kind old head. Then silently he floated up into the air, and left brother and sister alone together beside the tomb of the prophet, to say their farewells.

Now that the moment had come, Bowman found himself at a loss.

'I can't live without you, Kess.' It wasn't a plea. Bowman

understood what was to happen. It was a statement of his own conviction. 'If you die, I'll die.'

'But if you live, I'll live.'

She came up close before him, and he bowed his head, and they touched brows. Standing quietly in this way, as they had done countless times since they were very small, they let their fears and dreams join, and be shared.

'I'll never leave you,' she said to him. 'Feel me now.'

He felt her, entering her mind with his, deep, deeper than he had ever done before, deeper than he had thought possible, and deeper still. She opened before him, and fell away, emptying herself even as he sought her, until he was lost in her mind, and still he had not touched her. He no longer knew where to look. She was gone. The form of his sister still stood before him, his hands could hold her, but she herself, all that he knew of her, was gone.

'Kess! Where are you?'

'Here, Bo. Here.'

He turned like a fool, expecting to see her behind him, but there was no one.

'Where?'

'I'm with you!'

He found her then: so close that he couldn't see her or touch her or sense her in any way, except as part of what he saw and touched and sensed for himself.

'Do you feel me now?'

That was his own voice speaking, and yet it was Kestrel's. He looked at her, smiling before him, and saw her dear face: only it was his own face he saw, and he was seeing with her eyes.

'Yes. I feel you now.'

'We go together,' said her voice that was also his. And his voice answered, that was her voice,

'Always together.'

Hand in hand, they rose up into the moonlight, past the sheer rock walls of the cave, to the sloping hillsides of Sirene. Here the Singer people waited in their thousands, covering the slopes entirely, so that the island seemed to be formed of robed men and women, clustered close together. They looked west, towards the mountains of the mainland, and their song grew stronger all the time.

While Bowman and Kestrel had been down in the cave, the night had slipped away. Now behind them the first light of winter dawn was glowing on the eastern horizon. Then as they waited and watched and sang their wordless song, a wind came rippling over the sea. The wind flurried their robes and clattered the leaves in the olive trees.

'It's time,' said Jumper.

All together, like some vast flock of birds, the Singer people lifted up into the air and letting the wind take them, flew west over the water. Kestrel and Bowman flew with them, and Mist the cat, following the long stream of robed men and women as they skimmed the roiling sea to the far shore. As they flew, they sang. The ever-strengthening wind blew their song away, but no one cared. They sang not to be heard, but to be changed.

Bowman knew now he had no part in this. His life lay elsewhere. There were no more words to say. There comes a time in partings when all that is left to be done is to part.

'Are you coming, Mist?'

Bowman spun himself round in the air for one last look at Kestrel, one last salute, and then peeled away to the north, flying fast and straight like an arrow towards the mountain pass. Mist, taken by surprise, lagged behind for a while, mewling crossly as he paddled the air.

'Wait for me!'

The Singer people paid no attention to his leaving. The wind was come, they had begun their last journey, their eyes were on the mountains, their minds on their song. Only Albard, who had once been the Master, turned and watched Bowman all the way out of sight.

18

Into the beautiful land

Bowman flew over the snow-covered plains, a little higher than the treetops, driving himself towards the mountains as fast as he could go. He never stopped to think how strange and glorious it was that he could fly, that the woods and fields, farms and villages, slipped past below him almost as soon as they came into view; nor did he think of Kestrel, who he would never see again. Instead all his attention was on his people waiting at the mountain pass, who needed him; and on the suffering of the land he was passing, the unknown world unrolling below him.

This was the time of cruelty, cruelty beyond control, cruelty that fed on cruelty and begot cruelty. Village after village was burned and looted. Haystacks still smouldered in the snow-bound fields, and cattle lay dead, abandoned, prey to carrion birds. Here and there Bowman saw people moving through the ruins, but they were scavengers, not survivors, and even as he flew past overhead he could smell their violence and their fear. He passed over a large farmstead that had not been destroyed, and saw that its terrified owners had turned it into a fortified camp, and huddled within its walls, not knowing when the marauding gangs would attack again. Not far from this farm, a brake of trees was burning, a stripe of bright fire across the snow. Beyond the burning trees, some children were making their way up the high road, small children, no more than six and seven years old. Bowman felt the waves of panic that surrounded them, but he could do nothing for them. He flew on, knowing the misery below was too great for his own small powers, but he felt sick and angry at the waste of the world, and longed for the coming of the wind on fire.

Now as he flew he saw a column of mounted soldiers, and riding after them a ragged following of men on horseback. He saw them ride into a village, and torch the houses. He saw the hiding villagers come running out, and saw the horsemen ride them down, and heard their screams of terror as they fell. This was one of the free companies, the remains of defeated armies, that now roamed the land destroying all before them. Here was the horror of these times: that men killed and burned not for gain, not for power, not even for pleasure, but because they craved destruction. They had lost everything. Now they were determined that everything should be lost. If their lives were ravaged, let the world be ravaged. They who had received no mercy gave no mercy. As their victims screamed, so the killers screamed, until it was impossible to tell who was suffering the more.

So Bowman passed over the grieving land, his sensing mind reaching down to embrace all the people below. He let himself feel not only the fear, but the hatred; not only the grief of those whose loved ones had been killed, but the passionate anger of their killers. He wept for those who suffered and for those, almost equally helpless, who inflicted the suffering. I understand you all, he called down to them. I am the guilty one who will be saved for you and with you, so that the world may start again.

Ira Hath sat in her litter, framed by the V of hills, and looked out over the homeland. The red sky of dawn was gone. The snow cloud, with its flurry of slow-falling flakes, had blown by. But she had seen it, just as in her dream, and now she could go. It had been hard holding on for these last days. She had become so weak at the end she had not been able to eat, and she drank only because Hanno poured water over her mouth. Most of it trickled away down her chin, but some passed her lips. Now, as if her eyes had waited only to see the homeland, she found she was losing her ability to see. People's faces were blurred, and although she knew the sun was rising, the sky seemed to be growing darker. She could hear, when Hanno spoke to her, or Pinto, but she could no longer speak in reply. She lacked the strength. How surprising to find that mere speech required so much work from so many muscles. So instead, to show she heard and understood, she gave a very slight pressure, with the tip of one finger. Hanno sat beside her, her hand in his, and he could feel her movement and understand her. The code they had established, without ever once discussing it, was this: a movement of her finger meant yes. No movement meant no.

Ira felt her own dying very clearly now. She was not

afraid. She had played her small part in life, and she was willing to go. Her body felt light, no longer under her control. She could not stand upright unaided, and even if she had been able to, this rising wind would have blown her away like a winter leaf.

So it was come now. She too must sing her song to the end. It was hard to leave her dear Hannoka, and her children; but harder still to stay. And why linger? Her little ones were grown big, she must move aside, so that they could blossom into life. This is why we have children, she thought, smiling to herself. So that we can die gracefully.

Hanno saw that passing smile, and squeezed her hand. 'Not yet,' he said.

Pinto sat beside him, filled with a strange mixture of grief and excitement. Every time she looked at her mother, she wanted to cry. But every time she looked ahead, towards the homeland, she felt a fierce thrill of joy. She had never seen it before, but she recognised it. This is where my life will begin, she thought. This is where I'll grow and be strong and do great things. This is where I won't be a child any more.

There was no way to reach the homeland. The cliff was too high, too steep. The rest of the Manth people sat in bewildered huddles, utterly defeated by this one insurmountable fact. Coming as it had, when they were so close to the end of the journey, when their hopes had risen so high, it was a crushing blow. But not to Pinto. She had no answer to the problem. All she knew was that the homeland was found, the prophecies were true, and her life lay before her.

Her mother's dying was all muddled up inside her with this final impassable obstacle, the cliff. There was no logic to the thought, but it seemed to Pinto that when the first impossible event occurred, the death of her mother, the second would follow in its course, and they would enter the homeland.

She said as much to Mumpo.

'Ma has brought us here. She'll lead us the last mile. You'll see.'

Mumpo believed her. He was learning to respect Pinto's pronouncements. She was a special person, and it was his task to look after her for all of them. Also, she loved him, and that seemed to Mumpo to be a gift of great preciousness.

Those among the Manth people given to forming opinions took a gloomier view. To Branco Such, and Silman Pillish, and Cheer Warmish, it was all too clear that their journey was over, and had ended in failure. Their prophet was on the point of expiring, and their leader had no answer to their dilemma. At the same time, there were plumes of smoke rising in the sky to the west, and the glow of unnatural fires. The world seemed to be ending, so they might as well sit on the cold hard ground, eat what was left of their food, and despair.

'We should never have left,' grumbled Branco. 'No good ever comes of leaving.'

'Never left where?' said Silman Pillish.

'Anywhere,' said Branco, irritably aware that it made no difference where they were if the world was ending; and that the place he wished he had never left was the past.

'Everything will work out. You wait and see.'

This was little Scooch.

'I won't,' responded Cheer Warmish. 'I won't wait and see. I've done enough. Why should I suffer? It's someone else's turn.'

'Hush!' said Lea Mimilith, nodding towards Ira Hath. 'At least you've got your health.'

'And for what?' demanded Cheer Warmish. 'What use is health when the world's about to end? What have I done to deserve it, I'd like to know?'

'I suppose,' murmured Scooch, 'that the world is about to end for everyone else too.'

'Oh yes, go on, make it worse. I know I'm nobody special.'

The young men, Tanner Amos, Miller Marish and Bek Shim, had gone off exploring the ridge to see if there was a way down the cliff further on. Now they returned with bad news. The sheer vertical face seemed to extend the full length of the mountain range. No doubt there was a way to the homeland back down the mountains, along the river, and round by the sea. But would they be given the time?

The wind was rising. They all felt it now.

Sisi remained apart from the others, even from Lunki. She was not concerned by the cliff, or the homeland, or Ira's dying. She was listening. She had told Bowman she would wait for his return, and she was waiting. Sisi made no claims to prophecy, but she had a strong will, and she trusted her will. Bowman would come back to her because she wanted it so much. So she listened, and waited.

She didn't know that the Hath family were waiting for

Bowman too: but both Ira, in her weakness, and Hanno, in his patience, understood that he would return. It was fitting, it was the only way, therefore it would happen. Both of them, faced by the immensity of death, had given up seeking to understand the reason for things, and were content with the lesser knowledge, of what was likely to happen. For Ira it presented itself to her in the simplest of terms: she would not die without saying goodbye to her son.

The little children, unaware of the seriousness of their situation, were becoming over-excited. The sight of the cliff frightened and fascinated them. They took it in turns to creep to the edge, look over, and then run back screaming. As they became more confident, they developed the game. They took little runs at the cliff, as if to jump off, stopping short, with a sharp scream, a few yards from the edge.

When Miller Marish saw what they were doing he was appalled.

'Fin! Jet! Stop that!'

'Why? It's fun!'

'Because you'll go over the edge.'

'Who cares? Everything's blowing up anyway!'

'I care! I don't want to lose you!'

'Everyone's going to lose everyone. Look!'

The little girl pointed to the sky. The smoke plumes were rising in the west, and shoots of bright flame fringed the horizon. There was a distant rumble of thunder, and a heaviness in the air. The children were half-intoxicated by the strange sensations, and by waiting for the end.

Creoth sat with his three cows. No longer able to tell

himself stories of the life he would lead in the homeland, he had fallen back on remembering the past.

'You'll never believe this, Dreamer,' he told the cow. 'I used to live in a palace, and eat chocolate buttons. Ah, how I loved those chocolate buttons! And yet, here's the oddity, I wanted them so much before I popped them into my mouth – so much that I scrabbled, I gobbled – but once they were in my mouth, even as I was eating them, I found I didn't really want them at all. What do you make of that?'

The cow swung its head slowly away, to look into the trees.

'Quite right. Foolishness, downright foolishness.'

Mrs Chirish waddled over to his side.

'Well,' she said. 'Here's a fine to-do.'

'And nothing to be done, eh?'

'Oh, I don't know about that. Things don't stay the same, sir. Events, that's the thing. They do keep happening. I say we wait for events.'

In their different ways, they were all waiting for events. Only, for Ira Hath, time was fast running out.

'Is it close?' Hanno whispered to her.

He felt the slight pressure of her fingertip. He leaned forward, and very softly kissed her sunken face.

'I won't hold you, my dear,' he said. 'Only your love. I'll hold your love. And you take mine.'

She pressed his hand.

'I've loved you for half my life,' he said. 'The best half.'

No movement from her finger. She refused to agree.

'Don't argue with me, woman.'

A shadow of a smile formed on her face. Then the

smile remained, but her eyes closed. Her hand lay still in his.

'Ira?'

No response. He leaned close to her nostrils, to feel if she was still breathing. Very faintly on his moistened lips he caught the movement of air.

'Pinto,' he said, looking up. 'Call the others.'

'No, pa,' said Pinto, not thinking what she was saying, which sprang unbidden into her mind. 'She can't go until –'

A sudden shiver went through them all. Creoth's cows jerked their heads upwards. The children froze in their game. The grumblers fell silent, mouths gaping. Sisi looked up, feeling tall and strong and full of certainty. And Pinto said no more, her eyes staring above her –

Bowman was circling them, high above, finding the precise spot for his descent. He had appeared so fast that to many he had come from nowhere. Now, treading air with his bare feet, he let himself drop gently down to the ground, by the side of his dying mother.

As he touched her, her eyes opened again. She saw him, and smiled.

'My brave birds,' she murmured.

Bowman took her from the litter, held her thin body in his arms, and kissed her face.

'You waited for us,' he whispered to her. 'You knew we'd come back.'

She looked on him one last time, and gave him her love, light now and faint, like the wind from a butterfly's wing. Then her eyes closed for ever.

At once, in angry exhilaration, still holding her warm

in his arms, Bowman kicked up into the air, straight up, higher and higher. When he was as high as he could go he kissed her again, and said goodbye, and let himself cry, up there in the secrecy of the sky.

Down he came, gently, gently, and gave her back to his father, her lover, her husband. Hanno took her and held her among her people. They were all still and silent, astonished by the two wonders they had witnessed, Bowman's flying, and Ira Hath's death.

Pinto kissed her mother, weeping. Hanno did not weep. He had made himself ready for this moment.

'We who are left behind watch you on your way.'

He spoke the old words without ever taking his eyes from his dead wife's face; as if he spoke to her directly, in the certain knowledge that she heard him. As he spoke, the others joined in with quiet voices.

'The long prison of the years unlocks its iron door. Go free now, into the beautiful land.'

He faltered, and fell silent. The others in respect fell silent too. For a few moments Hanno Hath remained still, his eyes gazing on his dead wife's face. Then he lifted his head to meet Bowman's eyes. He did not need to ask the question aloud.

'Soon,' said Bowman. 'Very soon.'

Hanno completed the words, his gaze fixed once more on his wife's face.

'Forgive us who suffer in this clouded land. Guide us and wait for us, as we wait for you. We will meet again.' He kissed her. 'We will meet again.'

Bowman turned towards the cliff edge, towards the homeland far below. As he turned back, his eyes met Sisi's, watching him from the back of the crowd of Manth people. Very slightly, he inclined his head to her, and very slightly, she inclined her head in return. It was enough.

'We wait for the wind,' said Bowman.

19

The wind on fire

Kestrel stood singing among the Singer people, losing herself in the song, becoming one with the thousands who had gathered here from all corners of their world. The sun was rising behind them, pouring sharp winter light over the barren ground, laying their shadows long and thin before them. The fire that raged in the sky carried no terrors for them. It was the roaring of a caged beast, venting its anger and frustration before a power greater than its own. Kestrel felt it in every nerve, the astonishing power of the Singer people. The more they sang, the greater this power grew. She was part of it, she was sharing that power, she was contributing to it. She sang joyously, because by singing she sent her life force out to join the others, to form this mighty engine of change.

She felt the wind on her back, and shivered with wonder at what was to come. She lifted up a little, pushed by the wind, she was so light now, and dropped down again. All over the plain she could see it was the same for the others, rising and falling like boats on a rolling sea.

They would all rise up soon enough: but not yet.

There came a crack that was thunder and earthquake together. The ground buckled beneath her feet, and in one great wave of movement, she and all the Singer people lifted up into the air. From the plains ahead came deep groaning sounds, then a cracking and a ripping, as the ground fissured and crazed before their eyes. The song of the Singer people grew stronger, to be heard above the exploding land. Now, within the weave of sound, Kestrel heard a new note: thin and far off and desolate.

She looked towards the mountains, and saw a lone figure walking out of the trees. Distant though the stranger was, Kestrel felt with certain knowledge that they had met before. It was a slow moving, frail, elderly lady with pale eyes. She seemed weak and helpless amid the heaving earthquake, but she did not concern herself over the destruction of the land. She walked on towards them, passing over fissures great and small, through the smoke that now hissed from the hot cracks, her pale eyes fixed on the way ahead.

The Morah was come again.

No power this time, it seemed to Kestrel. What need to destroy this pitiful creature? And yet that was what they were gathered to do. The vast might of the Singer people would surround her, and take her life, and in doing so they would give their own.

'Find the flame!'

It was the soft voice of Jumper in her ear. She turned and saw him, far away, but his mind was close. She understood. It wasn't hard, now that she saw what was happening to those around her. They had begun to glow, as Jumper had done before, on the barge.

Like dying, but not dying.

Kestrel didn't need to ask how, or why. She needed only to sing the song.

As she sang, gladly, eagerly, she felt the cool flame form round her, like a space close to the skin. The sensation was in no way painful. It was calming, and made her body feel lighter, and her senses keener. And yet along with this sharper vision and keener sound went the feeling that such things had happened long ago and far away.

She was watching the old lady. She was nearer now, and she was changing. At first she seemed to be losing focus, becoming blurred at the edges. Then the blurring resolved itself into two figures, one peeling away from the other. Then these two divided in their turn, becoming four. The Morah was multiplying. Human forms burst out of human forms, more and more, not all old now, not all female: there were men emerging, and boys, and girls, peeling the one from the next, spreading over the smoking earthquake-riven land. The Morah was unfolding into the legion that was her true being: not one giving birth to many, but the force that had always belonged to the many now redistributing itself into its original parts.

Kestrel felt the flame grow more intense around her as she sang, as through the shimmering air she watched the multitude form before her. She was amazed by the numbers, for every wave replicating itself brought a doubling, a redoubling, until it seemed the whole visible world would be filled by – what could she call it now, this enemy she had come to destroy? – not monsters after all, not devils – but by nothing less than mankind.

At the same time, the wind blew more strongly against her back, and the flames intensified, so that the thousand upon thousand of Singer people, hovering over the coast, began to shimmer like the winter sunlight on the sea. Kestrel knew the flame she was making with her song was formed out of her own life energy, but she felt only a deep, sweet joy. Soon now her flame would touch her neighbour's flame, and all the flames would become one.

A howl of pain sounded ahead, a shriek and a groan, repeated many times. Out of the cracks in the earth had risen up clouds of tiny whining insects, too small to see, but where they flew they stung, and the people they stung cried out. Now all the shuffling multitude that was the Morah howled in rage and pain, as the passion flies burrowed into their hearts. In a mounting lament that grew into a chorus of misery, Kestrel heard all the anger and fear, the envy and mockery, the hatred of happiness and hunger for pain. She heard screams that were racked with laughter, and saw the contorted faces of the people, and heard their sobbing cries, and she knew, *This is me, this is us, this is mankind.* This was the world of hurt and loss that must die, for the time of kindness to come again.

The clouds of passion flies spread out like a miasma over the land. As they reached the waiting ranks of the Singer people, they struck the aura of flame and burned, popping in tiny flashes of bright light, so many at once that they made a cascade of pinprick stars.

As the multitude that was the Morah advanced howling and sobbing across the plain, the Singer people changed their song once more, and the flame that wrapped each one of them glowed more intensely still. Kestrel let herself go, gladly, knowing the flame was now stronger than she was, that the more intensely it burned, the more she was fading. She felt the wind blowing ever more strongly behind her, and saw the Singer people rise up, sails in the wind, and let herself rise up with them. So close now, their separate flames nudging at each other, licking each other, flurrying in the wind –

Soon now.

Do you feel me, Bo? Soon now!

Bowman stood on the cliff top, with his mother's body in his arms, light as a sleeping child. He too felt the wind strong on his back, and knew what he was to do. On one side stood his father. On the other, his sister Pinto. Beyond them, and behind, all his people, and the cows, and the horses, and the cat. All looked to Bowman, who had returned to them, and who possessed powers they couldn't begin to understand.

Bowman heard the wind, and it sounded like his sister Kestrel, though there were no words he could make out.

'Soon now,' he said. 'Trust the wind.'

The thousands upon thousands of Singer people now let the wind drive them forward, slowly at first, like the shadow of a passing cloud. Kestrel flew with them, still singing the firesong, feeling the way the wind made the flame that was herself burn more brightly still. She did not resist. She opened herself, her body, her mind, her heart. She poured herself out into the flame, and the more she emptied, the lighter she became, and the more she was swept and scoured by joy. Knowing the end was very close, she cried out through her song,

I love you, Bo! I love you all! All my loves!

The wind drove them faster now, they were racing, the Singer people aflame, sweeping over the land, their song unstoppable, deep and far-reaching. The stronger the wind, the more they flared in the air as they flew, and the fiercer burned their flame. Now the wind whipped and gusted, hurling the mournful cries of the multitude that was the Morah back into the shivered ground. The wind raged like a hurricane, and the Singer people burned into dazzling brightness, the wind and the flames converging into a sky-wide sheet of roaring heat that sucked the air from the world.

The last Kestrel felt was a wild singing, a white-hot melting glory. She was falling into the light, for the last time, never to return. The flame was consuming her now, and she was lost in bliss, lost in the thousand flames that now burned together as a single flame, carried on the charging wind –

Up on the mountain cliff top, the Manth people felt the wild wind hit them like a blow. Bowman stepped off the edge, with Ira Manth in his arms, and the wind took him. At once, without hesitation, Pinto followed him, stepping into nothing, into the thousand-foot drop, but she did not drop. Sisi too, her eyes on Bowman, stepped into the air in perfect faith. Like leaves on an autumn day, they fell, slowly, circling as they went, sustained by the turbulent wind.

Seeing that they came to no harm, the others now followed. Some screamed as they jumped, in terror or delight, but all jumped. Creoth was puzzled as to how to persuade his cows to do something so unnatural, but to his astonishment they ambled off the edge of their own free will. Mumpo jumped boldly, arms outreached. Miller Marish held his little girls' hands and they all jumped together, with their eyes shut. Cheer Warmish gave a great scream, but didn't jump, so the teacher Silman Pillish took her hand and simply pulled her off the edge.

Once they had jumped, it was easy. They found themselves floating down, quite slowly, and were able to converse as they fell. It was a long way down.

'Beard of my ancestors!' exclaimed Creoth. 'This is the way to travel!'

Out on the plains the wind on fire roared down on the hordes that crawled over the land, and into the smoking cracks and caves, and on into the forests and mountains, and everywhere it touched the spirit of the Morah was turned to ash and was swept into nothingness. There was no time even for the howling masses to cry out at this new ordeal before the intense heat had blasted them into oblivion. On swept the wind on fire, scouring out all the fear and all the hatred, and leaving behind after the passing of its purifying fury a cool, sweet stillness across a silent land.

Bowman dropped gently to the ground at the foot of the great sheltering cliff, his dead mother still safe in his arms. The air was calm here. The ground was lightly covered with snow. Nearby flowed a broad river, winding its way to the sea. Eastward, the sky was clear.

One by one, his family and friends came dropping down, unharmed, and silent with wonder. Mist the cat, turning as he dropped, contrived to land on Bowman's shoulders, just to make sure he'd not been forgotten.

The Manth people shook themselves as if they were in a dream, and looked round at the land to which they had come in so strange a way. They saw low wooded hills, descending to a broad coastal plain. They saw two rivers, that looped lazily through water meadows still covered in snow. They saw the ocean beyond, calm and bright in the winter sun. They had arrived in a virgin land, an unknown land. And yet every one of them was struck by the same thought at the same time: I have been here before. I know this place.

Hanno Hath came to Bowman, and held out his arms for the body of his wife.

'I'll take her now,' he said. 'Now that we're home.'

Epilogue: A betrothal

Pinto was angry. The date of the ceremony had been agreed, long ago. It was to be seven days after her fifteenth birthday, which was today. So why had they not come? Unable to stop herself, she ran yet again down the long shingled spit of land that reached out from the harbour, and stood at its furthest tip, gazing east over the sea, into the dazzling summer sun. The sea was calm, there was a light wind. Why had the ship not come?

Lunki came looking for her. She waddled out onto the spit, wagging her plump hands in dismay.

'Scooch has burned the cakes! What are we to do?'

'It doesn't matter,' said Pinto. What did she care about cakes?

'The poor man is in tears. He says you specially asked for honey-cakes. It wasn't his fault. He fell asleep. And now he's in tears.'

'Tell him I don't mind,' said Pinto, feeling even more annoyed. She wasn't annoyed about the cakes, she was annoyed about Scooch crying. Now she would have to go and be nice to him, and there were too many other things to do, and Bowman still hadn't come.

'Has the ship come yet?' said Lunki.

This was too much.

'I don't know, Lunki. Can you see a ship?'

'No,' said Lunki, looking round.

Pinto walked back down the spit as fast as she could go, leaving Lunki peering into the distance. She took the path that ran round the back of the village square, hoping not to meet anyone. As she went, her brain seethed with angry thoughts. Why must Bowman and Sisi live so far away? Obagang sounded horrid, crowded with stupid people who did nothing but cause problems. Everyone said Bowman made a fine ruler, but was that what Bowman himself wanted? Or Sisi, for that matter? They'd only agreed because Sisi was a princess, and the people of Gang had pleaded with her, and Bowman had been flattered. And now they lived in a palace hundreds of miles away, and were going to be late for her betrothal.

Muttering crossly to herself, she ran straight into Silman Pillish, who was teaching his little class of children in the open air. He was rehearsing them in a song.

'Where have you gone, little chicks, little chicks?' he sang. 'Oh! oh! and oh!'

With each 'oh!' a child was supposed to peep out from behind Pillish's skirts. Pik Shim and Gem Marish jumped out; but five-year-old Harman Amos had not got the idea at all.

'Harman! You're the third oh!'

'Pongo,' said the little boy from behind the teacher.

'Harman! Here's Pinto, whose betrothal we're singing the song for, and all you can say is a silly word!'

'Pongo pongo pongo,' said Harman stubbornly. 'Stupid pongo chicks!'

'You don't have to sing if you don't want to,' said Pinto. 'And anyway, my brother hasn't come yet, so I expect we'll have to put it off, and everything will be spoiled.'

'Oh, I hope not! We've worked so hard. Pia! Lea! We don't pull each other's hair.'

'We asked each other first,' said little Pia in an injured voice.

'We don't even pull each others' hair if we've asked.'

Pinto went on her way. She made a wide circuit round Scooch's bakery, though the smells drifting out through the open door were very tempting. Beyond the bakery, in the middle of the square, she caught a glimpse of two men clinging to a wooden platform, assembling the wind singer. Not a real wind singer, of course; no one had made such a thing for a hundred years. This was a model that Tanner Amos and Miko Mimilith had been building for months and months. They had failed to have it ready for the betrothal of Fin Marish and Spek Such, and were now determined to get it up and working for Pinto and Mumpo. She could tell even at this distance that it was not yet functioning. The men had a frantic distracted look, and kept colliding with each other on the narrow platform. The scoops were in place, and air was passing through some of the pipes, but the resulting rattle could not be called singing.

Pinto did not care. Everything was going wrong anyway. She stamped on across a field of maize, the topmost cobs higher than her shoulders; past the line of shelter trees that Creoth had planted eight years ago, feathery-thin silver birches, now twenty feet tall; and on past the open front of Creoth's cow barn, where he had nailed up Cherub's crumpled horns. She meant to walk on by without stopping, but from the hayrick there came a shrill wailing sound. She went to investigate, and found little Milo, Red Mimilith's baby boy, trying to get out. Milo could crawl, and did crawl, at startling speed, and so was always disappearing and having to be rescued. Pinto hauled him out of the hay and shook her finger at him.

'You're an evil little rat-child,' she said.

Milo gazed back at her and chuckled, as if to say that this was both true and satisfactory. Pinto put the baby on the ground, pointed him towards the square, and off he shot, his bottom raised, wagging as he went like a clumsy puppy.

Creoth was out in his yard, churning butter.

'Not come yet, then?'

'No. Not yet.'

He kept churning as they spoke. Summer butter was a tricky beast. It could turn on you if you didn't keep after it, and then all you had for your trouble was lumps of grease swimming in whey.

'My wife should be doing this, but she won't,' he said.

'Takes a strong arm,' said Pinto.

'Takes getting out of bed, that's what it takes.'

Pinto began to feel less agitated. The baby and the cowman between them somehow put her into a better humour. She liked it that they had their own concerns, that didn't include her.

'I'm going to go and talk to ma,' she said.

'You do that. Tell her good day from me.'

Pinto followed the path to the river. Here, in a little meadow ringed with stones, the Manth people had made their graveyard. Seldom Erth had been laid to rest in one corner, when he died three years ago. There were markers for others who had died before, put up by friends or family: stout wooden posts, on which the names were cut in vertical columns, one letter above another. The Warmish family had placed a memorial to Harman, though as Ashar Warmish said, his true memorial was her little boy, called Harman after him. Tanner Amos, Ashar's husband, had placed a memorial post to his first wife, Pia Greeth. There was a post for Rufy Blesh, erected by Bowman before he left; and Mumpo had placed a marker for his father Maslo Inch, who long ago had been Chief Examiner of Aramanth.

The grass in the graveyard needed cutting. It was long and lush and yellow with buttercups. Pinto pushed on into the middle of the meadow, where four round stones marked the corners of her mother's grave. They had buried Ira Hath here on first coming to the homeland, and carried the smooth boulders from the beach to lay them on the raw earth. Now grass had grown up round them like a nest, and moss clung to the grey stone, and the grave itself was a thicket of clover and daisies and dandelions. Hanno Hath let it grow wild because he said Ira had always been on the wild side.

Pinto sat herself down on the stone in the south-west corner, which was her stone, and looked from the grave to the meadow, and from the meadow to the river, and from the river to the sea.

'Why do I get so cross, ma?' she said aloud. 'Pa says you were always getting cross and shouting at people. But all I remember is you being quiet.'

She let her thoughts settle down into quietness within her. This was what she came for: talking to her long-dead mother was a way of seeing the anxieties of the moment in a longer perspective, both of time and space, which made them seem smaller and less burdensome.

'I love him so much,' she said. 'That's all that matters, isn't it? The cakes are burnt. The wind singer isn't finished. The children hate their song. Bowman hasn't come. But we'll still be betrothed today. What else matters?'

The gentle wind flurried the grasses, and rippled the water of the river, and the whole homeland seemed to answer Pinto in her mother's voice.

Nothing else matters.

She sat and thought about being fifteen; or to be exact, fifteen and seven days. Her mother had been betrothed a week after her fifteenth birthday too.

'Did it feel strange? Did you feel like you weren't old enough? I don't. I feel like I've been old enough for years.'

She thought about having children. She'd never really been interested in children before, but now that it was coming closer, it seemed to her to be something rather extraordinary. The baby would grow from nothing inside her, like a part of her body. She shivered at the idea.

'It seems to me like my baby would be me, only I could love her,' she said. 'Is it like having yourself to cuddle?'

Mumpo wanted to call their first boy Mumpo, which she thought would be confusing, but of course she had agreed. If it was a girl she had wanted to call her Ira, but to her irritation Bowman had taken the name for his third child. Baby Ira was a boy, which was even more confusing. And now they were going to be late for her betrothal.

She heard footsteps, and there was Mumpo, striding steadily across the meadow towards her. She watched him approach, and all that was left of her crossness fell away. He was so tall and strong, and his face was so good and kind. It seemed to her that he never thought a bad thought or did a bad deed. He was simple and clear and straight, all the way to the bottom, like a mountain pool.

'I thought you'd be here,' he said.

She got up off her stone and kissed him.

'Sun's shining for us,' she said.

'Of course it is. So what are you fretting about?'

'Who says I'm fretting?'

'You only ever come here to fret. I should think your mother's tired of you.'

Only Mumpo could have such a notion, thought Pinto, smiling back. She turned to the grave.

'Are you tired of me, ma? There. She's not.'

She took Mumpo's arm, to return to the village.

'Bowman's late.'

'He'll be here.'

'Scooch burned the cakes.'

'He's cut the burned bits off. They're fine.'

'The wind singer isn't ready.'

'It will be.'

'So according to you, nothing can go wrong?'

'Nothing,' he said. 'This is our day. Whatever happens is right.'

As they stepped out of the ring of stones, Pinto turned back to call to her mother.

'Creoth said to say good day.'

The ship dropped anchor out in the bay. The harbour was deep enough for the fishermen's yawls and the merchants' barges, but not for the full-keeled three-masted schooner from Gang. The villagers came pouring from every building to line the harbour spit and wave to the sailors on the ship as they reefed in the sails. Pinto stood not waving, feeling cross and happy, her father on one side and Mumpo on the other. The ship's boat was winched down to the water, and then the crowd on shore saw Bowman himself come out on deck and wave. Then Sisi followed, and she also waved: two tiny figures surrounded by a crowd of servants and mariners.

Gem Marish was disappointed.

'They're wearing ordinary clothes. They don't look like emperors at all!'

'Emperors are nothing special,' said Creoth.

'Where's the baby?' asked little Pia Amos.

'Look! That man behind them! He's blue!'

'There's little Siri! There she is!'

'I want to see the baby!'

'Ah, she's a beautiful sight,' said Miller Marish, meaning the ship, as he dandled little Milo in his arms.

Now one of the sailors was in the bobbing boat, and holding up an arm to help Bowman down. Bowman then reached up and took a bundle in his hands, and held it safe. Lunki, straining to make out the details, caught sight of a little pink face in the bundle, and squealed with delight.

'My baby!' she cried. 'My baby's baby!'

The older children followed Bowman into the boat: Falcon, already four years old, insisted on climbing down the ladder by herself; then the Johdila Sirharani, known as Siri, who was six-and-a-half. Then came Sisi herself, and the blue man, and another very small man, holding a basket.

'I know that little fellow!' said Lunki, struggling to remember.

The landing party crossed the bay and was rowed to shore. Pinto threw herself into Bowman's arms, forgetting all her anger, and held him tight. Lunki took Sisi in her arms, and overcome with emotion, burst into tears.

'My precious,' she sobbed. 'My little one.'

Sisi was now a striking woman of twenty-four, tall and slim and elegant. After she had hugged Lunki, she looked round at the friends she hadn't seen for two years now, until her great amber eyes came to rest on Hanno Hath. She bowed to him, and he returned her bow. Little Pia Amos came up to her and tugged her robe.

'Your face is funny,' she said.

'Yes,' said Sisi, smiling. 'Are you Ashar's little girl?'

'Of course I am,' said Pia.

Sisi looked round for her own little girl, and found her with her face shyly buried in her skirts.

'Fal, this is Pia.'

Falcon refused to come out.

'Let me see my baby's baby,' begged Lunki.

Bowman reached out the bundle.

'Don't mind if he cries,' he said. 'He's hungry.'

Lunki took the baby, and all the little children crowded round to see, except Siri and Falcon.

'It's only a baby,' said Siri with a shrug.

Hanno now stepped forward to embrace Bowman.

'Good to see you, Bo. My dear.'

'Pa. You look well.'

'I am well.' He bent down to talk to Falcon, his favourite. 'Good morning, Fal. How was your journey?'

'Too long,' said the child.

Hanno embraced Sisi.

'Sisi. We miss you. I hope your parents are well?'

'Getting old,' said Sisi. 'My mother worries about everything, and my father does nothing at all.'

'He's very happy,' said Bowman with a smile. 'He eats and he sleeps, which is all he ever wanted to do, anyway.'

Bowman greeted all his old friends, as slowly and chaotically the crowd moved back up to the village. Here Scooch and Creoth had laid out lunch on trestle tables in front of the schoolhouse. Tanner Amos was still frantically bolting together sections of the contraption on the platform.

'A wind singer!' exclaimed Bowman when he saw it. 'Does it work?'

'Not yet,' said Tanner, shaking Bowman's hand. 'And anyway, it's only a model.'

'Good to be home, Tanner.'

'I thought home for you was a grand palace, with servants and gold plates.'

'No,' said Bowman quietly. 'This will always be home.'

Lunki had worked out by now that the blue man was Ozoh, and the little one was Lazarim, both of whom she had known in the old days in the imperial court of Gang. Ozoh, it now emerged, had abandoned augury and become a wine maker. A barrel of his best wine was even now being ferried from the ship, along with crates of trade goods ordered by Branco Such for his general store.

Ozoh was not shy about his wine.

'You wait till you taste it, ma'am. A glass of my Golden Yanoo is generally agreed to be the closest a body ever comes to paradise, without the inconvenience of dying.'

'I'll tell my Scooch. He'll want some of that.'

Lazarim, once a dancing master, was now tutor to the imperial children: for, improbable as it seemed to the Manth people, Bowman and Sisi ruled the great empire of Gang. Their realm reached from sea to sea, encompassing the ruined city of Aramanth, the territories of Gang itself, the former Mastery, the mountains, the forests, and even the homeland. In Obagang, where their palace stood, Bowman had taken on the title of the Bowmana of Gang, Lord of a Million Souls.

'You're not lord of my soul,' said Rollo Shim every time he heard this. 'So you can subtract one from your million.'

Sisi had become the Sirhardi, Mother of the Nation.

Now, surrounded by her friends Ashar and Red, Seer and Sarel, all young mothers like her, she dismissed her titles with a laugh.

'It's all nonsense,' she said. 'But as Bowman says, someone has to rule, and it turns out to be us.' In a lower voice she added to her friends, 'Bo is amazing! You'd think he'd been born to it! He's so grave and wise you'd never recognise him. But he likes it best here.'

Lazarim sat quietly on his haunches, his sharp eyes watching the girls. He had set his basket down on the ground. Falcon now came over to the basket, and reached inside.

'We're on land now, Mist,' she said, stroking the grey fur of the cat curled up inside. 'You're like me, aren't you? You hate boats.'

Mist looked back at her through clouded eyes. The cat was very old, and minded very little any more. However, he reflected to himself, the girl is right. Living is a tiring enough affair as it is. Going about in boats only makes it worse.

Baby Milo Marish made a bid for freedom, crawling off at speed towards the bakery. Red Mimilith chased after him, and carried him back to the group of young mothers.

'This is my smallest. I swear he'll drown before he can walk.'

'Hello, little Milo,' said Sisi. 'I hear your big stepsister Fin is betrothed. Where have the years all gone?'

Mumpo found a moment's quiet to speak to Bowman.

'Well,' he said. 'Pinto and I seem to have got there at last.'

'I'm very happy for you both.'

'Do you think Kess would approve?'

'I know she would.'

'How long will you stay?'

'A month. No more. Then we must return. But you'll come and visit us in Obagang, both of you?'

'Of course.'

The two men looked over the cheerful crowd, now clustered round the lunch tables.

'We're lucky to be living in this time,' said Bowman.

'I know it,' said Mumpo.

Ozoh's barrel was broached, and the wine glasses were handed round. Siri and Falcon lost their shyness, and raced round the wind singer with Harman Amos, Gem Marish, and the Shim twins. Teacher Pillish watched Falcon play, and said to Sisi, 'That girl is the mirror of you, my lady.'

'Except for the scars,' said Sisi. She caught Bowman's eyes looking on her, and smiled for him. Often and often she saw him gazing at her like this, and she felt his quiet love and gratitude, and it was all she wanted.

Lunki gave her back her baby boy. For the moment the baby was quiet, interested in all the new faces round him. Sisi put him in the basket with Mist.

'Oh. You again,' said Mist.

Little Ira reached out a tiny hand and poked at his fur. It couldn't be called stroking, but the cat didn't mind. Although the baby never spoke, Mist had a strong suspicion that he understood him. As a result, he regarded little Ira as his own baby, and gave him advice, and told him stories.

'I used to fly when I was younger,' he said. 'I was a flying cat. I'll teach you when you're bigger, if I'm still alive. You'll like it. Though it's like everything else, once you've done it for a while, you lose interest.'

The baby gurgled at him, and prodded him again.

'That's the trouble with life,' said Mist. 'In the end, you lose interest.'

Pinto now emerged from the schoolhouse, looking radiant in her betrothal dress. All conversation stopped. Then everyone clapped, and Pinto blushed. Miko Mimilith, who had made the dress, stood behind her watching her with a gaze that combined critical dissatisfaction and bursting pride. Sisi felt tears sting her eyes. Pinto looked so like Kestrel. The dress was like the white sheath made for her wedding in the Mastery, the dress in which Kestrel had danced the tantaraza. Pinto didn't share Kestrel's features, but there was so much of her older sister in her manner, in those quick movements and those bright eyes.

Then she heard her baby crying.

'What have you done now, Mist?'

'Me? Nothing. When did I ever do anything?'

Sisi lifted the baby out of the basket and put him to her breast, and the nuzzle and tug of the little mouth on her nipple calmed her. Her oldest child, Siri, came up by her side, and touched her mother's scars, as she often did.

'I wish I had scars like you. You're so lucky. They make you special.'

'You're special too, darling.'

'No, I'm not. I just have special clothes.'

Sisi sighed, and held her baby close to her breast, and let her mind be filled by his simple need, that her body could so simply satisfy. It got so much harder so quickly, as they grew up.

Bowman made sure he had greeted everybody, and that Lazarim had his eye on the little girls. There was still a little time to go before the ceremony. He moved quietly away from the gathering, and took the path Pinto had taken earlier, to the graveyard. No one followed. They knew he would want to be alone.

As he walked, he looked round at the fields and rivers, reminding himself of the familiar landscape, happy to be back. *This is the time of peace,* he said to himself, *and the time of forgetting. Don't let me forget too much, for too long.*

When he reached his mother's grave, he sat down on one of the corner stones, as Pinto had done, and spoke to his mother.

'Did you foresee our happiness, ma? Is that why you were able to leave us?'

A strange noise sounded from the village. He turned his face and shaded his eyes to see. Tanner Amos had finally got the wind singer to work, and it was swinging round, catching the wind, and letting out a comical groaning sound. The people in the square were all laughing. Bowman smiled. He thought of the old wind singer in Aramanth, and then of its silver voice, and then of Kestrel.

It all seems so long ago. Did you ever think it would lead us to this?

Of course, said Kestrel. *What else was it all for?*

Liar, said Bowman. *You had no idea.*

Once Bowman had rejoined the gathering, the children sang their song with Teacher Pillish, and everyone laughed and clapped as the little chicks popped out. Then Hanno Hath took Pinto's hand in his and led her to stand before Mumpo. There in the sunlight by the wind singer they clasped hands and looked into each other's eyes and spoke the words of the vow.

'Today begins my walk with you.'

The children fell silent, sensing the solemnity of the moment.

'Where you go, I go. Where you stay, I stay.'

As he spoke, Mumpo looked into those fierce black eyes, and he marvelled that anyone could love him so much; he who had been the bottom of the class, the one who never understood, the lonely one.

'When you sleep, I will sleep. When you rise, I will rise.'

Oh, it's taken so long, thought Pinto. But now it's come at last.

'I will pass my days within the sound of your voice, and my nights within the reach of your hand, and none shall come between us.'

That's all I ask, thought Mumpo. Not to be alone.

That's all I ask, thought Pinto. To love you till the day I die.

Baby Ira gave a loud chortle of delight. A ripple of laughter ran round the gathering.

'This I vow.'

Mumpo took Pinto in his arms, and they kissed.

Bowman watched, and looking out through his eyes, Kestrel watched with him. They remembered dawn sunlight piercing winter trees, a promise that had not been broken.

Why should it ever end? Why shouldn't we love each other for ever?

They remembered too a greater light, that had for a moment touched all things. The memory now reached out from them, here at the betrothal, as if that long-ago light was bathing and transforming this crowd of laughing friends, and the laden tables, and the creaking wind singer, and the homeland, and the ocean beyond, until all was turned to light, themselves too, and the dazzling moment hovered weightless, astonished, beautiful, ravished by the song that never ends.

The End